Broken Dreams

Nick Quantrill

Joe Geraghty, Private Investigator, is used to struggling from one case to the next, barely making the rent on his small office in the Old Town of Hull. Invited by a local businessman to investigate a member of his staff's absenteeism, it's the kind of surveillance work that Geraghty and his small team have performed countless times. When Jennifer Murdoch is found bleeding to death in her bed, Geraghty quickly finds himself trapped in the middle of a police investigation which stretches back to the days when the city had a thriving fishing industry. As the woman's tangled private life begins to unravel, the trail leads Geraghty to local gangster-turned-respectable businessman, Frank Salford, a man with a significant stake in the city's regeneration plans. Still haunted by the death of his wife in a house fire, it seems the people with the answers Geraghty wants are the police and Salford, both of whom want his co-operation for their own ends. With everything at stake, some would go to any length to get what they want, Geraghty included.

Broken
Dreams

Fiction aimed at the heart
and the head...

2

Published by Caffeine Nights Publishing 2010

Copyright © Nick Quantrill 2010

Nick Quantrill has asserted his right under the Copyright, Designs and
Patents Act 1998 to be identified as the author of this work

Published in Great Britain by Caffeine Nights Publishing

www.cnpublishing.co.uk

British Library Cataloguing in Publication Data.
A CIP catalogue record for this book is available from the British Library

ISBN: 978-0-9554070-2-4

Cover design by
Mark (Wills) Williams

Everything else by
Default, Luck and Accident

Dedication:

For my Dad - Jeff Quantrill, 1948 – 2009.

4

Acknowledgments:

Writing is often considered to be a solitary business but I've learnt nothing could be further from the truth. I owe a huge debt of gratitude to the following for all their help and inspiration:

Cathy Quantrill, my wife, for everything. And for letting me off chores.

Paul Thompson for the amazing example set over the years. Keep on shining.

Darren Laws for the opportunity to work with Caffeine Nights and the unwavering belief in this book.

Roland Standaert and Beth McGann for the amazing photography work on my websites.

Jason Goodwin for sterling work in creating a website from the scraps of information he's given to work with.
www.hullcrimefiction.co.uk

Mac and Stephany NJC for gamely taking up proofreading duties without complaint.

Cilla Wykes and the team at www.thisisull.com for opening the door.

Tim Roux at www.a63revisited.com and all of Hull's writers, poets and playwrights for their advice, enthusiasm and friendship.

Mum and Dad for their support and encouragement throughout.

Everyone who's read one of my stories on the Internet over the last four years. It's what keeps me going. You know who you are.

Broken Dreams

6

One

'**You** didn't hear or see anything?'

I shook my head. It's not every day you're accused of murdering a client. I checked myself in the mirror; the cuts on my face leaving a bloody mess and a bottom lip twice its normal size. It didn't look clever. The phone call had woken me and after listening to the message, I washed down some painkillers, threw on an old tracksuit and stepped out into the night. The taxi arrived quickly and drove me through the deserted streets of Hull towards my office in the Old Town. Ten minutes later I was sat in my chair, waiting for Don to say something. He was my business partner, but more importantly, my mentor. I explained that I'd been jumped as I'd walked home.

'Are you sure?'

'Nothing.' All I knew was my mobile had been taken. It sounded feeble, given the state of my face.

Don towers above me, so I always feel like a naughty child when he tells me off. Although I'm in my early forties and still in reasonable shape, I know when to keep my mouth shut.

I heard the toilet flush and looked at Don, who was refusing to meet my eye. I turned and watched Detective Sergeant Richard Coleman walk into the room.

'Joe Geraghty, Private Investigator' he said, still drying his hands on a paper towel.

I nodded a greeting. 'Make yourself at home, why don't you?'

He sat on the top of the table opposite me. 'I'll get to the point; Don said you were outside of Jennifer Murdoch's house tonight?'

'I didn't make it.'

'No?'

'No.'

'What did you do tonight?'

'Went to the pub.' I stared at him, assuming he might know why I'd felt the need to get drunk tonight.

'With anyone in particular?'

I shook my head. He was oblivious. 'Why do you ask?'

'She's dead' Coleman said, staring straight at me, 'She put up quite a fight, but I can't go into the details.' He paused to look at me before changing the subject. 'Don tells me you were watching her on behalf of her employer.'

'A false illness claim' I said, before he had chance to go on. 'She claims she was suffering from stress and was unable to work. Her employer disagrees. Perfectly normal.'

'Don tells me she's the company's accountant, right?'

I nodded.

'Any luck with it?'

'Not yet.' We'd only been on the case for a couple of days and didn't have the necessary proof.

'Notice any one else watching her?'

I shook my head. I asked if Terrence Briggs, her employer, had received the news.

Coleman confirmed he'd be speaking to him. Another fee gone, I thought but didn't dare say.

'Do you want to tell me what happened?' asked Coleman, pointing to my face.

'I was attacked on my way home. Lost my mobile and what money I had on me.'

'Who by?'

'No idea.'

'Report it?'

'No.'

Coleman sighed. 'Did you see the man?'

'No.'

'Local?'

I thought about it. 'Sounded it.'

'Where did it happen?'

'The tenfoot near my flat.'

'No witnesses?'

'I don't think so.'

Coleman looked from Don to myself. 'Upset anybody lately?'

Don stared at me, looking for confirmation. I shook my head. 'No.'

'Your story is you were attacked by an assailant, identity unknown, and you weren't anywhere near Jennifer Murdoch's house tonight?'

'Correct.' I sipped the coffee Don had made and tried to read Coleman's face.

'I'll need a statement from you tomorrow.' He pointed at my cuts and bruises. 'You might want to think about reporting the assault, too.'   Coleman stood up and told Don he'd be in touch. He looked at me again before leaving.

'What the fuck are you playing at?' Don asked me, once he'd shut the door on the policeman. He didn't swear very often.

'I was attacked.' It sounded weak.

'And you're telling the truth about not being near Murdoch's house?'

It was my turn to be indignant. 'Of course I am.'

'We're not pissing about here, Joe.'

I nodded. It doesn't come any more serious than murder, so I knew the police would be throwing some resources at it. I sat up, my head feeling clearer for the caffeine. 'Did you tell them?' He would often tell the police when and where we are performing surveillance as a professional courtesy. If the police knew we had a genuine and legitimate reason for following an individual, it was supposed to prevent future misunderstandings. As I was learning, the system wasn't perfect.

Don shook his head. 'I hadn't got round to telling them.'

I considered the situation. They'd obviously seen my car outside of Murdoch's house the previous day. 'They were watching her?'

'Or her husband' Don suggested. He took my empty mug off me and shook his head. 'You'd best report the assault.'

I said I would, but it would be pointless. The truth was I didn't know who had attacked me. Losing my mobile was a pain but I could get a new one easy enough. What was occupying my mind was the fact the police knew I had been carrying out surveillance outside Murdoch's house. I looked like I'd been involved in a fight and had no alibi to speak of. It was a chance I couldn't take; people have been arrested for much less. I knew I was going to have to find out why Jennifer Murdoch had been murdered.

Two

A shower and strong coffee had me feeling almost human again by mid-morning. I'd walked to the nearest supermarket, bought a cheap pay-as-you-go mobile and topped it up with credit before meeting Don to talk to Jennifer Murdoch's employer. Only he was in his boardroom talking to the police. The company was based on Sutton Fields, an industrial estate to the east of the city. The middle-aged woman stood behind the reception desk wanted us to come back some other time.

'Maybe you could help us' said Don, explaining why we were there.

She'd thought we were salesmen before introducing herself as Sheila Chester, Briggs's PA. She directed us to her office. I gave her what I hoped was my winning smile, but with the cuts and bruises, I wasn't sure it was working.

'Take your time.' Don said, as she sat down.

Her hand was shaking slightly, the earlier confidence disappearing. She lifted her mug and slowly drank a mouthful of tea.

'We understand this is difficult for you, Sheila.'

And given the visit from Coleman, I wanted some answers.

Don lent in close to her. 'We're here to help.'

She nodded. I'll do my best.'

'How long have you worked for the company, Sheila?' Don asked.

'Nearly twenty years.'

I could see the pride in her face, so I smiled. 'You must have seen some changes, then?'

'One or two, I suppose.'

'How long had Jennifer been with you?'

'It must be about ten years now. She used to work for our auditors, so Mr Briggs offered her the job when her predecessor retired.'

'And before her illness, how was she was doing?'

She looked reluctant to answer the question. I tried to help her out. 'Whatever you say stays between us. It won't go any further.'

'Her alleged illness.'

'Right.'

'I know you shouldn't speak ill of the dead, but I didn't like her, to be totally honest with you.' Unburdening this seemed to enable her to relax. She looked me in the eye. 'Either as a colleague or as a person.'

'Was she difficult to get on with?'

'Very much so. We were very different people, you see. I've never married, never travelled very much or led what you might call an exciting life. I have what I have, and I'm very thankful for it. I'm not the type of person who always wants more. Jennifer, on the other hand, was very different. She wanted everything, and I suspect that was only to say she had it.'

I encouraged her to continue.

'If it wasn't a flash car, it was holidays abroad and designer clothes. It put a few backs up, that's for sure.'

'I assume she could afford these luxuries?'

Sheila nodded. 'She was well paid and her husband has a good job. He's some sort of business hotshot, but I don't really know the details. Besides, most people these days use credit cards to get what they want, don't they?'

I tried to hold a smile. 'It's often the way.'

'I remember when people used to save up for things they wanted.'

I half-heartedly agreed, anxious to keep her talking to us.

'How was Jennifer as an accountant?' asked Don, getting us back on track.

'Generally, I'd say she was fine; certainly to start with.'

'To start with?'

'I assume you were told about the incident with her assistant?'

Don and I shook our heads. 'No.'

Sheila didn't hold our stare. The nervous Sheila had returned.

'It won't go any further' said Don, encouraging her to continue.

She placed her hands on the table and took a deep breath. 'A couple of years ago there was a spell when money seemed to be going missing.'

'Going missing?'

'I don't think all the petty cash cheques made their way into the actual petty cash tin. The auditor brought it to Jennifer's attention and she sorted it out. Mr Briggs was on holiday at the time and she never told me about the problem.'

'What happened?' It was obvious she had felt put out by her lack of involvement.

'Her assistant, Sonia Bray, left, and Mr Briggs considered the matter closed. Jennifer had told me how difficult it would be to get the proof for a conviction, so there was no point involving the police. She also claimed she'd worked out how much Sonia had allegedly stolen and made sure Mr Briggs got the money back.'

I sat up. 'I assume you're not convinced Sonia was behind the theft?'

'No. Not at all.'

'Any idea where we could find Sonia?'

'I think so. I'll let you have the details.'

Don thanked her.

'How about Jennifer's supposed illness?' I said. 'Do you know anything about it? Mr Briggs said you'd seen her when she was meant to be at work?'

'My friend had seen her, shopping in Princes Quay when she was supposed to be here. Sheila laughed and shook her head. 'Her illness? Jennifer might be many things, but I doubt she had been stressed. As I said earlier, she had loved flaunting her money and telling everyone what a great life she had.'

Don nodded to me that we were done. Whether or not she was simply bitter at Jennifer Murdoch's lifestyle, I didn't know, but I was taken back at the spite of the woman. The suggestion Murdoch had stolen from the firm and that Terrence Briggs might have an ulterior motive for sacking her was interesting. Before we had chance to consider it further, Terrence Briggs walked into the room.

'Sheila was helping us out while we waited' I said to him. Briggs nodded to his PA, who quickly left the room. 'What do you think you're doing?' he asked us.

'Our jobs' said Don.

'Under the circumstances, you don't have a job. I won't be needing you anymore.'

'The police have already spoken to us.'

Briggs walked across the room and opened the door in the far corner. 'We'll talk in here.'

The boardroom featured photographs of building developments the company had been involved with over the years. Briggs had been involved in the construction of several well-known buildings around the city. On the opposite wall were black and white photographs of Hull's fishing past.

'Fisherman in a former life?' I asked him.

'My brother.'

I nodded and asked if he was keeping busy.

'Plenty on at the moment. I've got the bread and butter stuff around the estates, maintenance work for the council and there's still the regeneration projects on the go.' He opened his drawer and placed a manila file on the desk. 'I suppose you can take it back.' It was the initial report we'd prepared for him on Jennifer Murdoch. It contained all the background information we'd pulled together, including her educational details, family background and anything of interest we'd learnt. We left it sitting there.

'What did the police have to say?' Don asked.

'What's it to you?'

'You'd asked us to do a job and now she's dead.'

'We're done then, aren't we? How much do I owe you?'

He looked flustered. I assumed the police had rattled his cage.

'You told us you wanted her out of your life.' I reminded him. 'Whatever it took, I think you told us.'

'I didn't mean I wanted her dead, for crying out loud.' He pointed at me. 'Look, I set this place up by myself over thirty years ago, built it up from nothing. I got nothing given to me on a plate. Several years later, here I am with one of the city's largest building companies. I'm not having someone like her take the piss out of me. It's not going to happen. All I said was that she was on long-term sick and I didn't reckon it was genuine. Don't be twisting my words.'

'The police will see you as having motive' said Don.

'I only wanted her out of this place.'

'It's still the beginnings of something. She was costing you a lot of wasted money, it makes you angry, you know where she lives, you want rid of her. It's a thought process they'll be following' I said.

'What's your point?' asked Briggs. He picked the file up.

'You've still got a few hours left on the clock and we don't like loose ends.'

Don was waiting for me in the reception of Queens Gardens police station, talking to the officer on front-desk duty. I'd taken his advice and called Coleman to arrange reporting the assault. He'd told me to come to the station and, though he'd led me to believe it would be over with quickly, it had taken a couple of hours. When Coleman eventually saw me, I'd kept my composure and answered the questions as honestly as I could. Even though I had nothing to hide, the situation felt like it had been made as uncomfortable and awkward for me as possible. For all that, I was left in no doubt should I learn anything about the murder of Jennifer Murdoch, I was to inform him immediately. Coleman had assured me I wasn't being treated as a suspect, rather a witness with some useful background information, but I wasn't so sure. Maybe I was being paranoid, but I didn't like the situation I found myself in.

I was glad to be out of the building and getting some fresh air. We walked towards a pub close to our office. I needed a drink to calm my nerves. I showed Don the leaflets I'd been given whilst I waited for Coleman.

'Investigative Officers,' I explained, 'cheap detectives, basically.' The force was recruiting civilians to assist the detectives with interviewing suspects and gathering evidence. It was policing on the cheap.

Don laughed and passed me my drink. 'Cheeky bastards. Did they tell you anything?'

'Nothing. I don't even know how she was killed.' I'd asked but they'd refused to tell me. They would be releasing details later during a press conference.

'What about the assault on you?'

'They weren't interested.'

Don said he wasn't surprised and turned the conversation back to Jennifer Murdoch. 'You'd have thought there would be some forensics, wouldn't you?'

'They didn't tell me if there was.' We both knew it was only any good if you had a match on the database. I also knew it could take days for the police to confirm a match. They hadn't asked me for a sample, as they didn't have the legal grounds to, but they could have asked me to volunteer if they had really wanted to.

Don asked me what I had made of Terrence Briggs.

'I don't like him.'

'He's still got a bit of credit left; we should see what turns up in that time.'

I agreed. Although we still had the regular bread and butter work of serving legal papers from solicitors, we weren't that busy.

'I don't like him.' I repeated.

'Why not?'

'Rude, unpleasant, take your pick.' I'm usually a good judge of character and something about Briggs jarred with me.

I moved our glasses to one side to allow Don to open the file on Jennifer Murdoch. He started to read to me.

'Okay, so she's in her mid-thirties, married and lives in North Ferriby with her husband. Overall salary package is somewhere in the region of £40,000. She's worked for Briggs for close to ten years.' He passed the file over to me. There were details of her education and previous employment; father worked the docks, standard education in a local secondary school; nothing unusual.

'Not such a great employee, though.' I took a look at the doctor's notes we'd previously copied from Briggs.

'Any thoughts?' Don asked me.

I leant back in the chair and swallowed a mouthful of lager. 'She's his accountant, right? She controls the purse-strings. Maybe there had been a falling out between them? Maybe over the money theft?'

Don shrugged. 'Enough to kill over? I don't see it.'

Sometimes I'm too inquisitive for my own good. Or rather, our good. Don was good at focusing in on the task at hand. All we'd been asked to do was look at her claim to illness; see if her absence from work was justifiable, and if we could, offer some evidence to her employer.

Don closed the file. 'I'll get on with checking her out tomorrow; see what else I can find.' He looked at his watch and stood up. 'We'd best hurry up. Sarah's going to be waiting for us.'

As we walked into the office, Sarah was showing a woman out. The woman wore a head-scarf, partly obscuring her face and didn't make eye contact as she left. Sarah walked back in and sat down without saying a word.

'Who's picking up Lauren?' Don asked.

'John.'

I'd not met her ex-husband, but his reputation preceded him. Sarah was in her mid-thirties and hadn't had much luck with men since. Usually, Don collected his grand-daughter from the childminders if Sarah was held up, but we'd been too busy with Briggs and Coleman. I asked who wanted a drink and busied myself in the kitchen.

'Potential client?' I asked, my back turned to them.

'I think so' Sarah replied.

I walked across to them with three cups of tea balanced on a tray. 'What's her story?'

Sarah opened her notepad. 'That was Maria Platt. She needs our help to find her daughter.'

Should be a straightforward task, I thought. 'How long's she been missing for?'

'Nearly ten years.'

I sat back in the chair. It'd either be a simple job or a total nightmare.

'Did you explain our fee structure to her?' asked Don.

Sarah looked away and said nothing. I looked down at the floor, knowing what was coming.

'You didn't, did you?' he said.

She shook her head. 'Not really. Look, she's desperate. I said we'd help her.' She passed a cheque over to Don. 'I've got this.'

Don looked at it and passed it to me. £200. It wouldn't go very far in paying the bills.

'I thought we could see how it goes' said Sarah, smiling apologetically at us. 'She's really desperate.'

'Why?' I asked.

'She's dying of cancer.'

Once we'd played out the ritual of Don trying to feign anger with Sarah, we all sat back down together to discuss what we could do to help the woman. I smiled at Sarah. The job wouldn't make us any money, but I admired her spirit. You could never say her heart wasn't in the right place. Don also knew that, and being his daughter, he was probably all the more proud of her. Besides, it wasn't like we were inundated with other jobs and it made life interesting.

'What's her daughter's name?' Don asked.

'Donna Platt' said Sarah. She'd photocopied her notes and passed them across to us. '29 years old.'

'No contact at all?' I asked.

'None at all.'

'Not even birthday or Christmas cards?'

Sarah shook her head. 'Nothing.'

Don looked up from the notes. 'How about family? Her father?'

'Died three years ago. Cancer. There's a brother who's three years older, but apparently he's had no contact with her either. I've got his details. He'll talk to us, if need be.'

'Why did she disappear?' I asked. 'What triggered it?'

'The official line is she wanted to be a singer, so she was going to head off to find fame and fortune. She was in a band with her friend, regulars on the city's club circuit.

We've got the name of a friend she sang with, but she wanted bigger things. She'd spoken about moving to London, but we have no idea whether she made the move or not. Other than that, she had a part-time job in a local shop to help pay the bills.'

'Didn't her mother try to contact her to tell her about her father's death?'

'She put a notice in the paper asking her to get in touch.'

'Nothing?'

'Nothing.'

'I assume she was reported to the police?' I said.

'Her husband wouldn't allow it.'

'Wouldn't allow it?' What kind of father wouldn't do everything he could to find his daughter, I wondered?

'I got the impression she was scared of him.'

'It's going to be a tough task' said Don. He stood up and walked over to the window. 'We've not got a lot to go on, have we? Or much time to do it, given the financial constraints.'

'Maybe we should start with the brother and friend? See if we can shed some light on it?' Sarah suggested.

I looked away. It was going to be a total nightmare. And that was assuming Donna Platt was still alive.

Three

Don walked over to my desk and placed a pile of print-outs in front of me. 'Jennifer Murdoch.'

I flicked through them. He'd been thorough, but that was his speciality.

'There's more to come, but that should keep you going for now.'

I grunted some form of reply. 'What do we know?' I asked him.

'Not too much more than we already knew.' He flicked through the paperwork he'd quickly put together and passed me what he was looking for. 'Take a look at her husband.'

His face was familiar, but I had to scan the text to refresh my memory. 'Christopher Murdoch.' He was a local businessman involved in many of the large ongoing regeneration projects around the city. The article I was reading described him as a 'consultant to the local council', but as to what he actually did, I didn't really know. The one thing I was certain about was that he was a major player on the local business scene. If he attached himself to your project, it was likely to be a success.

'It's background information' said Don, reading my mind. From a financial point of view, it suggested Jennifer Murdoch didn't need to work, but it didn't explain anything else. I was sure the police would be taking a look at him, though.

'I'm waiting to hear back from some people.'

It's surprising how much information is a matter of public record, but we earn our money by uncovering the pieces of information which aren't so readily available.'

'Are you helping Sarah?' he asked me.

I walked over to the kettle and poured myself a re-fill. 'Meeting her there.' It'd be a distraction from Jennifer Murdoch, if nothing else.

Don nodded his approval. 'I've got a warrant to serve once we're through. A rush job, as per usual.'

I watched him gather his papers together as we prepared to head out. I took it as my cue to put my mug down and collect my stuff together.

I sat down next to Sarah, huddled around a small table, legs touching. The pub was hidden away on Bankside, an industrial area situated on the outskirts of the city centre, dominated by the type of light engineering enterprise that employed Gary Platt. The place was almost empty, only a handful of lunchtime drinkers sat at the bar. I'd read the area had at one point been populated by Irish immigrants, though any houses were long gone. Chances were my family had lived in the area.

'Did your mother explain to you about us?' asked Sarah.

He stared at us. 'How much are you charging her?'

'Excuse me?'

'I don't like the thought of you taking advantage of her, not in her state. How much are you charging her?'

I took a deep breath and leaned forward. 'Frankly, Gary, it's not enough.' I didn't want to sound callous, but I wasn't about to take a lecture from him. Sarah dug me in my ribs with her elbow.

'What he means, Gary, is we're working for very much less than our usual rate.'

'£200, Gary. That's all' I said, interrupting. 'And frankly, if it wasn't for Sarah insisting we'd help, I would have said no. Now, if you think it's too much money to maybe find your sister, then fine, we'll walk away right now. We'll use the money pursuing other avenues, and when it runs out, which will be very quickly, we'll draw a line underneath it. Otherwise, you could show us some gratitude and try to help us.' I was angry but maybe I'd gone too far. 'Look' I said, hoping to sound more conciliatory, 'We want to see if we can find Donna, so your mother finds some peace.'

Gary nodded. 'I'll try to help you.'

'Good.'

Sarah took over the questioning. 'Obviously we didn't want to push your mother too hard, so we were hoping you could fill in some of the blanks.' She opened her notepad.

She'd pre-prepared some questions. I only had one question for him at this stage - why had Donna suddenly disappeared?

Gary shrugged. 'I don't know.'

'Was there an argument, or disagreement?' Sarah suggested. 'A falling out?'

Gary laughed. 'There were always arguments. We were a family.'

'Anything specific around the time she left?'

'I don't think so. It's such a long time ago now.'

'We appreciate that, Gary. What about her music?'

'What about it?'

'Did your dad approve? It must have been difficult for Donna. She wanted to be a singer, but I'm sure most parents would want their children to get a steady job, build a career.'

I wondered if Sarah was talking from personal experience. I can't imagine Don's burning ambition for her was to become a private investigator. I picked at my ham salad sandwich. It was disgusting. The lettuce looked days past its best, the bread bordering on being stale.

'As I said, I don't think our dad cared for it all that much, and what he said, went.'

'What did he do for a living?' I asked.

'Fuck all. He used to work the trawlers, but when it all went to shit, he couldn't find another job.'

I knew what he was talking about. My uncle had worked in the fishing industry but that was probably thirty five years ago. Once the jobs disappeared and nobody wanted his skills, he'd worked in factories, making ends meet until he retired. I took the hint that Gary didn't want to talk about his father, so I asked him if he had any idea where Donna had run to

'No idea. She'd spoken to people about moving to London, to improve her singing, but I knew Donna, she wouldn't have made it to London.'

'Why not?'

'For a start, she was always skint. She wouldn't have been able to get to Leeds, never mind London.'

'What about her other friends?' I looked at the name his mother had given us. 'How about Lisa Day, the girl she sang with? Did she know anything, or suggest where she might have gone?'

'Nobody knew anything. We asked her. I'm telling you, she just disappeared.'

'And the police were no help?'

'Said she was an adult and could do what she liked. They fobbed us off with some of those lost-people charities, but they did nothing for us, either.'

'What about boyfriends?' asked Sarah.

Gary shook his head. 'She didn't have one.'

'Ex-boyfriends?'

'Only the one I knew about and she got rid of him. Dad didn't want her bringing men home, so I can't really help you there.'

'Did Donna have a job, other than the band? Any workmates who would have missed her?'

'She worked part-time in a shop, nothing serious.' He looked at his watch. 'I never heard anything from them. I guess they got someone in to replace her.'

I sighed and pushed my sandwich to one side. It sounded like nobody had really made the effort to find her.

Sometimes working as a mixed-sex team is useful. If I'd been alone when I'd knocked on Lisa Day's door, I doubt I would have got my foot in the door, especially looking like I did. Sarah smoothes the rough edges off and her pleasant manner invariably gets us invited in. Like a lot of council properties, Lisa Day's house had been neglected to the point of no return. It needed decorating from top to bottom and an overall maintenance upgrade; the gas fire looked like it had seen better days and the thin carpet was worn in patches. Lisa was juggling two children. The one on her lap slept while the other child ran freely around the room. Sarah, as ever, was great with them and helped Lisa keep the older one under control as she asked the questions.

'It's been years since I saw Donna' she explained to us. 'I'm not sure how I can help you.' She looked at her watch. 'I've got to pick the eldest kids up from school soon.'

Lisa was in her late-twenties, around the same age as Donna. I guessed life hadn't been too kind to her, but I didn't ask.

'We know it's been a long time' said Sarah. 'We appreciate your time. Donna's mum really needs to contact her.'

'Why?'

Her suspicion was tangible. A mistake. She looked away from us.

I glanced at Sarah. 'Mrs Platt has cancer' I said.

'Bad?'

I nodded. When was it ever not bad?

'Poor woman. I really liked her.'

'How well did you know Donna?' Sarah asked.

Lisa composed herself. 'We were best friends. We lived next door to each other, went to school together. All that kind of stuff.'

'Mrs Platt mentioned you sung together?'

She looked embarrassed before answering. 'Yeah, we had a band. Not a proper band, mind you. It was just us two using backing tapes. We played the local pubs and clubs. It was alright; we made some cash and we had some fun for a bit. We called ourselves *2's Company.*'

I thought I sensed something in her voice. 'What happened?' I asked.

'Frank Salford happened.'

'Frank Salford?'

'He was our manager.' She looked at Sarah and then me. 'I don't want to talk about him.'

'Why not?' I asked.

She shrugged. 'I don't want to get involved with him again.'

Sarah nudged me. It meant shut up. We'd take a look at him in due course. 'Did Donna have a boyfriend?' she asked.

Lisa looked relieved at the change of subject. 'Nobody she took seriously. There was always one or two on the scene but nothing that was going anywhere. It was difficult for her, living at home. She couldn't take them home. Her parents didn't approve.'

It might be something worth looking into. She clearly knew more than Donna's brother. I leant forward. 'Why did Donna leave, Lisa?' There had to be more.

'I don't know.'

'No idea at all?' I asked.

'Donna had big dreams.' She shrugged. 'She was always saying we should go to London because that's where it all happened. She seemed to think Salford could help us.'

'You didn't want to go to London?' asked Sarah.

Lisa shook her head. 'We were too young for all of that. I've got family here, so I couldn't swan off to London, even if I wanted to.'

'Is there anywhere else Donna might have gone? Anybody else who might be able to help us?'

Lisa shook her head. 'Singing was her life. It was all she wanted to do.'

'Do you think she went to London?'

'Doubt it. Donna talked a lot, but I don't think she had it in her to leave Hull, to leave her mam.'

'Did you ever try to contact her?'

'I couldn't. It was down to her to ring me because she knew where I was. I had no way of finding her.'

'What did her parents think about the singing?' I asked, changing the subject.

She shrugged. 'Don't really know. Her mam always supported us and offered to help with costumes and stuff.'

'What about her father?'

'What about him?'

'Did he take an interest in the band?'

'No.' She laughed and looked up. 'He never took much interest in anything other than his drink and horses. He didn't approve of us singing.'

'Was it a problem for Donna?'

'What do you mean?'

'If her mother was interested in helping her, and her father wasn't, did it become a problem? Did they fall out over it?'

Lisa shrugged her shoulders. 'It was none on my business.'

Sarah nodded to me that we were about finished. She was probably right but I wasn't happy with her response about Donna's father. Maybe it was something for another day. I opened my notebook and made a note of their manager's name. 'Any idea where we might find Frank Salford?'

'No idea.'

I wanted to speak to Salford. We stood up to leave.

'Will you let me know if you hear anything?' she asked us.

'Sure' I said. I turned back to her. 'Do you still sing?'

She looked at me properly for the first time. 'Only to my children.'

I leant down and placed the flowers I'd bought earlier on the grave. It was late afternoon and the light was starting to fade. It was my favourite part of the day and the time I liked to visit. Set back from the main road, it felt peaceful. Even though I knew it word for word, I read the headstone, as if on automatic pilot. It had been two years, but it felt much, much longer. My mobile vibrated in my pocket. I looked at the screen and disconnected the call. It was Don calling. I'd left him a message earlier to check out *2's Company's* manager, Frank Salford, but it could wait. He told me to speak to him before I did anything further. I sensed somebody stood close to me and turned around.

'Alright, lad.' The man was old, I guessed in his seventies.

'Alright.'

'It doesn't get any easier, does it? It never goes away.'

We stood there for a moment in silence, looking at the headstone, detailing dates of birth and death. I could tell he was doing the maths.

'I think I've seen you here before' I said to him.

'I visit every week.' I followed his finger to where he was pointing to. 'My wife's over there. Nearly ten years now but I still miss her every single day.'

There wasn't much I could say. We stood there silently, bound together by our respective losses.

'38 is no age.' He was pointing at my wife's grave. 'No age at all.'

I didn't make a habit of daytime drinking, but it had been that kind of day. The Queens Hotel on Princes Avenue was my local and close to my flat. Princes Avenue was the place to be seen in the city. Everywhere you turned, there were bars and restaurants, all trying to sell the illusion of continental relaxation. Hull was a tough town but however well you covered over the bruises, the true nature of the place was never far from the surface. Queens is situated well away from the rest of the bars and I like to think it has a well-kept secret feel about it. It certainly doesn't appeal to the kind of people who mistake the trendier bars for catwalks, so I was happy enough. I paid for my lager and headed over to an empty table to read the evening paper. I was about finished with the sports section when I noticed I had company. A man of similar age to myself was stood over me.

'It's Joe, isn't it?' he asked.

I nodded but had no idea who he was.

'I thought so. Joe Geraghty.'

The man sat down and extended his hand to me. 'Dave Carter.'

I shook it, still none the wiser.

'You used to play rugby with my brother, John.'

I wasn't in the mood for taking a trip down memory lane.

'I saw your debut for Rovers, when was it...1986?'

I nodded. 'Castleford.' I scored a try as well.

'That's right. I remember. You were the best teenage scrum-half I ever saw. It's a shame injury did for you, otherwise I reckon you'd have gone on to play internationally.'

I mumbled some sort of agreement. I hadn't played enough rugby to know how good I could have been. I'd signed for the club I supported, Hull Kingston Rovers, back in 1985 when I was sixteen. Within six months, I'd made my debut for the first team, which was no mean feat, as the team was superb at the time. It was a dream come true for me. A lot of people were tipping me for bigger and better things, not that I really thought there were bigger and better things, but as often happens with youngsters in sport, my performances dipped and I headed back to the youth team to learn my trade. The dip couldn't have come at a worse time, as the team reached the Challenge Cup Final at Wembley. As great as it was, I was only there as a spectator. I travelled down with the squad, but I knew I was never going to be selected. I went away that summer and worked hard on my fitness, so when I returned for the next season, I'd never miss out on such an occasion again. I fought hard and won my place back for the league game at St Helens. Within five minutes of the game starting, I was hit with a tackle so hard, my knee collapsed under me. I'd never known pain like it. I'm told I drifted in and out of consciousness on the pitch, as well as vomiting several times. Eventually I was taken to a hospital on Merseyside, where I was told I'd never play again. The doctor was right. I never played again. Telling Dave it was nice to meet him, I quickly finished my pint and left the pub.

My flat was on one of several tree-lined streets off Princes Avenue, which somehow had become the trendy part of the city. I'd rented in the area for no other reason than a lot of property was available. It was easy and made sense. I looked at the photograph of my wife, which sat on the windowsill in a place I'd always see. Other than that, there was a chair, stereo and a television in the front room. I walked over to the stereo and looked through the small pile of CDs. All I had were my favourites. The rest had been lost. I sifted through them and found The Specials debut album. I was a big punk and ska fan, thanks to my older brother. He'd been old enough to go out and see them all when they'd come to town. I was too young, but inherited his collection when he'd left home. The flat was rented. The capital left over from the house sale sat in a savings account I didn't want to touch. I was alive, but not really living. It was how I liked things to be. I kept my wedding ring wrapped in a tissue and every so often I'd take it out to remind myself of what I'd once had. I needed to remember, but by not wearing it, it reminded me I needed to attempt to move on and start over. I had fallen asleep, if only for a short while, but the incessant drone of my doorbell brought me round. Sarah was stood on my doorstep, holding a pizza and a four-pack of lager.

I picked up another slice of pizza and carefully transferred it to my plate. 'Thanks, Sarah.'

'What for?' she asked, mouth full of food.

'For coming here.'

She smiled at me. 'Not a problem.'

I smiled back. I was glad she was here and pleased Don had been good enough to look after Lauren for a few hours. My initial reaction was to send her away. I thought I wanted to be on my own, but she stood her ground and told me I'd only get drunk, listen to bad music and generally mope. It wasn't healthy for me to be alone. She probably had a point. She told me Don wanted to speak to me, but it could wait.

'I thought you might be able to use the company.' She looked around. 'When are you going to furnish this place, Joe?'

I shrugged. I liked the sparseness of the flat. I wasn't ready to make it feel like a home. It was still too soon.

Four

I woke up late, nursing a hangover, my front room littered with empty beer bottles and pizza boxes. I sat down on my settee and pushed a hand through my hair. My flat was a mess, but I was pleased Sarah had thought of me. If she hadn't, I'd have most probably sat in the dark, drinking and brooding. I'd arranged with Don that I would go into the office later on today. The only urgent work for the morning was the delivery of a warrant to a business address and Don was quite capable of dealing with it. I stood up and moved over to the stereo and flicked through my CDs. Finding nothing remotely quiet amongst my ska and punk, I put The Clash's debut album on. As 'Janie Jones' burst through the speakers, I knew it would either kill or cure.

Moving into my small kitchen, I filled the kettle and popped some bread into the toaster. Settling back in my chair with my breakfast, I started up my laptop. As usual, my first stop was the local sport message boards. I'd started going to games again recently for the first time in years. It felt right again. The gossip and rumour on these sites was always good for passing five minutes. I logged into my emails and settled back to read what Don has sent me about Frank Salford.

The email was brief, but he'd done his homework. Salford had come to the police's attention in the early 1980s, when he was landlord of several notorious pubs and clubs around the city. It appeared there had been more than one investigation into Salford's business affairs, but he'd always managed to avoid prosecution. More recently, Salford had moved away from pubs and clubs and now ran a massage parlour on the edge of the city centre. Don's email concluded with the warning Salford was a nasty bastard. He wanted to meet me in the office, where he'd give me the detailed version. I reached across for my mobile and punched in the office number. All I got was the engaged tone. Finishing my coffee, I eased myself up and headed for the shower. The Clash were still hammering their way through those glorious early tunes. I was beginning to perk up.

I'd tried the office and Don's mobile again, but there was still no answer. I'd thought about tackling some domestic jobs; my flat needed a clean and the cupboards were empty. The thought filled me with dread, so I'd found myself looking up the address of *The Honeypot*, Frank Salford's massage parlour. Clearly, he wasn't a subtle man. I had nothing better to do, so ignoring Don's warning, I found myself walking towards the city centre, trying to use the fresh air and exercise as justification for my actions.

The massage parlour was every bit as seedy and dirty as I expected it to be. There was nobody working the reception desk, so I casually picked up the brochure which had been placed there. It detailed the parlour's employees, with photographs and brief summaries of their vital statistics. I heard someone cough. A man sat in the small waiting area. He smiled at me, but I turned away without acknowledging him.

'Alright, love.'

I nodded to the woman stood behind the reception desk. She was looking me up and down, presumably unsure whether I was a customer or the police. She noticed I had the brochure in my hand and smiled.

'That's an old brochure now. We're in the process of having the latest recruits photographed. At the moment we've only got two girls on. You can see either Kerry or Anastazja.' She nodded to the man sat in the waiting room. 'If you want to see Anastazja, you'll have to wait. The prices are in the brochure, anything else is negotiable with the girls, okay?'

'I'd like to see Mr Salford, please.' I wanted to get it over and done with. The place made me feel sick.

'He's not in, love.'

'Not his Jaguar outside, then?'

She stared at me. 'No.' She smiled. 'If you'd like to leave your number, he could call you back?'

It was my turn to smile. I didn't think Salford would be the kind of man who returned telephone calls. 'I won't take up too much of his time.'

'He's not here. If you'd like to leave your details.'

I passed her a business card. 'I'm trying to find a missing woman. Mr Salford used to manage her singing career.'

Her eyes narrowed, as she read my details. 'Which girl?'

'Donna Platt. Her mother is trying to find her.'

She shook her head. 'I don't remember a Donna Platt.'

'You used to help Frank manage the bands?'

'None of my business.' She passed me my card back. 'It's a long time ago. I doubt Frank will be able to help you.'

I tried to pass it back to her. 'If you could get him to call me.'

She turned around and shouted for some help. The help was a man-mountain, far bigger than myself. He didn't return my smile.

'I've told you. We can't help.' She folded her arms and nodded to her help. 'Escort Mr Geraghty off the premises, please.'

Leaving Salford's massage parlour, I headed to the pub for a couple of hours. I didn't need any more alcohol, but strong coffee and a read of the newspaper had me feeling human again. Sarah rang me on my mobile, partly to see how I was feeling after the previous night, partly to tell me she'd arranged a meeting with Katie Glew, the third member of Donna Platt's band. I hadn't realised there had been a third member of the band, and it didn't make much sense of the band's name. I drank up and collected Sarah from her house before heading to Katie's flat. Sarah explained to me how Donna's mother had remembered Glew. A quick call to Lisa Day confirmed the details and Glew had called Sarah to agree to a meeting. The flat was in a tower block on one of the city's largest council estates and in a similar state to Lisa Day's house. It needed a good clean and some decoration, but nothing that couldn't be sorted with a bit of effort.

'Thanks for agreeing to see us' said Sarah. 'We appreciate your help.'

Katie lit a cigarette and shrugged. 'No skin off my nose.'

'We're looking for Donna Platt' explained Sarah.

'She's missing?' She looked surprised.

'Has been for several years. When did you last see her?'

'When I left the band, but I'd heard she had a job in a factory on Sutton Fields a few years back.'

'How long ago are we talking about, Katie?' I asked.

'I'm not sure, to be honest.'

I removed my wallet from my pocket.

She looked at me. 'Three, maybe four years ago. I've got a mate who works there. It was her who mentioned it.'

'Are you still in touch with this mate?'

Katie nodded and asked if Donna was in any trouble.

'Not at all' said Sarah.

'My friend wouldn't lie to me.'

I smiled at her. 'We're not implying that. It's all very helpful information for us.

'I'll text her, if you want to meet her?'

I nodded. 'If that's okay.'

'It's fine.'

'How well did you know Donna?' I asked.

'Not that well, really. I saw an advert for the band and after I auditioned, they asked me to join.'

'How about Lisa Day? Do you know her?'

'Not really. I was only in the band for a bit. We'd rehearsed as a three-piece for a while but it wasn't working, so I left. Donna and Lisa just carried on as a duo.'

Which explained why it was *2's Company,* I thought. Sarah smiled at me. She'd obviously had the same thought.

'Why did you leave the band?' I asked.

Katie fell silent. 'It's a long time ago now.'

I wasn't sure if she was hoping I'd increase what I paid her. 'Didn't you get on with Donna and Lisa?' I asked.

She shrugged. 'We got on alright. Donna brought along this guy, Frank, who she wanted to manage us.'

'Frank Salford?'

'That's him.'

'But you weren't keen?'

'I didn't like him.'

I nodded. 'Why not?'

'He was a sleazeball. I never felt comfortable around him or his people.'

I wondered if I'd done the right thing trying to see him earlier today. I might have tipped him off to our interest in Donna. Maybe he had something to do with her disappearance. I cursed myself.

'What did he do for the band?' I asked.

'Not a lot. When he got bored, he dropped us. The gigs stopped and I left.'

I leaned forward. 'Where did Donna go, Katie?'

'No idea. One minute she was here, the next she was gone.'

'She didn't tell you anything, you were in a band together?'

She laughed. 'We sang in shitty pubs and clubs. It wasn't like The Beatles had split up. They carried on for a couple more months and I got on with other things.'

'Did you ever hear from Donna again?' Sarah asked.

'Never. I heard she owed Frank some money and did a runner.' She shrugged. 'Maybe she did.'

'Maybe' I said, thinking it was a bit of an extreme reason to leave. But then again, I'd not met Frank Salford. I took a £20 note out of my wallet and placed it on the coffee-table along with my card. 'If you think of anything, give me a call.'

She nodded, turned away and said she would. I offered to buy Sarah lunch, once we were done with our next appointments. It'd delay telling Don what I'd done.

Sonia Bray was in her late thirties and without wishing to be unkind, she was the very definition of mousey. We'd agreed to meet in Queens Gardens. I found an empty bench and made sure I was holding the newspaper in my hand, as arranged. She sat down next to me and explained her office was only a five minute walk away.

'Thanks for meeting me' I said, offering her a smile. 'I appreciate it.' I told her what had happened to Jennifer Murdoch.

Bray nodded and composed herself. 'Obviously no one deserves to be murdered, but I've moved on. I told Sheila I'd try to help you if I could.'

I looked at the notes I'd made. 'Sheila said you had to leave the company.' I left the question open-ended, to encourage her to explain in her own words.

'Jennifer Murdoch,' she started, 'took advantage of me. I had personal problems and I couldn't think straight. I'm not proud of what happened but I couldn't stop it.'

'Something about missing money?'

She nodded and put her drink down. 'The auditor found some discrepancies in the accounts. I'm only the person who inputs invoices and payments and such like, but I can't sit here and pretend I understand how accounts are prepared. What the auditor was saying didn't make sense to me but Jennifer started saying it was my fault. With all the problems I was having, I couldn't think it through. Eventually, Jennifer said the auditor has completed their investigation and there was a problem. She said she had no choice but to sack me. If I left quietly, she'd make sure I received a severance package and a good reference. If I didn't go quietly, she'd recommend to Mr Briggs that I was sacked.'

'Not a pleasant position to be in' I said, knowing she'd chosen to leave quietly.

'I didn't think I'd done anything wrong but I couldn't be sure, either. My mother was ill and I didn't want to upset her unnecessarily.'

'And you didn't want Briggs to become involved?'

She shook her head. 'Jennifer said he'd call the police.'

'What's Mr Briggs like to work for? We only met him a couple of days ago. He struck me as the kind of man who

36

doesn't suffer fools lightly. Would you say that's reasonable?'

'Very much so. Some people think he's a bit mean, but he's not. He expects you to do the job he pays you to do. It's perfectly normal, surely?'

'Of course. What was the severance package?'

'Jennifer gave me £1,000 and told me to go. She'd make sure there was no further action and I got the reference I needed.'

'And that was the end of the matter?'

'Until Sheila said she had her suspicions and I started to think it through. We meet occasionally for a drink. She told me about the holidays Murdoch was taking with her husband, the designer clothes she was wearing and the expensive jewellery.'

'Christopher Murdoch's a successful businessman. I assume they could afford things like that if they wanted them?'

She shook her head and smiled. 'I was always taking telephone calls on her behalf from people chasing her for money. Obviously I can't be sure, but I don't believe they were as wealthy as she made out.'

I thought I knew where she was heading. 'And you'd think if the auditors thought there was a discrepancy, they'd have an obligation to tell Briggs?' I said, partly thinking aloud.

'Exactly.'

'But Jennifer dealt with it all?'

'She did.'

'Did she pay you the money with a company cheque?'

'No. Cash.'

Untraceable. I sat back and thought about it for a moment.

'But how would it work? Why didn't the auditors blow the whistle to Briggs?'

'Jennifer used to work for the auditors.'

Of course. I smiled to myself. I remembered Sheila telling me that. 'She knew the person the auditors sent, didn't she?' I said, smiling to myself.

Bray looked me in the eye for the first time. 'That's right.'

Sarah had beaten me to the cafe, so I quickly read the menu and ordered our drinks and food. I went for a much needed shot of caffeine and a BLT sandwich, Sarah opting for a healthier juice and salad combination.

'How did you get on?' I asked.

Sarah put her drink down. 'Yeah, interesting. She worked with Donna, but she didn't really know her that well.'

I wasn't surprised. The difficulty in this job was judging whether people were able to help you, or just wanted to take the money. Maybe I was more cynical than Sarah, but I'd back myself to sniff-out a time-waster and I hadn't been impressed with Glew when we'd met her, even though she'd immediately set up a meeting between her friend and Sarah.

'They'd worked on the same production line, packing aerosol cans' Sarah explained. 'They weren't really close friends, more mates you see at work. This was just over four years ago and she's not heard from Donna since.'

'Where did she go?'

'She didn't know. Apparently, she walked out and didn't come back.'

I thought about it. 'Why? It doesn't make sense.'

'That's what happened. No swapping of phone numbers, no leaving drinks, nothing.'

'What could she tell us?'

'Not much. There was a boyfriend on the scene but she never met him. He worked at the factory as well.'

'Still there?'

She nodded. We'd be talking to him.

'We're not much further forward, are we?'

Sarah shrugged. 'We know Donna was definitely in Hull a few years ago. She might still be here.'

'Without her family knowing?'

'It's a big city.'

That was true. It was big enough to get lost in if you wanted to. 'Did you get any other leads at the factory?' I asked.

'No.'

'But we got the boyfriend's name?'

'I've already rang it through to Dad.'

It was something. Don might be able to dig something out.

'I also went to the shop on Hessle Road where Donna worked' Sarah said.

'Which shop?'

'The one her mother told me about. She worked part-time in an off-licence. I went on the off-chance somebody remembered her. It's a horrible place; one of those which has its employees behind a big Perspex screen and you have to shout to make yourself heard.'

I knew the sort she meant. They were everywhere nowadays. If there was an off-licence, it was likely there would be groups of kids hanging around outside. And that usually meant trouble. 'Any luck?' I asked.

'I spoke to the owner. She remembered Donna. Her son, who'd also worked in the shop, had dated her for a while, but they've not heard from her once she left the shop. She dumped the son and that was that.'

'And that was before she formed *2's Company*?'

'Around the same time. I got the details of the son, though, so we can speak to him. I think they'd like to know what happened to Donna, too.'

The food arrived and as we started to eat, I turned my thoughts to Jennifer Murdoch. What concerned me most was that the police themselves were watching the house. I was embarrassed I'd been seen there, but Don wasn't the kind of person who dwelt on such things. He didn't need to say anything. The lesson has been learnt. So far, our inquiries into Murdoch had produced little. Certainly not enough to give an insight into the police surveillance. If the police weren't looking at her, it made sense that they had to be watching her husband.

'Still with us?' asked Sarah, placing her knife and fork down.

I apologised and told her I was miles away. I didn't want to voice my suspicions about Christopher Murdoch yet. I wanted to know more about him first.

Five

As I expected, Don had gone ballistic. I'd sat in my chair and let him tear a strip off me. He'd thrown the file he'd put together on Frank Salford at me. Since leaving the licensed trade, Salford had been busy. His massage parlour was well known to the police and several undercover operations had been mounted, though nothing had stuck. There was also the suggestion he was linked to organised crime, through the Eastern European women he employed. I thought back to the women who were working in the parlour and knew he wasn't somebody you messed with lightly. I had no idea what I was getting myself involved in. After Don had calmed down, I told him what we'd learnt about Donna Platt. Although we hadn't found her, we knew she'd been in Hull much more recently than we had thought. Sarah had trawled public records and hadn't found any reference to her death, so we had to assume she was still alive. Don was pleased with the progress, but mindful of the lack of money coming in. I'd decided it was his problem. If he wanted to take Sarah to task on the matter, that was his business. I looked at my list of phone calls to return and decided I wasn't in the mood.

'I need to know what happened to Jennifer Murdoch' I said to Don. I was chewing the end of a biro. 'I spent a couple of hours being questioned.'

'But they won't have you down as a serious suspect.'

'I don't want to be any kind suspect.'

Don pulled up a chair and sat down. 'It's procedure. Nothing to worry about.'

'I'm not worried' I said, though I didn't necessarily believe it.

'It needs to run its course, that's all.'

'What do you really know about Coleman?'

'Not much. I'm waiting to hear back but word is he's a decent guy. All I know about him is that he transferred in from Sheffield a few years back. I know you don't like him, but from what I can gather, he won't mess you around.

Don picked my mug up and asked if I wanted a coffee. I nodded and thought about things. Whether or not Coleman is on the level, I don't want to be under suspicion. Don carefully placed the steaming mug on my desk. 'I'm going to take a look at Murdoch's husband' I said. 'If the police were watching the house, it seems reasonable to assume they were looking at him.'

'Because we've not turned up anything on Jennifer Murdoch?'

I nodded. 'It seems logical.' I'd done some more research.

'Managing Director of FutureVision Limited. Jennifer Murdoch is also listed as a director and company secretary.'

'Doesn't necessarily mean anything, though, does it? She could be involved for tax reasons?'

I nodded my agreement and passed over some print-outs, including several newspaper articles. Christopher Murdoch had become a local celebrity, never far from the headlines. 'He formed the company five years ago, just as the regeneration boom started to take grip around the city. Before that, he'd led government funded organisations in delivering similar projects. I assume he discovered the private sector was more lucrative.

One thing you had to say Murdoch possessed was vision. He had a clear picture of how the city should develop and what it needed to rival Yorkshire cities like Leeds and Sheffield. Not surprisingly, this ability, together with a seemingly effortless charm, made him a man in demand

and he now seemed to be a consultant on every major project undertaken in the city.

Don handed me the information back. 'A man in demand.'

'Has he been interviewed yet?' I asked.

'I'm sure he will have been but I might find out more a bit later on. I'm meeting Bill for a drink.' Bill was an old colleague of Don's who'd stuck at it when everyone else was getting their years in and leaving. Their friendship went back decades and was invaluable to us on a professional level. Although he'd stop short of giving us the inside track on the investigation, he'd mark our card for us.

'So we don't know about the forensics either?'

'No.'

'Or potential suspects?'

Don shook his head.

I told him about my talk with Sonia Bray.

'And you think she would have sufficient motive for killing Murdoch?'

I was far from convinced myself. It didn't feel right, but I've known such things happen for less. I could tell Don was sceptical but at least he was showing some interest. 'I don't know whether Bray was stupid or naive but the implication that Murdoch and the auditors were acting together is interesting. She was bitter, but she also suggested the Murdochs weren't as well off as you might think. It also made Briggs's attitude easier to understand.' I told Don I'd take a more thorough look at Bray but even if she wasn't involved, she might give us a lead on the underlying cause of Murdoch's murder.

Don stood up and walked across to the telephone. I organised my print-outs on Christopher Murdoch and hole-punched them, ready for filing. I needed to know more and I knew who to ask.

Don sat back down. 'Timewaster.' He passed me a folder to put my print-outs in. 'Sarah rang me earlier and mentioned Donna Platt, but it was only in passing, we didn't get chance to really talk about it.'

'She was definitely in the city more recently than we first thought.' I told him what Sarah had learnt about her working in a local factory.

Don passed me over a sheet of paper. 'The boyfriend from the factory' he said.

I glanced through the information. Once again Don had come up with the goods - convictions for assault stood out.

'I've got us an appointment with someone I used to work with to tell us more about Salford' he said. 'The name makes me nervous. I want to know more about him first hand.'

'When?'

'About an hour's time.'

The telephone rang again. Don answered it, and covering the mouthpiece, told me it was Terrence Briggs. That made it my turn to put the kettle on. I made the usual coffee for myself and a milky tea for Don. I walked back into the office and waited for him to terminate the call.

'He wants to know what's going on.'

'I assume the police have spoken to him again?' I said.

'Dragged him out of a meeting, which upset him, as you can imagine.'

I smiled. 'What did he say?'

'They wanted to run down his alibi. Obviously he can't deny he's got issues with the woman.'

'I suppose not.' I drank a mouthful of coffee and quickly checked my mobile for any new texts.

'Just being thorough. They've got to run down every possible lead.'

'Was he sounding off?'

Don nodded. 'Pretty much. I don't think he's a man who takes very kindly to being questioned. And apparently it's our fault.'

'Why is it?'

'Because we told the police about him.'

'Of course we did. What does he expect?'

'He doesn't think we should be getting him involved.'

'Tough. He is involved. He asked for our help. If he's that bothered, he should have said it to our faces.'

'If I didn't know better, I think being questioned rattled him a bit; put him under pressure.'

Makes two of us, I thought.

'Did you ask him about Sonia Bray?'

'He said Jennifer Murdoch had dealt with it when she sacked her. He was on holiday at the time. He knew he wouldn't get the money back, so he let it drop.'

I wondered if there was more to the story than we knew. Briggs didn't seem like the type of employer who'd be so laid back about an employee stealing from him. I half-listened to Don, as he continued talking, but I had turned my thoughts back to Christopher Murdoch.

We sat in the corner of the pub, well away from the other customers. Although some parts of the city were now overrun with stylish cafe-bars, Anlaby Road remained resolutely old-school. We were waiting for a former colleague of Don's, Gerard Branning, to arrive. Branning had worked in CID all his life before taking early retirement five years ago. Don told me Branning had been involved in several investigations into Frank Salford throughout the last 30 years. He was the man to ask. Don's involvement with Salford had been limited and his knowledge limited to hear-say. Branning still liked to patrol his old stomping ground, so the pub was the best venue. Spotting us in the corner, he ordered a drink and joined us. Don stood up and shook his hand. I did likewise.

'Thanks for coming, Gerard' said Don. 'We appreciate your time.'

Branning sat down. 'When you said it was in relation to Salford, I couldn't resist.'

Don had already briefed me on the history. Salford had been the one who had got away. Seemingly, every detective had one. Despite Branning's efforts, he'd never secured a single conviction against Salford.

'His name's come up in one of our investigations' I said.

'We're looking for someone. She disappeared about ten years ago, aged nineteen. She was in a group managed for a while by Salford.'

'What was the band called?'

'*2's Company*.'

Branning shook his head. 'Doesn't ring a bell, but I remember Salford having a dabble in the music industry. He owned a club for a while and had singers on and the like. It was the place to be seen for a while, if you're into that scene.'

'He runs a massage parlour now' I said.

Branning nodded. 'Amongst other things.'

'I went round there and asked for him' I explained. 'I was escorted off the premises.'

'Sounds about right for our Frank. He's zero tolerance. Even these days. Has Don told you about him?'

I shook my head. Don hadn't had much direct involvement with investigations over the years into Salford's affairs. We'd agreed it was best to let Branning explain.

'Whatever else you might hear, Salford's a career criminal' he started. 'He first came to our attention in the mid to late seventies as one of the top lads in the hooligan gangs. There was a surge in football hooliganism around this time. You'd get gangs from around the city, like the Bransholme lads and the Avenue lads going to the matches, and they were mad. They'd be off their heads on cheap drugs; amphetamines and the like and they travelled around the country on double-decker buses. The traditional rivalry in the city was drawn down the lines of which rugby league team you followed, so the football gangs needed someone to draw it all together. Once Salford had done that, he cashed in on his hooligan kudos. He offered to run the doors of some of the city's nightclubs. Sometimes the offers were made more forcefully, depending upon the owner's attitude. Once he had a way in, he started to control the supply of drugs in these places. His football activities gave him the contacts he needed to get the stuff. As time moved on, he stopped his direct involvement in the football trouble. He knew we were on to him, and frankly, we'd have taken any arrest, even a public disorder offence. In 1979, as the drugs trade became more serious, one of his major rivals in the area disappeared. And when I say disappeared, I mean, totally disappeared. We investigated, as did this man's people. Although the word was Salford was behind the killing, we never came remotely close to building a case. His speciality for dealing with those who crossed him was either burying them alive or throwing them overboard at sea. Not that we ever recovered a body we could connect to him.'

I didn't dare look at Don.

'We had to wait until 1998 for our chance' Branning continued. 'By then he was a major player but he stepped out of line and beat up his mistress, a woman called Julie Richardson.' Branning put his pint down and lent in closer. 'She was known to us as a high end prostitute, so she was given the option of walking away from the game if she agreed to give evidence against him. We had her in a safe house, outside of the city and we learnt more about Salford's business activities in those few weeks then we'd learnt in years.'

I was absentmindedly drumming my fingers on the table top. I'd guessed the ending to the story.

'We got the case to court' said Branning. 'He was charged with GBH and he was looking at some serious prison time and that would have given us an opportunity to really go to work on his empire. But on the first day of the trial, she withdrew her statement. Just like that. We thought we had her safe but he got to her. The bastard got to her. The case was out of the window and he walked out of court a free man. He even came up to me and shook me by the hand and wished me better luck next time. After that he tightened up his operations and we never got anywhere near close to him again.'

'That's when he moved into other areas?' I asked.

Branning nodded. 'He went legitimate on paper. Taxi firm, takeaways, a casino, even. See the link?'

I nodded. 'Cash businesses.' As is the massage parlour, I thought.

Don took over and opened a file. 'I'm still working on this, but it appears he's branched into property in the last few years, becoming some sort of slum landlord.' He passed over some paperwork to Branning, who shook his head.

'I've not heard about this.'

'It's post your retirement, Gerard. And it's low key.'

Branning continued to look at what Don had discovered. 'Usually the guys at the station keep me in the loop. They know what it means to me.'

I quietly sipped at my drink. I wasn't going to be the one who told him his day had been and gone, that his ship had sailed.

Don continued with his outline. 'At the moment, it's a mass of shell companies. It's proving difficult to pin down exactly what he's done, but he's certainly legitimate, on paper at least.'

I looked at the list of properties Don knew Salford owned.

Many of them were three and four bedroom terraced houses at the cheaper end of the market and they were spread across the city.

Branning passed the print-outs back to Don and stood up, ready to leave. 'You just watch yourself with him, son.'

Don and I returned to the office following our meeting with Branning. I tried to catch up on the paperwork, but I wasn't able to concentrate. Don was worried about Salford and told me to leave him to the police. I still felt like I needed fresh air, so I decided to call it a day and walk home. I'd headed down Spring Bank and turned onto Princes Avenue, stopping only for a pint of milk and a night paper. My flat was only a further five minute walk if I hurried. Keeping my head down, I pressed on.

'Got a light?'

I looked up to see a man stood at the top of the tenfoot which snaked around the back of the house containing my flat. When they were first built, the houses were owned by rich, middle class families but now many had been converted into five or six self-contained flats, with large communal grounds to the rear. I didn't recognise him, but the people who lived in the area changed almost monthly. I fished around in my pocket until I found my lighter. I didn't smoke, but I found it useful to carry one in case I spoke to someone who needed a cigarette to calm themselves down. I handed it over and waited for him to light up. Catching me off balance, he grabbed hold of me and I was pulled down the ten-foot and out of sight of the main road. Before I had time to react, a punch to my stomach winded me and I was on the floor, trying to breathe through the pain. Trying to keep my focus on the man, I didn't see the kick to my back coming and I screamed out in pain. His mate must have been waiting further down the ten-foot. I couldn't see him, but he pulled my head up by my hair. The man with the cigarette spat and threw a punch that landed square on my nose. Tasting the blood in my mouth, I knew it was broken. The man behind me pulled me back to my feet. He forced my head around until I was looking directly at the man who had punched me.

'Think of this as the friendly warning, knob-head' he said, before punching me for the final time in my stomach. I collapsed in agony and rolled on to my side, vomiting over the newspaper I'd bought. Closing my eyes, I heard the mens' shoes on the pavement start to fade as they walked away. I checked my pocket to make sure my wedding ring hadn't fallen out and then rolled over.

'Joe.' Sarah looked at me and lent on the frame of her front door. 'It's late.' She was dressed in her pyjamas; I'd woken her.

I nodded. She was right. I'd picked myself up, staggered into my flat and attempted to clean myself up. I wasn't able to settle.

'What happened to you?' she asked.

'It's a long story.'

She sighed. 'You'd best come in, then.'

We walked through the hallway and I heard Lauren shouting, wanting to know what was going on. Sarah ushered me into the front room and said she'd be back once she'd settled her back to sleep. I felt bad. I had no right to be coming here in the middle of the night, waking them up. I'd got myself into this mess, so it was my responsibility to get myself out of it. The truth was, I had nowhere else to turn. More than anything, though, I was frightened.

48

Sarah poked her head around the door and said she'd put
the kettle on. She'd also put a dressing gown on. I looked
around the small room. On top of the television was
several framed photographs of Lauren; some with her
posing with Sarah in the park, some with Don at a theme
park. I smiled; she was a great kid. I jumped when
Buttons, their cat leapt onto my knee. I stroked her on the
top of her head, just as she liked and listened to her purr.
At least somebody was pleased to see me.

'There you go.' Sarah passed me a cup of coffee.
'Decaff.'

'They're great' I said pointing at the photographs.

Sarah looked at me. 'Hopefully she'll settle back down
and be ready for school tomorrow.'

'I'm sorry' I said, noting her displeasure.

'What happened?'

I touched my face. The cuts still stung a little, though
the swelling was already starting to reduce, to be replaced
with bruising. 'I got jumped on my way home.'

'Jumped?'

'A guy asked me for a light, attacked me and I was
dragged down the tenfoot near the flat.'

'Why?'

I shrugged.

'Frank Salford?' She told me she'd spoken to her father
earlier in the evening.

'Makes sense, I suppose. They told me to take it as a
warning.'

'Does dad know?'

'Not yet.'

'He's right, you know. You can't go around trying to
square up to dangerous people like Salford. It's pointless if
it's not done properly. You've got to think things through
and plan accordingly.'

I smiled. It was like listening to Don. I had to agree with
her, though. I told her I was still concerned about the
police's interest in me, and how that didn't exactly
encourage me to speak to them. There had been no official
developments in the investigation into Jennifer Murdoch's
murder.

Sarah tried to reassure me. 'What motive would you have? It's ridiculous. They're just tying up loose ends.'

'They're going to want somebody for it. Her husband is an important man. He'll know the right people to talk to.'

'They're hardly going to fit you up, though, are they? It's not the 1970s. Dad knows them. He won't let that happen.'

She was right but I couldn't think straight. She squeezed my hand and told me I was being paranoid. It didn't make it feel any better.

'Here' she said, passing me a duvet. 'We'll get these cuts cleaned up first and then you can sleep down here.'

I nodded. There was no point in arguing with Sarah. I hoped she was right.

Six

'**What** kind of business do you own, Mr Geraghty?'

'It's a private investigation bureau' I replied.

'Sounds fascinating.'

I smiled. She was trying not to stare at the state of my face.

'Sometimes. It's amazing what you learn.'

'I dare say.'

She passed me her business card and some publicity literature. I briefly looked through the information about Clancy, Knight and Capebourne Chartered Accountants. Her card read Natalie Buckle.

'Is there anything you need to ask me, Mr Geraghty? Any of our services you're unsure about?'

I looked up from the brochures. 'I need to ask you about Jennifer Murdoch.' I watched Buckle's eyes widen. 'You do know her?'

She nodded. 'I can't believe she's dead. It's terrible.'

'I assume you knew her pretty well?'

'Not really. We worked together, that's all.'

I leant forward. 'I'm going to try to help you, Natalie, so don't lie to me, please.'

She looked shocked. 'I'm not lying to you.'

'Okay' I said, hoping to relax her. 'You knew Jennifer through work?'

'She doesn't work here anymore.'

'That's right. She worked for one of your client's, Terrence Briggs.'

Buckle nodded. 'She left here to go and work for him. It's not unusual; clients often poach staff from us.'

'You're not tempted?'

She shook her head. 'No. I like it here.'

'And I suppose with people like Jennifer leaving you get the chance to advance?'

'That and the fact I passed my exams and work hard.'

I nodded. 'Of course. I didn't mean to suggest otherwise. You've obviously done well.'

'Thank you.'

I got to the point. 'I understand there was a problem when you audited Briggs's accounts?'

Buckle shook her head. 'I don't believe so.'

'Some pretty serious accusations have been made.'

'By Mr Briggs?'

'It doesn't matter who.' I leant forward again. 'So far I've not spoken to Mr Capebourne or Mr Briggs about this but I might need to change my mind.' Buckle turned away from me. I got up and closed the door.

'I was stupid' she eventually said. 'Please, you've got to promise me this'll go no further.'

I nodded, but hated myself for the lie. The truth was I didn't know what she was going to tell me, so I had no idea what I was going to do with the information.

'I went out there to do the audit as normal. It was one I was looking forward to because of Jennifer working there. When I'd been training, it was Jennifer who had taken me under her wing. She was the one who trained me and made sure I knew what I was doing. We also got on well away from work. She was like a big sister, I suppose.'

'What did you find in the accounts, Natalie?'

'It was a chance finding, really. I noticed the company had been drawing petty cash cheques almost every week yet their petty cash book said they only drew one per month.'

'Somebody was going to the bank and cashing these cheques? Walking out of the bank with the money?'

'Exactly.'

'What did you do?'

'I spoke to Jennifer about it.'

'Not Mr Briggs?'

'No. I thought it was more appropriate to go to her first. She was the company accountant.'

'What did she say?'

'She took me out for lunch.'

'Lunch?' Murdoch had some nerve, I thought.

'Away from other people listening. She wanted to do it privately. She told me she had a problem with one of her assistants.'

'Sonia Bray?' I asked.

'I don't know, I didn't ask.'

I told her to carry on.

'This assistant had been cashing the cheques and taking the money but she'd only just found out about it. Jennifer said she'd been having some personal problems, stuff with her husband, that kind of thing. So she'd taken her eye off the ball, so to speak. She'd never opened up to me before, so I was flattered she was telling me, I suppose.'

'What was the problem with her husband?'

'Money problems, arguing, the usual kind of stuff. She confessed to me that she wasn't really doing a good enough job and she'd let this assistant get away with it.'

'And you believed her?'

Buckle didn't answer.

'You know what it sounds like, don't you? Why didn't you report the matter to Mr Briggs or your manager? Surely you had a responsibility to do that?' She was upset, but I had little sympathy.

'She asked me for some time, so she could sort it out. The next day she said she could get just under £10,000 back, about half the amount. She said she'd sacked the assistant, so it wouldn't happen again.'

'And you accepted that?'

Buckle was barely whispering. 'She offered me half of the money to not mention it to Briggs.'

I was trying to process the information. 'Why would she do that?'

'Because she said Briggs would sack her if he found out.'

'But she wasn't doing her job properly?'

Buckle shook her head but offered nothing further.

'If it had been her assistant, she didn't really have to worry too much, surely? You went along with her story, despite knowing it wasn't true. It doesn't make sense. You let someone else take the blame. Why would you take the money? You've got a good job.' I shook my head. 'You're a qualified accountant; you could lose your qualification, couldn't you?'

'I needed the money.'

'Sorry?'

'I needed the money. Me and my husband had bought a house, just before the property collapse. Our mortgage deal was about to end, he'd lost his job as a builder and we were struggling. Jennifer offered me a way out. I didn't question it. I suppose I just heard what I wanted to from her.' She sat up straight and held my stare. 'We all have money problems, don't we? I might be lucky enough to have a good job but it's expensive just getting by.'

I thought about Sonia Bray. She'd carried the can for Murdoch and had been taken advantage of.

'Why did Jennifer need the money?'

'I don't know.'

'I think you do. Even if you were complicit in her deception, you must have wanted to know why. You were putting yourself on the line.'

I watched her stand and pace around the room. She was biting at her fingernails. 'What are you going to do?'

'How do you mean?'

'Are you going to tell Mr Capebourne? If he finds out, he'll sack me. I'll lose my job, my qualification, everything.'

I stood up. 'I need to know why Jennifer needed the money.'

'She was gambling. She'd joined a casino. I think her husband had taken her there once and she'd got the bug for it. She told me she'd got into some trouble but her half of the money would clear her and she'd seek help. I wanted to help her.' She turned to me. 'What are you going to do now?'

I shook my head. 'I don't know. I really don't know.'

'You've got a nerve, Joe.'

I flashed her what I hoped was a winning smile but she was right. Jane was sort of an ex, and I hadn't spoken to her in a long time.

'You messed me around, never returned my calls and then you pitch up here expecting my help. Unbelievable.'

I passed her a menu. We were sat in a quiet corner of The Corn Exchange, a pub close to the office. It was late afternoon and I'd spent the last couple of hours delivering warrants. The kind of bread and butter work which keeps our heads above water. I wasn't hungry but it was the only way I could get her to agree to meet me. 'I hear the fish and chips are good.' I placed my wet coat on the back of my chair. So much for the sunshine.

She shook her head. 'You certainly know how to treat a girl, don't you?'

I sipped at my diet coke. 'I know...I should have called you.'

'Save it, Joe.' She flashed a smile at me. 'Water under the bridge.'

I hoped it was true. A mutual friend had introduced us and I'd felt pressurised into asking her out on a date. In truth, I'd had mixed feelings about it. On one hand Jane is an attractive divorcee in her late thirties with everything going for her. On the other hand, it all felt far too soon after Debbie's death. The date had been set up with good intentions, but I was surprised how unprepared I felt. The body was willing but other parts of me less so. When I remembered Jane worked for Christopher Murdoch, I'd made the call. It had felt embarrassing but needs must.

'Let's get one thing straight, though' Jane said. 'I'm still angry with you. I'm only here because I want to help Christopher.'

I nodded and took our order to the food counter. I had about twenty minutes before it arrived. Sitting back down, I asked her how Murdoch was doing.

'As you'd expect,' she said, 'he's in pieces. His wife has been murdered.'

'How about the police? I assume they're in close contact with him?'

I stumbled over my words but Jane cut across me. 'If you mean, are they treating him as a suspect, I don't know. What's your interest?'

I told her I'd been investigating his wife. 'Do you know her?'

'Not really. I'd met her at functions but I wouldn't say I knew her.'

'How was their marriage?'

Jane put her drink down and stared at me. 'I know what you're doing.'

'What am I doing?'

'For whatever reason, you're fishing. I don't know why and I can't say that I want to know. I know how you make a living, Joe, and frankly, I find it a bit strange. All I want to do is help Christopher as much as I can, so whatever it is you want to know, can we get to the point?'

I nodded. Definitely business not pleasure. 'How long have you worked for him?'

'About five years. I met him when we both worked for the council. When he set up on his own, he asked me to come with him.'

'What do you do?'

'I assist him. Work on projects, meet people. It's not a specific job.'

'I assume you two get on?'

'Absolutely. I wouldn't work for him otherwise. He treats me well; I'm well paid, given interesting projects to work on and I'm left to get on with things. And I get to help shape the future of the city. It's perfect for me.'

'And away from work?'

'We don't really socialise too much. We both have lives away from work but I have nothing bad to say about him. He's a decent guy who people warm to. Feel free to ask others who know him.'

I assumed you had to be likeable in some way if you were trying to bend people to your way of thinking. If you're fronting regeneration projects, it's also inevitable you're going to face opposition and be unpopular. 'Has he said anything about his wife's murder?'

'Like what? Do you think he did it?

'I don't know.' I shrugged. 'It wouldn't be the first time it was the husband.'

'Don't be ridiculous. Christopher isn't capable of such a thing.'

I lent closer. 'I'm trying to level with you, Jane. These sorts of things don't happen by accident. If I accept he didn't do it, then it means one of them has seriously pissed someone off. Does he have any enemies?'

'Of course not. He's a businessman, not a gangster.'

'Does he have an alibi?'

'Not that I'm aware of, though he shouldn't need one. He didn't do it.'

She put her drink down and smiled at me. 'How about you? Anybody new on the scene?'

I wondered how she could be so certain about him before telling her there was no one special in my life. The food was brought to our table and we ate in silence.

I was happy to have the excuse of a meeting with Donna's boyfriend from the factory to escape from Jane. It had been a mistake talking to her. As I waited for the barman to give me my change, I picked up my drink and looked around. The pub was run down and practically empty. Shabby, nicotine stained wallpaper adorned the walls, reminding me how much the smoking ban had cost places like this. There were few people in the place, but one or two who'd probably been there since opening time. The old man stood next to me at the bar continued to stare as I walked away. I spotted who I was looking for in the corner and walked across the room.

'Simon?'

He looked me up and down before nodding.

'Joe' I said, introducing myself.

'How did you find me?'

I looked at the man who Donna had met at the factory. He was wearing an out of date Manchester United shirt and dirty jeans. I guessed he was about 40 years old. 'I'm a private detective.'

He snorted. 'That doesn't answer the question.'

'I rang the factory and asked for you.' Sometimes it really was that easy. I got to the point. 'Tell me about Donna Platt' I said.

'Not much to tell.'

He was going to be hard work. 'Did you meet Donna at the factory?'

'Where else?'

The pool table was the only sign of life in the pub, with two teenagers in caps laughing loudly at each other's shots. I looked at the black and white photographs of the local area on the wall whilst I waited for him to elaborate.

'She was on the line I supervise' he eventually said. 'And it just sort of developed.'

I nodded. 'People meet at work and things happen.' My mobile vibrated in my pocket but I ignored it. 'What was Donna like?' I asked.

'Different.'

'Different?'

'Vulnerable. She needed some company, someone to talk to. I suppose I liked being that person.'

I wasn't sure whether his answer was uplifting or just plain creepy. I wondered if he'd taken advantage of her. 'Where did you do your talking?'

'Sometimes in here, sometimes at her flat.'

'Her flat?' I asked him for the details. 'Did she ever talk about her singing career?'

He turned to look at me.

'What singing career?'

'She used to sing around the clubs. She was in a band called *2's Company*.'

He laughed. 'She was a singer?'

I nodded.

'I had no idea.'

'She never mentioned it? I was surprised. The band had been her life.

'Why are you asking me about this?' he asked.

'I need to speak to her.'

'Why?'

'Her mother wants to know she's alright.'

'Can't help you, I'm afraid.'

'You've not heard from her recently?'

'Not since we split up.'

'When was that?'

'Three, four years back. A long time ago.'

'Any idea where she went?'

'None at all.'

'Apparently she just upped and went. Was it because you hit her?'

'What did you say, cunt?'

'Did you hit her?' We were eyeballing each other.

'You best watch your mouth.'

I removed a post-it-note from my pocket. '1992, conviction for assault followed by another in 1995. Charges dropped in 2000. It looks like a habit to me, Simon.' Don had done good work. 'Do your employers know about these?'

'Get fucked.' He'd turned away from me. There was no venom. He was beaten. 'Did you hit Donna?'

'I never laid a finger on her and that's the truth.'

'Where did she go, Simon? I need to know.'

'Look, you can throw your weight around all you like, but I still don't know. Once we finished, I had nothing to do with her. It was easier that way.'

'What about at work?'

'She said she was going to transfer to another shift. I didn't see her and after a while I assumed she'd got herself another job.'

'Away from work?'

'I never saw her again.'

'Why not?'

'My wife found out about us..'

Lauren skipped out of the kitchen, smiling and headed in the direction of the front room.

'It's a good job you can do maths' said Sarah.

I smiled. 'It's maths for nine year olds. Besides, you're supposed to be our book-keeper.' I needed to catch up with Sarah and going to her house was the easiest option. 'I don't remember learning that stuff at nine.'

Sarah playfully punched me on the shoulder. 'It's hard stuff.' She collected up the plates from the dining table and placed them in the sink. 'Sure you're not hungry?'

I said I wasn't and told her not to change the subject. 'It's only percentages.' She'd text me earlier in the evening, asking if I wanted to come round to help with Lauren's homework. The text said I owed, but I was pleased to help. I was pleased not to be sitting by myself in the flat and was determined I'd take the leftovers home with me. I was passed a coffee refill. "You're exaggerating' I laughed. 'It's not quite that difficult.'

'You want to try explaining why you can't help to her teacher.'

'Not at all..' Everything's easy if you know the answer, I thought.

I took the coffee off her and set it down on the kitchen table. Sarah switched the television off.

'Donna Platt's first boyfriend' she said, passing me over a neatly typed report.

I glanced at the in-depth information. 'Tell me about him' I said.

'As we know, Tim Nicholson met Donna at the shop his parents own. They both worked there part-time. Donna was seventeen when they met, Tim was twenty. A bit of a difference when you're that age, but he tells me it wasn't a problem to them.'

'What does Tim do now?'

'He's an account's clerk for a local builders merchants.'

It didn't sound too exciting to me. 'I'd have thought he would have stuck with the family business.'

'They've got three off-licences around the city but he said he wanted to strike out on his own. To be honest, I think he was under his parents thumb in the shop and he wanted away.'

'Did they approve of Donna?'

'At first, but it became fraught. Tim was quite open about it. When they first started dating, everything was fine. Once the band started, her attention turned to trying to be famous. It turned his parents off. His father had worked on the docks as a bobber, unloading the fish off the trawlers when they came home. When the work dried up, he used the money he'd saved to put a deposit down on the first shop. I don't think they had much time for Donna's dreams. They were more traditional. Hard work got you what you wanted. You didn't achieve it through pipe-dreams; that kind of thing.'

'What did Tim think about it?'

'They drifted apart. She wasn't the girl he first started dating. She changed; she became high maintenance. She was loud and difficult for him to deal with. He didn't like what she had changed into.'

'Who dumped who?'

'She dumped him. Said he was too boring for her.'

'Did he get to meet her family?'

Sarah nodded. 'He was a regular visitor to their house.'

'How did he get on with them?' I wanted to know more about Donna's background.

'He said it was difficult at first. Donna's dad, Ron, was part of a crew that'd go out to sea for weeks and come back loaded up with fish. Because Tim's dad worked on the docks, they vaguely knew each other.'

'Did he approve of them being together?'

'Tim said he was keen to see his daughter settled down; married with children. He was quite traditional in that way.'

'Presumably her singing in a band didn't sit well with him, then?'

'No. He didn't approve and apparently they often argued about it. He didn't like the way she dressed, the places she went, or who she was hanging around with.'

'Sounds like he pushed her away.'

'Sounds like it.'

I was intrigued by Ron Platt and wondered what kind of role he had played in forcing his daughter's disappearance. I wanted to know more about the man.

Sarah stood up and checked on Lauren. I heard them go upstairs and get ready for bed. I flicked through the newspaper which was on the table before Sarah came back into the room with a bottle of wine. 'Shall we?'

I nodded and smiled.

'Truth is Joe, I'm under pressure.'

I shrugged. Coleman's problems weren't my concern. I'd considered not answering his call earlier, never mind agreeing to meet in a near-by pub after I'd left Sarah's house.

I wasn't in a rush to go home, and although Don and Sarah had reassured me to a point about not being a potential suspect in Jennifer Murdoch's death, I was intrigued to hear what he had to say.

'We should be working together' he said to me.

'Why?' I wasn't in the mood to make it easy for him.

'We both want the same thing here, don't we? We both want the truth. We might be coming from different angles, but it's the same bottom-line.

I sipped my drink and continued to stare around the bar

Coleman turned to face me, clearly angry. 'For fuck's sake, Joe. I'm not pissing around here. I know we've had some differences in the past but we've got to move forward. Some co-operation might go a long way. I'm sure there are things we can work on together.'

'Work together? My wife is dead.'

Coleman put his drink down and lowered his voice. 'We did our best, Joe. We really did. Nothing got overlooked; everything was given our full attention.'

It was my turn to sigh. I knew I was being unfair, but it was hard to admit it. I couldn't bring Debbie back and though the cliché about time being a great healer contained some truth, I still harboured bitterness towards the police and in particular Coleman. I wasn't surprised he was under pressure to make a breakthrough. On the face of it, Jennifer Murdoch was an upstanding member of the local business community. It was the kind of case which could quickly become the police's worst nightmare. I sat there and said nothing, letting Coleman take the lead.

'It's a chance to start again' he continued. 'I'm sorry for what's happened in the past, really I am.'

'Sorry?' I cut in. 'I lost everything. You didn't.' My hands were ripping up the beer-mat they were holding. I needed to get a grip.

'We can't keep going over old ground, Joe. I know you're still working the Jennifer Murdoch case and I might be in a position to help.'

'How do you know what I'm doing?'

'It's my job to know.'

62

'How's the wife?'

Coleman sighed. 'We don't need to do this.'

'How's your wife?' I repeated.

'She's fine.'

'She was pregnant when we met.' I was going to add, when you were implying I had a hand in my wife's death.

'A girl. She's nearly two now.'

'Congratulations.' I drained my glass and placed it on the bar. 'Be seeing you, then.' I got up and walked out of the pub. I didn't care what he thought we were doing. To me, we were just two men talking, passing the time of day.

Coleman followed me out and shouted. 'Come on, Joe. You know you need me if you want some answers.'

I ignored and him and continued walking, my night ruined.

The drink had made me hungry, so when I returned home, I made myself pasta surprise. The surprise part of the recipe was whatever vegetables were left available in the fridge. I'd stirred in a tin of chopped tomatoes and with the aid of some herbs and pepper, it had at least been edible. Actually making something had helped pass twenty minutes and I still had Sarah's left over lasagne for tomorrow. I switched the stereo on and The Clash leapt out of the speakers. I pressed skip, as they tore into 'I Fought The Law'; it wasn't appropriate.

I thought about the hours spent in the station with Coleman and how I'd let Don down. I'd messed up by going direct to Frank Salford without knowing the full story. It contradicted everything Don had taught me. Not only had I compromised an investigation, I'd paid the physical penalty. I couldn't prove it was Salford's men who had attacked me, but I knew it had to be his doing. More than anything, letting Don down hurt more than the beating. When I had been drifting, it was Don who took a chance on me, who saw the potential in me. He'd treated me like a son, picking me up and putting me back together when I was in pieces.

Our partnership had started about three years ago. Don was a seasoned private investigator with over thirty years police service under his belt. By contrast, I'm still very much learning the ropes. After spending countless years in dead-end jobs, I'd sort of fallen into the profession. To my surprise, I was good at investigating. Although I could do the work, I had no idea how to run a business. And that was when I was introduced to Don. Don was looking towards retirement and wanted to hand his business on. He needed some fresh blood to help him with the work, and had even started to advertise himself as 'Ridley and Son', in an attempt to give the impression the business was more than just one ageing man. It's an unusual profession, and one that Sarah hadn't shown any interest in. With a never ending supply of the desperate, the needy and the downright nasty to deal with, it's certainly not glamorous. Over the last year or so, she'd relented and started to work part-time for us, initially as administration help. When we had needed female help with a surveillance job, she'd proved herself to be a natural. As I fell asleep on the couch, I knew I owed them everything. I needed to get some answers.

Seven

We'd battled through traffic and made good time for our appointment with Maria Platt. She'd agreed to meet us before she went to the doctors. Her illness meant we couldn't be choosy when we spoke to her.

Don had rung me on my mobile as Sarah was driving, to tell me about his drink with Bill, a veteran detective still working the cases, despite being officially retired. Like all forces, Humberside was so short of experienced detectives, it was re-employing retired detectives on short-term contracts. Judging by the leaflet I had been given the previous day, they were desperate. I'd watched the highlights of the police's press conference on the local news bulletin whilst I ate my breakfast. Jennifer Murdoch had drowned in her bath water. She'd put up a fight but to no avail. The detective in charge of the investigation had been interviewed to camera, appealing for anyone who knew anything to come forward. It sounded like Don and Bill had cagily exchanged information last night. Bill told him Murdoch's killer had seemingly gained access by breaking a window, but there was doubt as to how genuine this appeared to be. I assumed from that they meant they were looking at her husband. There were still no DNA results, but that wasn't unusual. These things moved slowly, even in urgent situations. Don had told Bill what we knew about Jennifer Murdoch's life, which admittedly still wasn't a huge amount. The police hadn't been aware of Sonia Bray and her link to Murdoch and I felt guilty thinking about the storm I could have brought down on her. She was fragile enough.

Walking down Hessle Road, I could see the decay of the area. When Hull had been a thriving port, with plentiful employment, this area was the city's heartbeat. Now, it was run-down and being slowly abandoned. Many of the residents had left and those who remained suffered from anti-social behaviour, with some parts of the area all but out of bounds to non-residents. Shop units which hadn't been left to stand empty were generally run down and shabby. A few major chains still remained in the area, some I knew had been there since its heyday, but it was mainly local traders scratching out a living. It was the kind of area which seemed to lack hope and had been allowed to just wither away. It made me angry.

Maria Platt's house was as I expected; old-fashioned but neat and tidy. It was situated on one of the many rows of terraces, which ran like spiders legs off the main drag of shops. The furnishings and electrical goods were out of date, but that was the least of her problems. We sat down on the settee and she introduced us to Derek, her brother.

'Have you got some news?' she asked us. 'I want her back here with me. I know I've not got long left and I can't begin to tell you how that makes me feel.' She looks terrible; underweight and gaunt. Her voice raspy and thin.

Her eyes still have a sparkle of hope but I shake my head. 'I'm sorry. Not yet.'

Sarah took over. 'We've been speaking to some of Donna's friends; the girls she was in the band with. They suggested Donna didn't get on too well with her father.'

Derek cut in. 'Ron loved his kids. Donna was always the apple of his eye.'

'I'm sure he had their best interests at heart' I said, hoping to sound diplomatic, 'but we need to at least discuss it. If we can understand how Donna was thinking and acting, then it might help us find her. It's surprising how the smallest detail can help.'

The room was silent. Maria Platt looked at her brother and nodded before turning back to us. 'Ron loved our kids. It was like Derek said.'

Sarah and I sat quietly, allowing her the time to tell her story.

'It was difficult raising the kids. It was difficult for me with Ron working away for weeks on end. I was at home trying to bring them up right; keep them on the straight and narrow. Because Ron got paid depending how much fish they caught, I never knew how much money he would bring home. Sometimes it was next to none. It was tough to run a house under those conditions.'

'A three day millionaire?' I said.

Derek smiled. 'Those were the days, alright.'

I'd read that when the trawlermen returned to Hull, they'd often pick up substantial pay packets. The men worked hard and played hard, taxiing around the city and spending their money in the pubs of Hessle Road, before heading back to the docks for another trip.

'Ron had a family to look after' Maria said.

'But he was a drinker' said Derek.

Maria tutted and looked away.

'They need to know how things were' he said to her. 'If it helps to find our Donna, you've got to tell them how it was.'

Maria nodded. 'He liked a drink. He didn't always arrive home with the money.'

'And I was as bad as anyone' Derek said. 'We'd go drinking, and once we'd started, we wouldn't stop.'

'Did you have a family to support?' Sarah asked.

He shook his head. 'Not at the time, no.'

Maria had turned away. It was obvious she hadn't approved of their behaviour. I asked her what her husband had done once the trawler industry disappeared.

'He never worked again.'

'Never?'

'Just the odd days here and there; working on a building site, you know, that kind of thing.'

'I suppose it was difficult, given the skills he had' said Sarah.

'There was nothing for most of the men around here once the fishing went. I learnt to get by on his dole money.' She shrugged and looked at her brother. 'It's what we had to do.'

I knew it wasn't true because Donna's boyfriend's parents had opened an off-licence and made a decent living. I mentioned his name to her.

'Tim was a nice boy' she said. 'I liked him.'

'Did your husband approve of them?'

'Oh yes. He thought Donna should go steady with him and settle down; buy a house and start a family, like we did.'

'And Tim was a good bet?'

'His mam and dad have done well for themselves. He saved his money and they eventually opened themselves a shop. They've done well.' Sarah had told me about the shop. I assumed Maria Platt was ignoring the gangs of youths who congregated outside of it and the necessity of Perspex glass within the shop. It didn't seem like paradise to me. Her voice contained a trace of bitterness. Reading between the lines, it sounded like her husband had wallowed in self-pity whilst others used their money more wisely. I wondered how bitter that had left him, what kind of man he became.

'What happened with Tim?' asked Sarah.

'Our Donna chucked him; said he was boring. A mistake, if you ask me.'

'Boring?' I repeated.

'She said they were stuck in a rut, always going to the same places, seeing the same people. Donna wanted a bit more from life than just getting married and becoming a housewife.'

Sarah said nothing and neither did I. Life had been disappointing for Maria Platt and she wanted better for her daughter.

'How did your husband feel when she dumped Tim?' I asked.

'He wasn't best pleased' Maria Platt eventually said.

'Did they argue about it?' I asked.

She nodded. 'All the time. They fought like cat and dog. He'd lose his temper and tell her she was stupid. He thought she should get a steady job. She'd tell him it was none of his business; it was her life and she'd please herself. I was stuck in the middle, trying to keep the peace.'

I sat forward. 'Did he threaten her, Maria?'

Derek lent forwards. 'I don't like where you're heading with this.'

I held my hands up. 'I'm sorry. I don't mean to imply anything. I'm trying to understand the state of her relationship with her father.' I turned to Maria. 'What did he think of her being in a group?'

'He hated it. He didn't understand it, I suppose. He didn't like the thought of her being in nightclubs, having the men in the crowd leering after her. He hated it all, the whole thing, I suppose.'

'Did they argue about it?'

She nodded. 'All the time. He tried to ban her from being in the band. She just laughed at him.'

'Did she ever mention Frank Salford?'

'Why would she?' asked Derek. Sarah stared at me. I got the message.

'He used to manage the band' I said.

Maria Platt looked at her brother before shaking her head. 'She never mentioned him.'

I had to ask. 'Do you think your husband knew the band had a manager?'

'I doubt it. I'd have been the one to know, and if I'd known, I'd have told him.' She searched for a new tissue. 'Should we know this man?'

I shook my head. 'No. Not at all.'

Maria Platt waited for me to sit back down and looked me in the eye. 'I just wanted Donna to be happy.'

But your husband drove her away, I thought. 'Why didn't you report her as missing?'

She didn't respond. Sarah moved over to comfort Maria Platt. I didn't feel great about what I'd said, but we were getting somewhere. Donna had obviously been opposed to her father. Derek looked at his sister and Sarah huddled together, nodded to me and suggested we went for a walk.

Derek clearly intended our walk to take us no further than the nearest pub, which had just opened for the day. It was the kind of place where new faces weren't very frequent, or particularly welcome. Derek nodded silent greetings to a few of the men stood around the bar, but no one acknowledged me. The walls were decorated with old black and white photographs of Hull FC from days gone by and photographs of old trawlers. One of the 1980 Challenge Cup Final team caught my eye. I recognised all the faces; even knew some of them back in the day. I'd learnt how to play the game alongside and against them as a boy. I wondered what they were all doing now. The rivalry between the two Hull clubs is still intense and as a former KR player, I was very much in enemy territory. I'd only ever played in one derby match, and that had been at Craven Park, our home ground. The noise had been incredible, the game so much more intense. I can still hear the individual voices calling out; encouragement from my fans, abuse from the opposition.

'Cheers' said Derek, taking hold of the pint I'd bought him. He steered us over to the far corner of the pub, away from the handful of other drinkers.

'Cheers' I replied. I waited for him to put his drink down and gather his thoughts.

'I remember when you'd come back from sea and the pubs would have pints already pulled, ready on the bar for you. That was some sight, I can tell you. All the glasses lined up neatly, full to the brim.'

'Must have been quite a sight.'

'It was.' He placed his glass down and looked at me. 'Mr Geraghty' he started.

'It's Joe' I said.

'Joe, then. I wanted to talk to you away from the house. Try to explain a little better that Ron wasn't a bad man, but Maria doesn't understand what it was really like for us at sea.' He put his drink down and continued. 'It was hard work on the trawlers; unbelievably hard work. We'd work eighteen hours a day and there was no time for niceties like washing or eating properly. Even sleeping was difficult on the boats. We'd often be six men to a small room and the bunks were so small, you just wedged yourself in, which was no bad thing, given the conditions. As for the noise, it was 24 hours a day because you were often next to the engine room, and that was before the weather conditions. You'd get thrown about the place and the noise and coldness as you sailed through ice was beyond belief.' He looked at me. 'It was beyond horrible.'

I just nodded. I couldn't begin to comprehend what it must have been like working under those conditions. 'Did you work on the same trawlers as Ron?' I asked.

'We did for a while, but he left to join another company. We were both deckies. We'd haul the fish into the boats, gut them and pass them down to the storage area. The tough thing was, we'd only get paid if we got a decent catch, so it was a competitive carry-on. If the skipper found us a decent fishing spot, we'd milk it all we could. We'd work slightly longer and even in dangerous conditions. Anything to bring home a decent catch so we got paid. There was once when Ron and me came home with absolutely nothing after our food money and what not had been deducted by the bosses. It was a bit of a one-off as there were always alternatives available to you. We'd remove the livers and boil them to make cod liver oil to sell when we returned home. It was our bonus, if you like. Of course, if you were Ron, you'd try and make your bonus from playing cards. When you weren't working that hard, like when you were sailing out to the fishing waters, the place to go was the canteen. We'd smoke our cigs, talk and listen to foreign radio which piped in new music we'd not yet heard. It was great, just spending time with your mates.'

'Ron was a card player?'

'There was always a card school on the go, but Ron wasn't the best at it to be honest. He'd often leave a boat owing people money, which wasn't the plan, or something our Maria was very happy about.'

Hardly surprising, I thought.

'Ron could usually make it up a bit at Christmas when the Christmas Crackers would go out. You'd make excellent money if you had a decent catch, but it was a risky business, alright. Because most of the regulars wanted to spend Christmas at home, the crews would be padded out with anyone who wanted the work. Just chuck them onto the boat and get going.'

Derek glanced at his empty glass. It was my round again.

After his story, I needed the break. I knew you had to be tough to survive on the trawlers, but I never knew just how tough. I placed the fresh drinks on the table and asked him what it was like once the industry had disappeared.

'Harsh. We got nothing at all. Not a thing.' He held his left hand up. 'Didn't even escape with a full set of fingers.

'The Cod Wars?' I said, not wanting to look at the gap where his index finger once was.

'Once Iceland said we couldn't fish their waters, our government rolled over and threw the towel in without a thought to us workers. It was disgusting. We had our nets cut and Ron once told me a trawler he was on was rammed. Scary as hell that kind of thing. Our government sold us out. We were allowed to fish in their seas up to a certain amount, but it was a fraction of what we'd done in the past.'

'What did you and Ron do after that for work?'

He laughed. 'Work? What work? We weren't trained to do anything else. Nobody wanted to know us. I was one of the lucky ones. My brother-in-law ran his own business, so I got some work on building sites, just labouring to start, but it worked out alright and I was a foreman until I retired.'

'What about Ron?'

'Hardly ever worked again. I got him a few days here and there but it wasn't for him.'

'What about redundancy money? What did he do with it?'

He laughed again. 'There was no redundancy pay. I don't know how it worked, but we never qualified for any. In legal terms, we were casual labour. We had no rights.' He lent in towards me. 'If you owned the trawlers, you were fine. You received compensation for your boats not earning and what have you. They didn't suffer, believe me.'

'You got nothing?'

'We got something eventually. Ron worked for over twenty years on them trawlers, but because of the various legal loopholes, he only got a few hundred quid off the government.' Derek shook his head. 'A few hundred pounds, it's insulting.'

'Was he bitter?'

'Wouldn't you be?'

I nodded. Under those circumstances, I probably would be.

'And that was before the pension carry-on. When you went to sea, you had to pay in to a pension scheme. There was no choice. Ron and me thought we had some decent money coming to us. I was lucky, my pension was waiting for me. It wasn't much, but it helped. Ron wasn't so lucky. Because the companies who owned the boats disappeared, nobody knew how to get their money. I was lucky because the company I worked for continued to trade, but the people Ron worked for shut down. He got nowhere trying to get what he was owed. The pension people reckon they paid the money out to the companies for them to give to us, but they say there's no paperwork. I know most people have got their money now, but there's still some who haven't and the insurance companies have washed their hands of it all. Ron didn't live to get his money and Maria's in no state to fight these people.'

'So Ron had to bring up his kids on benefits?'

'Maria brought them up on benefits. Ron more or less gave up.'

'I assume it affected his relationship with them?'

I watched Derek finish his drink. 'Whatever happened, he loved his kids. They were his world. But I have to admit he was harsh to them at times. He sometimes took his frustrations out on them but I know he only wanted the best for them.'

'Like with Donna and her band? What was his problem? Surely it was a good thing? Showed she was determined and had a bit of ambition?'

He shrugged. 'I don't think he could relate to it all. He wanted Donna to be secure and that meant settling down and getting married. He didn't think she'd find that security by becoming a singer.'

'Were their arguments ever violent?'

He shook his head. 'Never. Ron was a decent man. He wouldn't do that.'

On balance, I believed him. 'How did his death affect the family?'

'As you'd expect. Maria and Gary were devastated. The doctors didn't catch the cancer early enough, so there was little they could do. If the stupid bugger had been a bit more willing to see them when he was ill, it might have been different. Maria nursed him at home, all the way to the end. It was tough on her, but it was the way she wanted things. Have you ever experienced it first-hand, Joe?'

I shook my head. 'No.'

'Try and keep it that way.'

We sat there in silence for a few moments until Derek told me he knew Frank Salford. 'I know what he is, too.'

'So do I. Don't worry about that. Just leave him be for now whilst we get what we need on him.'

I watched Derek take a mouthful of lager. 'Alright?' I said.

'Alright.'

'Why didn't Ron report Donna missing to the police?' I asked, changing the subject.

It took Derek a few moments to answer. 'Ron was a proud man, Mr Geraghty. I don't think he wanted to admit it was his fault, that his attitude drove her away. He always told me she was old enough to make up her own mind. If she wanted to come back, she knew where to find us.'

I thanked him for his time. Although I still didn't know why Donna had left, I knew more about her upbringing. Undoubtedly, it had been tough for her; her family had little money, and her father for all his faults, had endured a tough life at sea followed by disappointment when the industry died. What puzzled me was if she left the city to further her music career, why didn't any of her band mates know more? It didn't ring true.

'Did she tell you anything more?' I asked Sarah. I hoped getting Derek out of the house would make her more talkative. We were back in the car and heading towards Lauren's school where Sarah needed to be for a merit assembly. I was going to walk to the office from there and catch up on some paperwork.

74

'Not directly' she explained, 'but I'm convinced she was scared of her husband. He certainly ran the family. His word was always final.'

'Did she say anything more about not reporting Donna to the police?'

Sarah nodded before hitting the brakes to avoid a car pulling out of a side street.

'Wanker...sorry, what did you say?'

'About reporting Donna missing.'

She shook her head. 'Her husband's word was final. He insisted she'd come back when she ran out of money. Her opinion wasn't needed, or wanted.'

My mobile rang but I didn't recognise the number. I answered and listened to the caller, saying little in response. 'Can you drop me at the office, please, Sarah?'

She turned to look at me. 'Who was it?'

I said I'd be there inside of fifteen minutes before terminating the call. 'That was Christopher Murdoch. He wants to talk to me.'

Murdoch was waiting for me on the doorstep of our office. He stood staring at his mobile, clearly agitated. Don must have been called out. I introduced myself, shook his hand and took a moment to have a good look at him. From the information I'd pulled on him from Companies House, I knew he'd just turned forty. Even though he hadn't shaved for a few days or washed his hair, it was clear he was in good shape and looked like he took good care of himself. The passing of time had been kind to him so far. I invited him in and sat down behind my desk.

'What can I do for you, Mr Murdoch?' I asked.

He was looking at the floor as he replied. 'I need your help.'

I waited for him to lift his head. 'Why?'

'The police think I killed my wife.'

I let it hang there for a short while. My initial reaction was he didn't seem the kind to kill, but it takes all sorts. He was an obvious suspect. 'What brings you here, Mr Murdoch?'

'I heard you were already involved, that you were investigating my wife.' He held his hands up. 'I just know, ok?'

The police had told him. There was no other explanation.

'You're already up to speed' he continued. 'I didn't kill me wife and I need you to find out who did.'

I wasn't sure what it meant. I tried to think it through. If the police had told him about me and cut him loose, did they really suspect him of his wife's murder? Or were they looking to me do their job for them by proving Murdoch's innocence or guilt for them? He was too high profile to simply disappear. He had to make some sort of move. I shuffled some papers. 'I'm afraid I can't help you. We're snowed under at the moment.'

I watched him produce a roll of twenty pound notes. 'Will this help?'

'It's not about the money.'

He lent forward across the desk and placed the roll in front of me. 'I need to be in the loop. My legal team tell me I need an investigator to help me. I want to clear my name.' He shrugged. 'I don't care about all the other stuff. She was my wife. I need to know.'

I looked at the money. We could certainly use it but I wasn't sure. I also wondered what he meant when he said other stuff.

'I don't care what you think of me, Mr Geraghty. Look, just take the money and do the job I'm asking you to do.'

I pushed the money back across the table. The way he'd offered it to me felt like an insult, like he thought he could buy me. Putting aside the question of money, he hadn't offered me a single good reason why I should start digging about on behalf of a man the police suspected of murdering his wife. I escorted him to the door.

Eight

After throwing Murdoch out of the office, I'd had time to get some fresh air and buy a sandwich before meeting Julie Richardson. Don had reluctantly tracked her down for me using public records. She'd been keener to speak to me about Salford than I'd anticipated. I sat on a small chair in her front room. Her flat occupied the upper floor of a converted terrace property and was only a couple of streets away from where Maria Platt lived. I knew Richardson was in her early fifties, but she could have passed for several years older. Like the area, she'd seen better days and was in need of a make-over. She passed me a mug of coffee and sat down opposite me.

'You can ask if you want' she said and pointed to the scar on her face.

It had been the first thing I'd noticed. The scar stretched from just underneath her eye, went around her cheekbone and stopped just short of her mouth.

'A present from Frank' she said.

I nodded and wondered what I was getting involved in. She lit a cigarette and offered one to me. I shook my head and let her continue.

'What's your interest in him?' she asked.

I told her about Donna Platt, and how he didn't like me sniffing around. She explained she wanted her revenge, the reason being obvious. I asked her to start at the beginning.

She nodded and took a long drag on her cigarette.
'Frank was a bastard; an absolute bastard from the minute
I met him, but that's not to say he wasn't a bastard who
didn't have his moments. I was 21 when we met. Too
young to know any better. Frank was very much on the up
by then and I liked the money, the buzz, everything about
him. It was a turn on, I suppose. Like an idiot, I thought
we were going places, but Frank was just high on the
power it gave him. He controlled it well, as he was mainly
about the business, but if you crossed him, you knew
about it. It worked well for years. He was married, which
was fine. I knew from the start what I was getting
involved in, but that was part of the deal. He bought me a
house which I lived in and he bought me plenty of
presents. I kept a low profile; that was the deal.'

'Did his wife know about you?'

Richardson shrugged. 'No idea. Never met or asked
about her. It was an off-limit's topic.'

Branning had photocopied us a set of notes he kept, so I
already knew some of her background, but it was useful to
hear it first-hand. I asked her to explain about the work
she did for Salford.

'Basically, I managed one of his clubs. He'd opened a
string of them around the city. Frank always had a soft
spot for the kind of entertainment you got in a working
man's club. I don't know why, I thought it was shit and
even then it was a dying game. I got the North Hull club
and Frank let me oversee things; hiring and firing, booking
entertainment, that kind of thing. And of course it suited
Frank, as he knew where I was.'

'Did you know Donna Platt? *2's Company*?'

'The name rings a bell.'

'Frank managed them.'

Richardson laughed. 'He managed a lot of bands. I
wasn't stupid. I knew Frank was shagging anything that
moved, and the singers were more than willing.'

'I got the impression the other girls in the band didn't
like him.'

'Wouldn't surprise me. If he wasn't interested, he could
be pretty blunt.'

'Did he like Donna?'

'Are you asking me if they were fucking?'

I nodded. No point beating around the bush if she was going to be so blunt.

She shrugged. 'Maybe. It's a long time ago. I can't be sure. The name rings a bell, but that's all.'

I changed the subject. 'Why were you willing to give evidence against him?'

She lit another cigarette and composed herself. 'By then Frank had me running his massage parlour, but when I say massage parlour, I mean knocking shop. The police came for us and because it was my name on the paperwork, I was going to take the fall. The police had other things on me, so I was looking at some serious prison time.'

'So you cut a deal?'

She nodded. 'They said they'd look after me, make sure I was alright. They had this twat in charge, Branning, he was called. Didn't know his arse from his elbow.'

I told her I'd met him and he still carried the case with him.

'So he should.' Her hand went to the scar. 'He put me in a safe house and told me Frank would never find me.' She stood up. 'Do you want a drink? I think I need one.'

I shook my head and waited for her to return and continue.

'Frank obviously had someone on his payroll, because he found me. He told me if I gave evidence against him, he'd kill me. I knew what he was like, so I wasn't taking the chance.'

'And that's when he cut you?'

'No. He's not that stupid. He waited until the charges were formally dropped. He'd kicked me out of the house, of course, but I thought that was it. He'd won. The police were never going to get another chance like that. He was bulletproof. He tracked me down to a friend's house where I was staying and I was home alone. He sat on the doorstep for ages, talking through the letterbox. I sat on the bottom stair, I can still even remember the colour of the carpet, and listened. He told me how much he loved me, how he shouldn't have involved me in his business. Stupidly, I let him in. He said he wanted to talk and make sure I was alright after all that had happened. Like an idiot, I believed him. Once he was inside, he cut me.'

'Did you report it?'

She laughed again. 'What for? The police wouldn't do anything and I had no proof.'

I had to agree.

'But the thing is, I'm not scared of him now. I've got nothing on him now. Anything I knew is useless nowadays. I'd like to see him taken down. He's not going to pay for what he did to me, but if you've got something on him, I want you to make him pay.'

Following my meeting with Julie Richardson, I headed back to the office for some time to think. My talk with her had left me disturbed. I knew Frank Salford was unpleasant, it came with the territory, but looking at Richardson's face, I was surprised how unpleasant he was. What disturbed me even more was his name looming large in both inquiries. It seemed increasingly likely he'd had a hand in Donna Platt's disappearance, but we still had no idea where she was.

Rather than going to the pub, which had been my original plan, I decided to walk home and visit the supermarket in the St Stephen's shopping centre. It was the kind of superstore you could get lost in. It seemed to take an age to walk from one end of it to the other before I settled on my usual selection of staple items. I treated myself to a ham and mushroom pizza, and although it was hardly fine dining, it hit the spot. I stood at my flat's large bay window for a few moments, looking down on the street. A few students silently hurried by but it was a quiet night out there. With a couple of bottles of beer settling nicely and Steve Earle's masterpiece, 'El Corazon' on low on the stereo, the day spent inquiring about Ron Platt and Jennifer Murdoch was fading from my mind, if only on a temporary basis. My relaxation was interrupted by the noise of the flat's buzzer. I peered out of the window but saw nothing. If the person stood close to the communal front door, they were out of my eye-line. I left my door on the latch and walked down the stairs. I could see the silhouette of my visitor through the frosted glass of the door. I assumed if the visitor was hostile, they wouldn't be announcing their arrival. I opened the door and shook my head. Christopher Murdoch again.

'What do you want?' I asked.

'Your help.'

'I've already told you.'

He cut me off. 'I want you to work for me because I know you understand what I'm going through.'

He had my attention. 'What?'

'I know you've lost your wife. You know what it's like.'

'How do you know about that?'

'It's not important.'

'It is to me.'

'I've just heard, that's all.'

I didn't want to air all my dirty linen on the doorstep, so I took him up to the flat.

I pointed him in the direction of the spare chair. 'Heard what about me, exactly?' I asked. Murdoch looked uncomfortable but I was in no mood to play nice. 'What the fuck do you think you know?'

He held his hands up. 'Just that the fire wasn't an accident.'

He knew nothing. It wasn't a secret the fire my wife had died in hadn't been an accident. I went into the kitchen and made strong coffee to sober him up. It also gave me time to think. Despite his clumsy and shallow attempts at appealing to me, I was falling for it. He was giving me a reason. He wanted the same thing as me; closure. I asked him to tell me about his wife.

'She was the love of my life' he said. 'We met just over ten years ago and I knew straight away she was the one for me.' He looked directly at me. 'You just know, don't you? At first, she wasn't interested in me. It took some effort to get her to notice me, I can tell you. To cut a long story short, my persistence won her over and I eventually proposed to her at the top of the Eiffel Tower. We were very happy. She had her career, I had mine. Things were good for us.' His voice was barely a whisper. 'I don't know what I'll do without her now.'

I let him compose himself before starting my questions. 'Why was your wife off work?' I asked.

'Stress. She has a demanding job. She was a mess.'

I wasn't sure being an accountant for a local building firm qualified as being particularly stressful, but I nodded my head. 'Other than that, did she like her job, when she'd first started there?'

Murdoch nodded. 'I think so.' He laughed, but wasn't convincing. 'As much as you can, I suppose.'

'Did you help her?'

'As much as I could. I tried to give her the support she needed, but it was difficult to know what to do. She was on medication from our doctor, which was for the best. I thought the experts would sort her out.'

'Did she need to work, financially speaking?'

Murdoch shrugged. 'We could manage either way. It was her choice to work, and why shouldn't she? She worked hard to pass her exams; she liked her financial independence, so why would I stop her?'

I got to the point. 'What about her gambling problem?'

He didn't answer straightaway. 'I don't really know anything about it, to be honest. I knew she was spending too much time at the casino, but I thought she could handle it.'

'How deep was she in?'

'We never really spoke about it. She wouldn't. All I knew was that it was getting more serious. She was borrowing more and more from me and I think she was starting to wake up to how serious it was. I blame myself, really. She hadn't even been in a casino until I took her on a corporate event. We'd got to the stage where the casino was becoming more aggressive about the money she owed.'

'Which casino are we talking about?'

'Rischio. It's Italian for bet. It's owned by a guy called Frank Salford.'

I nodded and moved things up a gear. 'Where were you on the night your wife was murdered?'

'I was working.'

'Where?'

'In my car, on the motorway.'

'The motorway?'

'In a lay-by. I wanted to get a few ideas down while I had them, so I pulled over and used my laptop.'

'Wasn't it a bit uncomfortable, working in your car?'

He shook his head. 'Not at all.'

'How long was this for?'

'I was coming back from a meeting in Leeds. I'd eaten around there with a business associate and left about 6.30, pulled up near Ferrybridge Services at about 7.00, worked for three hours or so and then drove back to Hull. I went to the casino to unwind and I got the call on my mobile about one in the morning and was met by the police.'

'Why didn't you go into Ferrybridge? You could have worked in the canteen area, had a coffee?'

'I'd already passed it. I couldn't be bothered to drive to the next junction and double back on myself.'

As befitting a man in the public eye, it was difficult to read Murdoch's face. Parking up in a dark, isolated lay-by to use an expensive piece of equipment didn't ring true to me. It was possible, but it didn't feel right. A laptop battery would probably last that long. 'Did anyone see you?'

'There was the odd lorry parked up and a few cars came and went but nobody I specifically noticed.'

I went into the kitchen for beers. I needed a drink.

He took the bottle and thanked me. 'Pretty basic place this, isn't it?'

'It's how I like it.'

'I think they call it minimalist.'

I sat back down in the chair next to the window. The sky was darkening and promised rain.

'Did you have life insurance on your wife?'

'Do I have a motive for wanting my wife dead?'

I nodded. That was exactly what I meant.

He told me they had policies out on each other. I knew it wasn't uncommon for married couples to have such policies, so a surviving partner would have some financial security should disaster strike. I also knew money made for a powerful motive. The police would be looking closely at the circumstances surrounding the policy.

'What kind of marriage did you have?' I was asking blunt questions but it was the way things had to be.

'How do you mean?'

'Happy, stormy. What was it like for you?'

'It worked. That was the main thing.'

Murdoch looked embarrassed. I took a mouthful of beer and waited for him to explain.

'We had an open marriage' he eventually said. 'To be honest, it was more Jennifer's idea, but I can't say I was complaining. We set ground-rules. We'd only sleep with other people at this club we were members of. It kept the spice in our marriage, if you follow me.'

I nodded. A swingers club. I'd heard about such places, but half-thought they were urban myths. I'd led a sheltered life, obviously. 'Did your wife have any special friends, if that's the right way of expressing it?'

'One or two regulars, if that's what you mean.'

'Did those relationships extend beyond the boundaries of the club?'

'No. We had rules about that kind of thing.'

It was something to look into, though, however adamant he was. Motive was the key to understanding why she had been killed, and the club sounded like an interesting development. I always kept a notepad by the side of the chair and I scribbled down a few basic details about the place. The place to start would be their website.

'Why are the police watching you?' I asked. It was the question I was waiting to ask, but I wanted to settle him in first. I watched him slowly place his bottle in his lap and shake his head.

'What do you mean, watching me?'

He tried to look surprised, but I had the measure of him. He wasn't the most convincing liar I'd ever met.

'The police were watching your house.'

'How do you know?'

'It's what I do.'

'They weren't watching me.' He tried to sit upright, but the alcohol was taking effect and making him drowsy, as he slurred his words. 'Or my wife.'

He wasn't making much sense and I watched him fall asleep. Rain was now beating on the window, so I found a spare blanket and threw it over Murdoch. He could sleep himself sober and let himself out if he wanted. I sat back down and thought about my wife, and reflected on how

Murdoch saw us as having something in common. I didn't feel comfortable with it, as he was still a major suspect in the murder of his wife. I didn't know whether he was innocent or guilty. After a few moments of reflection, I stood up and paced the room. I had to get out for a while. I looked at Murdoch, snoring on my couch. He wasn't going to wake up any time soon. I threw my coat on and headed out.

From the outside, the Rischio casino looked inviting. Neon lights flashed as the rain came down and it looked like it would pass for a relatively up-market establishment. Once inside, it was clear it was all about the business. The decor was tatty around the edges, the carpets sticky underfoot, but it didn't seem to be bothering the handful of people stood around the roulette and blackjack tables. I looked at my watch; it had just turned ten o'clock. I nodded at the barman and ordered a soft drink. He couldn't have been much out of his teenage years.

'Terrible weather' I said. I looked around the room. 'Not too busy, then?'

'It'll get busier later. Once the pubs start to empty a bit.'

'Make the boss happy, I suppose.'

He stared at me and passed me my drink. 'I suppose.'

'Worked here long?' I asked.

'What's it to you?'

I laughed. 'Just making conversation.'

'Are you a journalist?'

'Private investigator.' Sometimes it's better to tell the truth.

'That's a first. There's been one or two journalists kicking about the place, as well as the police asking about the murdered woman. She used to come here.'

'Spoken to any of them?'

'Not me.'

'I could make it worth your while.' I could tell the kid was nervous. 'No harm done. Just a chat.'

'I knock off in ten minutes.' He lowered his voice. 'We're treated like shit in this place.'

I arranged to meet him in a near-by pub, thinking it was easily done.

Thirty minutes later I placed a pint of lager in front of him. His name was Sam Carver, Hull University student and part-time barman. I assumed he was also in need of money, as he was willing to talk to me for not much more than the price of a drink.

'Cheers' I said.

'Cheers.'

I picked it up where we'd left it. 'You were saying Jennifer Murdoch was a regular in the casino.'

'She was. The first few times I noticed her, she was with her husband. After a while, I started to notice she was coming in by herself. Not many women do, so she stood out a bit.'

'What did she play?'

'Blackjack mainly. Easy to play; easy to lose a lot of money at.'

'She mainly lost?'

Carver laughed. 'All the punters do. Basic rule.'

I accepted his point. 'Was it a problem?'

'Depends what you mean. If you mean, did she owe a lot money, then yes, she had a problem. If you're asking whether Mr Johnson thought it was a problem, then it wasn't a problem.'

'Who's Mr Johnson?'

'Dave Johnson. He runs the casino.'

'For Frank Salford?'

Carver confirmed he did. 'It's very rare we see him, though. Johnson runs the casino.'

'But she was allowed to run up debts?'

'Seemingly so. My mate works on the blackjack tables and he said he'd been told to give her whatever credit she needed.'

I pondered the information. I had to assume Salford was pulling the strings and approved whatever happened in the place. Why would he extend credit to Murdoch? What was in it for him?

'Did she have any friends at the casino? I asked.

'Friends?'

'People she met when she played, that kind of thing.'

He shook his head. 'I don't think she had any particular friends. She wasn't short of male company, if you follow my drift.'

'Did she ever arrive or leave with men other than her husband?'

'Sometimes. Left with them more than she arrived with them.'

'Any idea where she'd be heading for?'

'Afraid not. I suppose there was one man she was friendlier with than the others. Shit. I can't remember his name.'

'Another pint?' I said, hoping to jog his memory.

He nodded and sat there thinking whilst I went to the bar.

'I'm sorry. I don't know the guy's name' he said, when I returned. 'We call him Nose.' He shrugged, as if apologising for the childishness.

'He's got a big nose?'

'No. Just a silly joke between us. He was always popping into the toilets and coming out wiping his nose and sniffing.'

I understood. Cocaine. 'What about Jennifer Murdoch?'

'Did she know, do you mean?'

I nodded.

'Of course she did. She was no better than him.'

That was interesting. Jennifer Murdoch seemed to have the run of the place, with unlimited credit and licence to consume serious drugs on the premises.

'I need this man's name' I said. 'I'll drop in tomorrow when you've had chance to have a think about it, ask your friend if you need to.' I asked whether or not Christopher Murdoch's alibi stood up.

He shrugged. 'No idea, to be honest. I can't remember.'

I nodded and handed over a business card.

'I leave Hull tomorrow and I'm not coming back' he told me. 'I've finished my course and I'm all packed up.' He stood up and collected his coat. 'I'll give you a call, though.'

Nine

Don liked to call them 'case management reviews.' I viewed them as an early morning opportunity to grab a bacon sandwich from the indoor market and have a catch-up chat. I assumed it was a hangover from Don's days in CID, but I had to agree it was a good idea to have them, as it gave me a fighting chance of staying up to date. I'd beaten Don into the office by about an hour, as I wanted to use the time to check out the club Christopher Murdoch had told me he and his wife were members of. Their website proclaimed them to be a social group who meet every month in the West Hull area. The implication was clear, but the website contained very little concrete information. Reading between the lines, it wasn't too difficult to grasp what they were all about. A contact page allowed you to send your details to them and promised a reply as soon as possible. Discretion was the point, I assumed, and it was clear the club was pretty much invite-only. I bookmarked the webpage so I could come back to it later and closed the Internet connection. I assumed the club wouldn't be keen on accepting a single male into their gang. I'd have to persuade someone to come along with me, and that meant Sarah.

Don pushed his plate aside and finished chewing his sandwich. 'You're telling me Christopher Murdoch spent the night in your flat?'

I nodded. Murdoch was fast asleep on the couch when I returned from the casino, so I left him to sleep it off. When I awoke this morning, he'd left. I'd walked into the city centre and mulled over not telling Don about it before deciding honesty was the best policy.

'He wants to hire us?' said Don.

'That's right.'

'What did you tell him?'

'I said we'd do what we could.'

'Why would you say that?'

'He's paying us.'

Don shook his head. 'I don't like it. He's the police's major suspect. It's going to open a can of worms for us, I can feel it.'

I nodded. 'Or we might be saving an innocent man.' I didn't mention I felt some sort of affinity with Murdoch, with both of us losing our wives.

'Speaking of suspects, have we got anything else?'

Don burped and apologised. I thought about it. So far, all I had were suspicions and leads to work on. I explained what Briggs's auditor had told me.

'Do you think it's relevant to Jennifer Murdoch's death?'

It was a reasonable question. 'Difficult to say at the moment. It seems like she stole a fair amount of cash and cost Sonia Bray her job.' I tried to think it through. 'Is it enough to kill over, though?'

'What about Briggs?'

'What about him?'

'Do you buy the fact he didn't know about the theft? I find it hard to believe.'

I knew Briggs was an unpleasant individual, but would a successful businessman murder his accountant? It didn't seem like he needed the money that badly. I couldn't see it. Besides, the police said his alibi checked out.

Don stood up and made us another coffee. I checked my mobile for new messages while I waited.

'So what did Christopher Murdoch have to tell you last night' Don said, placing my mug on the desk.

'Frank Salford's name reared its head again.'

'Salford?'

I nodded. 'The Murdochs were regulars at his casino.'

Don sat back down. 'Means nothing.'

'Not on its own, maybe, but I paid the place a visit last night and got talking to one of the barmen. He told me Jennifer Murdoch had a gambling problem, but more interestingly, Salford didn't seem to be too bothered.'

'Maybe he thought she was good for it?'

'But it might go some way to explaining her theft from Briggs.'

'Murdoch also told me they had an open marriage.' I explained to Don about the club they were members of. 'She was also friendly with a man the barman called Nose. He couldn't remember the man's actual name; it's just a nickname he gave him because of his fondness of the Class A's.'

I watched Don write the name down. 'Doesn't sound like the behaviour of someone who's depressed. I'll see if I can find anything out.'

I leant forward. 'It's odd, though, isn't it? Why would Salford give Jennifer Murdoch the run of his casino?'

'It could be nothing. Don't get carried away, just yet. We know her husband isn't short of money and she was a qualified accountant. It might be coincidence that it's Salford's casino.'

I knew Don was right. It might well be a coincidence. But I was growing to believe there were no coincidences where Salford was concerned.

'Did he offer an alibi for the night his wife was killed?' he asked me.

'Not really. He was working near Leeds during the day; stopped for some food with a colleague and then pulled up in a lay-by to do a few hours work on his laptop.'

'Even though he was only, what, an hour's drive from home or his office?

I nodded. It sounded weak. 'And then he went to the casino for an hour to relax.'

'I suppose we could verify that part of his alibi at least.'

'He also said he had a life policy on his wife.'

Don mulled it over. 'I suppose it means little. Most people have their partners covered. But I doubt that's the way the police would see it.'

I knew the open marriage and money problems gave him motive. I looked up to see Sarah enter the office.

'Morning, love' said Don.

She glanced at the paperwork and plastic sandwich boxes.

'Case management review?'

'Joe was telling me about his new friend, Christopher Murdoch, sleeping over at his flat.'

Sarah looked at me, clearly surprised. 'I'll tell you later.' She pulled up a chair and joined us.

I tidied away the Jennifer Murdoch files and watched Sarah replace them with the Donna Platt files.

'What do we know?' asked Don.

I explained we'd spoken to Donna's mother and uncle. 'Tricky one. We definitely learnt more about her background, but ultimately we're not an awful lot wiser.'

'Her father is the key' Sarah said.

I agreed. 'Donna found him difficult to live with. They had different outlooks, different values.'

'He didn't seem a very pleasant individual, never mind father.'

'We've got to remember the kind of man Ron Platt was' I said. 'He obviously found it difficult to deal with what his daughter wanted from life.'

'So we think this friction was what caused her to disappear?' asked Don.

Sarah and I both nodded. 'Nobody will confirm it, but it seems likely' I said.

I explained to Don we knew for definite she was in the city three or four years ago.

'I think I'm going to talk to her friends again' said Sarah.

'So we've got some sort of paper-trail to follow.' He wrote the details down on his pad. 'I'll see what I can do' he said, before tapping his empty mug with his pen. I laughed. Hardly a subtle hint he was thirsty. We were done.

I knew it wasn't a good idea, but it was too tempting. I'd served a court warrant and realised I was only a couple of streets away from Salford's massage parlour. As I turned down the one-way street which led to it, I saw the manager I'd had the run-in with previously walking away from the building. I pulled into a parking space and quickly walked down the street. I wasn't sure what I could learn, but I wanted to see a bit more of Salford's empire first hand. Entering the massage parlour, it was as seedy as I remembered. I nodded to the man behind the reception desk. 'Who's working?'

'Anastazja. Massage is £25.'

I got my wallet out and passed the money over.

'Anything extra you negotiate with her, alright?'

I nodded. He pointed down the corridor which ran down the side of the reception area. I knocked on the door and waited. The door was opened by a dark-skinned brunette, probably in her mid-twenties, wearing a short silk wrap and I assumed little else.

'Anastazja?' I asked, wondering if it was her real name.

She nodded and invited me in. The room was small, overheated and fusty. If it was designed so you wouldn't want to hang around any longer than necessary, it succeeded.

'Please, make yourself comfortable.' She was gesturing to the massage table. 'You want massage?' she asked me.

I looked at the table and the collection of oils and eventually nodded. I'd have more chance of picking up some information if I played along.

'You want anything else from me?'

I shook my head. 'A massage is fine, thanks.'

She smiled. 'It's Okay. I have to ask this question, you understand.' She pointed to the table. 'We start now.'

I nodded my understanding. She was very attractive, but given that I could barely bring myself to date women, this type of situation was simply too much to bear. As I removed my coat, I fingered the wedding ring in my pocket and thought about Debbie and everything she had meant to me. I felt Anastazja go to work on my shoulders.

'Have you worked here long?' I asked her.

'A while now. How many times have you visited us? I do not remember seeing you before.'

'It's my first time.'

'I thought so. You are so tense.'

I tried to focus on the job in hand, though it became more difficult as her hands worked down my back. I suppose I should be pleased I could still feel like a man. I propped myself up and rested on my elbows. 'Where are you from?' I asked.

'I am from Romania' she told me.

'Long way to come for a job.'

'A very long way.'

'Are you here legally?'

She stopped the massage. 'Why all the questions?'

'I'm not the police.'

Anastazja folded her arms and took a step away from me. 'Why are you asking about me? I will give you massage. I will fuck you, if that is what you are really here for, but you have to pay me. I do not want to answer your questions.'

I weighed things up and decided to chance my luck. 'I'm a private investigator.' If she didn't want to talk to me, word would get back to Salford, but then again, so what? It was about time I had a chat with him. I told her I wanted to know about him.

'Okay, I will tell you. Just so long as you promise not to tell him I spoke to you. I will take a chance with you because you have told me the truth. Mr Salford offered me a job. He paid for me to travel to Hull.' She looked away, her eyes glazing over. 'I am very grateful to him.'

'Is this the job he promised you?'

'I was told Mr Salford owned a casino. I have never seen it.'

'How does he treat you?'

She shrugged. 'I have a house to live in, I eat, I have a job. I am paying my way.'

'Does he pay you a wage?'

'A little. I get to stay in a house with six other women. The money I earn is through what you call the extras. I get to keep some of this money but I do not see much of Mr Salford. He does not come here very often, but he is a quiet man. It is Mr Johnson I do not like. He is here a lot and expects you to do as you are told.'

I didn't inquire any further as to what she meant. I stood up and dressed myself and passed her some money.

I didn't want to spend too long in the room in case it aroused suspicion. 'Tell them you had some extras.'

'I can not take it. I have not earnt it.'

'Please. Take it.' I got out my business card and passed it to her. 'Could we talk some more about Salford, please? I might be able to help you.' I don't know why I said it. What could I do to help her?

She looked at the card. 'I will be finishing work early today; around six o'clock. We could meet then.' She insisted I had to buy her a meal.

I walked out of the massage parlour and onto the street. The parlour was situated on a busy shopping street and I felt people staring at me. I quickly headed for a newsagents a few doors away and bought an early edition of the local newspaper, wanting to read the latest on the police investigation into Jennifer Murdoch's death. Back outside, I stood on the pavement, newspaper open, scanning the pages for what I wanted.

Out of the corner of my eye I saw the manager of the massage parlour walking in my direction. More interestingly, Christopher Murdoch was with her. Tempting thought it was to ask why he'd left my flat in a hurry this morning, I didn't want to get caught. I casually stepped back and lifted the newspaper high enough to cover my face. Once I knew they were past me, I lowered the newspaper in time to see them walk into the massage parlour together.

After folding my newspaper away, I'd quickly walked back to the side street on which I'd parked my car. I turned my mobile back on and played back the new messages. The most recent call had been from DS Coleman, telling me we needed to talk. Urgently. He was at Hull Royal Infirmary and told me I was to meet him there or we'd do it later on in the day at the station. I checked the time of the message, called him back and headed for the hospital.

Situated on the edge of the city centre, the hospital is a concrete monstrosity, barely fit for purpose. Thankfully, I'd not had much reason to visit the place recently. Sarah has a friend who works as a nurse and some of the stories she tells are enough to convince you never to be ill. I spotted Coleman pacing around the entrance of the hospital, smoking a cigarette and talking into his mobile. Under pressure, I thought with a smile to myself. I hit the horn to grab his attention and he flicked the cigarette butt to the floor before jumping into the passenger seat.

'Drive' he said to me.

'Where to?'

'Wherever. Just get me away from this place. It depresses me.'

I signalled right and pulled out into the traffic, pleased to be driving away from the hospital. We were close to the KC Stadium, so I followed the signs and pulled into the empty car-park. Even though it wasn't match day, people buzzed around the stadium, going about their business. I switched the engine off and released my seatbelt. 'What can I do for you?'

'I want to talk about Sam Carver.'

'What about him?' I'd only spoken to the barman last night. How did Coleman know?

'I've just taken a statement from him. A member of the public found him last night close to where he works. He'd taken a good kicking. Professional, you might say. The doctors are worried about one of his eyes.'

Coleman turned to look at me. 'All he had in his pockets was his bank card and your business card.'

I felt sick. Carver hadn't been that bothered about talking to me. He was going to be leaving the city today. Salford had obviously been watching us.

'And it gets better, Joe. A patrol car was sent out to Rischio, the casino owned by Frank Salford, and coincidently the employer of Mr Carver, late last night. A man called Derek Jones was causing a scene, insisting Mr Salford knew something about the disappearance of his niece, which he told us you were looking into.'

Coleman turned to face me. 'I don't give a shit about this Jones guy, but you might want to get your house in order. Your name keeps popping up with some regularity in my investigation and I don't like it.'

I shut my eyes and lent back in my seat. What was Derek playing at? I thought he understood the worst thing he could do was to interfere.

'It's the Carver business which interests me, Joe. He told me you were talking about Jennifer Murdoch. Why are you working for her husband?'

I wasn't surprised he knew Murdoch wanted me to look into his wife's death. 'Because he asked me to. If he's paying, I'll try and help.' I wasn't going to talk about my wife to Coleman.

'He's a serious suspect for this, Joe. You're going to find yourself in the eye of a shit-storm if you're not careful.'

I shrugged. 'Innocent until proven guilty.'

Coleman laughed. 'It's not looking good, though, is it? Financial worries and a new life insurance policy on his wife, no alibi. It's the kind of thing which makes my superiors suspicious. The break-in to the house looks suspiciously staged, too.'

Murdoch had told me about the insurance policy, but he hadn't told me it was a recent thing. It might be a coincidence, but it didn't look good. 'No alibi?'

'The tapes have already been wiped. Company procedure, apparently.'

'Surely some of the casino's other visitors could vouch for him?'

'It seems not.' I asked him whether or not I was still a suspect.

Coleman shook his head. 'I was just testing you. You know how it is.'

'What about my face? You said she'd put up a fight.'

'Poetic licence.'

'Look, I've got a job for you, Joe. Well, you and Sarah, really. The Murdochs were involved in a wife-swapping club and we want to know if they were friendly with any one in particular.'

At least they were considering options other than her husband killed her. 'I don't see how we can help' I said, not wanting to volunteer for anything.

'You and Sarah are going to pose as a couple and become the club's newest members.'

I laughed. 'Not likely.' I didn't tell him I knew as much as he did.

'Like I said, Joe, it's about co-operation. It's difficult for us to go in and obtain admissible evidence. Anything you learn about is easier for us to use. Besides, if you don't help us, I'm told we might have to look at this Carver business a bit more closely.'

I got the message but sensed they were empty threats. They had nothing to gain from making an enemy of me. That said, I didn't want to push my luck. 'What's in it for me?' I asked. There had to be some exchange.

'Carver said you were asking about a guy he calls Nose? Apparently he was a regular at the casino and a close friend of Mrs Murdoch.'

I nodded. 'That's right.'

'I can tell you his name.'

'I can find it out. I'm a big boy.'

'He's a regular at this swinging club.'

'Why were you watching the Murdochs' house?' I asked. I wanted to know who Nose was, but if I needed to, I could find it out myself. It would just take me a little longer to do. The surveillance was more interesting to me. 'You had me falsely pegged as a suspect. You owe me.'

Coleman sighed. 'This didn't come from me, alright?'

I nodded. 'Fine.'

'Christopher Murdoch is under investigation on suspicion of fraud and corruption. Obviously, he has a lot of sway in respect of new building work, planning applications and what have you. There's been allegations he's not been behaving as you'd expect from a man in his position. Some of his applications for regeneration money are not being spent as they should be.' Coleman shrugged. 'It's not really my area and I'm not involved with it. But it looks like he's been a naughty boy.' Coleman paused. 'You had no idea, did you?'

I shook my head. 'No.'

'Plenty for you talk about with your client.'

'It seems that way.'

'I think we're done, then.'

'You didn't tell me the name of Nose.'

'He's called Steve Taylor. He runs a chain of estate agents. Look him up in the Yellow Pages.' He looked at his watch. 'I need to be back at the station. You can drop me near St Stephens and I'll walk from there. I doubt you'd want to be seen with me.'

I started the car engine and thought there were a lot of things I wanted to speak to Christopher Murdoch about.

Ten

I sat at my desk, thinking about what I'd learnt. I wasn't comfortable with Murdoch not telling me the truth about the life insurance policy he had on his wife. The fact it had been taken out recently was important, as it undoubtedly gave him a strong motive for wanting her dead. The fraud investigation was an altogether different matter, as it was entirely possible he was ignorant of it, but however I looked at it, he hadn't been straight with me. My initial reaction was to head straight to his office and confront him. It would have done no good, though. All it would have done was make my wounded pride at knowing less than Coleman a little more bearable. The time to talk to Murdoch would come, but not just yet.

'Ready?' asked Sarah. We'd arranged earlier in the day to catch up.

'Ready' I said. She'd spread the paperwork and timelines she'd worked in relation to Donna Platt over the table.

'Are you sure you're OK?'

'I'm fine. Just a little tired.' I didn't want to share what I'd learnt about Murdoch yet. Don hadn't been keen on me agreeing to represent him in the first place. If I was getting us into a mess, I wanted to be able to get us out of it.

'Right. Donna Platt. So we know when she first started seeing the boy from the shop she was working at, she was the average teenager, agreed?'

'Agreed.'

'But by the end of their relationship she'd changed, became fame-hungry?'

'Agreed.' I shuffled the paperwork around. 'And we know from the last boyfriend we've met, this guy from the factory, that she'd stopped singing altogether. The dream seemingly dead.'

'And we know her father would have disapproved. The fact is he drove her away.'

'Sounds about right but it doesn't get us any closer to knowing where she is.'

Sarah gathered the paperwork up. 'I'll let you know if I get anything more.'

'Somebody has to know something' I said, standing up to stretch my legs.

Sarah's mobile vibrated and she read the text message.

'Shit.'

'What's the problem?'

'Dad was babysitting for me tonight. But he can't now.'

'I could look after Lauren.'

'It's short notice. I'll cancel.'

'Cancel what?'

'A bite to eat with a guy from college.'

'I owe you one from the other night.'

'I couldn't ask.'

'It's fine, really. You go and enjoy your night.' I'd made arrangements to meet Anastazja but I could still be back in time.

'Thank you for bringing me here, Joe' Anastazja said, all smiles as she read the menu.

She insisted if she was going to talk to me, it would be over an Italian meal. It was still early, so the restaurant was almost empty, which was unusual for Princes Avenue. Other than ourselves, there were a handful of couples eating, I assumed on their way home from work. Not many people had money to be spending.

'It is very nice here. My friends and I have never had the opportunity to eat here. Thank you very much for bringing me here. It is very good of you.'

I was pleased she was enjoying herself. We both ordered pizza and settled back, waiting for the food to arrive.

'You wanted to ask me about my job' she said to me. 'I have not told anyone about our meeting.'

'Thanks.' I forced myself to focus in on what I needed to know. 'You told me Frank Salford isn't around too much.'

'That is correct. It is Mr Johnson who is in charge. He is a not a nice man.' She lowered her head. 'He makes us do things or he will tell the authorities about us. Sometimes he comes to our house.'

I understood what she was telling me. 'Do you think Salford knows about this?'

'I do not know. We do not see Mr Salford very often. If he comes, he speaks to Margaret. She is our manager and in charge of the reception desk.'

I nodded. Margaret. It was nice to put a name to the face.

'It is very hard work. I usually have to work from 12 o'clock midday to 12 o'clock midnight. We are not allowed a proper rest time if we have customers but today is not so busy so I was allowed to go.'

'How long have you been in Hull for?'

'Nearly three years. Before this I lived in Italy. I hoped it would be better here because England is a nice country.'

'Have you tried to get another job?' I asked.

'How would I get another job? I do not have the skills to work many other jobs and I would have nowhere to live. I have no friends to ask other than the people I live with.' She shrugged. 'I cannot go home as I do not have the money to travel and I would have to explain to my parents. I tell them I work in an office in the city centre. I have got used to life as it is.' She caught her breath and looked me in the eye. 'I have dreams, you know; big dreams. I will stop this life eventually.'

I'd read enough in the newspapers to know how the system worked. People like Salford brought vulnerable women like Anastazja into the country, usually under false pretences of respectable work. They would then have to work to repay their transportation debt, but the catch was it would never be paid. She had no money and no escape route. Anastazja might even be working legally, but it was no life to lead. Salford controlled her.

'I know it could be worse' she continued. 'The people I live with are nice, the city is nicer than back home. I do not have much but at least here I have some comfort. The worst thing is the job but I deal with it. The men are not too bad with me. Most of them are lonely men or men travelling for their job and only want massage. They are not nasty like Mr Johnson. I would like to meet a nice man, who will take me away to live in a big house. I would do shopping all day, like all the big stars in the magazines.'

I smiled. 'There's plenty of women who'd like that.' I changed the subject. 'As I was leaving earlier, I saw somebody I knew. Do you know Christopher Murdoch?' I described him to her.

'Yes. I know Mr Murdoch. How do you know him?'

'He's a business acquaintance' I said, which sounded almost like the truth.

'He is a friend of Mr Salford. We are told we must treat him well when he visits. We must do exactly what he wants.'

'Does he visit often?' I asked.

'Sometimes yes, sometimes no. Sometimes he comes two or three times a week. Sometimes we do not see him for a long time.'

'How long have you known him?'

'Since I start work.' Anastazja picked up a slice of pizza and smiled at me. 'Thank you very much, Joe.'

'What for?'

'For bringing me here. For being nice to me and treating me like a friend.'

I smiled back but it didn't feel convincing. Our talk had confirmed my suspicions but the circumstances left me feeling lousy. Murdoch was seemingly a regular and valued user of Salford's massage parlour. I also knew his wife had been allowed to accrue debts at Salford's casino. More worryingly, I knew Christopher Murdoch was under investigation for fraud and corruption. I wondered if there was a link. I wondered what I was getting involved in.

'It'll be fun,' Lauren said, as she jumped onto the settee. She laughed and hit me with the book she had in her hand. The cat, which was asleep next to me, woke up with a fright.

Sarah walked into the room, adjusting her earrings. I smiled at her. 'You look great.' She was wearing a short black dress and had her hair pinned up. I wasn't lying or exaggerating.

She pointed at Lauren. 'You just be careful with that book. It's heavy.'

'Uncle Joe said he'd read it to me.'

I hadn't said any such thing. I shook my head and smiled at Sarah.

'He'll do no such thing, madam. You know you've got to read the book yourself. You don't want to be in trouble tomorrow at school, do you?'

Lauren climbed down, complaining it was more fun if I read the book and made the appropriate noises for the characters and animals.

'I won't be late back' Sarah said. 'We're only going to the new Italian on Princes Avenue.'

'You can always ring me if you are.' I didn't mention I'd just eaten there.

'No need. The table is booked for 7.30; I'll be home for ten. Besides, you've been kind enough to babysit after Dad let me down.'

'It was the least I can do.' Hopefully it would go some way to making amends for disturbing her the other night and having her clean me up. 'You're sure? You don't have to rush for me.'

Sarah laughed. 'Definitely.'

'Be careful.' I don't know why I said it, or where it came from. 'Sorry. I'm talking rubbish.' I knew she could look after herself.

'I'll hardly be eloping, Joe.' She bent down to put a shoe on.

I smiled. 'I guess not.'

'Besides, I barely know him.'

'I thought you went to night-class with him?'

'That doesn't mean I know him, though, does it?'

'I suppose not.'

I watched Sarah hunt for her missing shoe. 'He's a nice guy, though. He's a good laugh' she said.

I nodded. 'Good.'

'You know what you're doing with Lauren?'

I told her I did. I knew what time she was supposed to go to bed, what she could eat and drink and what she was allowed to watch on television. 'I'll be fine.' I showed her the book I'd brought with me for when I had put Lauren to bed. I'd stopped off at the library on the way home to borrow a book about the city's trawler industry. I only knew the basic facts and the story Maria Platt and her brother told me left me wanting to know more. Sarah looked at the title and nodded. I also had plenty to think about after my meal with Anastazja.

'I can't believe they used to treat people like that' said Sarah, pointing to the book.

'Proper work, and no mistake.'

We heard a car pull up outside the house. Sarah pulled the curtains back to have a look. 'Taxi's here.'

'Enjoy yourself.'

'Thanks, Joe.' She was already halfway out of the room, looking for Lauren. 'And you behave yourself, madam.'

I heard the front door shut. The house fell silent. It was stupid, but I was sure I felt a pang of jealousy. I was jealous she was going out, having a good time, but more than anything, I was sure I felt jealous of the man she was out with.

Sarah was good to her word and returned home at the time she said she would. Lauren had behaved and gone to bed without too much of a fuss. I'd read her a story before she went to sleep but I'd probably enjoyed it more than she did. I didn't know why Don had cancelled, but he'd been the one who missed out on the fun. Once I was happy Lauren was settled, I'd read the book on the trawler industry I'd brought with me. Although it felt like I was getting a better understanding of the Platt family, it wasn't helping us find Donna. I was certain her father was the underlying reason for her leaving but for now I was happy to let Sarah take the lead in our investigation.

I'd lost myself in the book until I heard the taxi pull up. Sarah walked into the living room and theatrically threw herself down onto the sofa. She told me the night was still warm, so I decided to walk home. It was only a twenty minute walk and the exercise wouldn't do me any harm. I put the key into the front door and felt a thud on the back of my head. I was aware of a hand removing the key from the lock as things turned to black.

I could only have been out cold for a short period of time, as I was lying on the path leading up to my front door. In those seconds or minutes, though, my hands had been tied behind my back and I had gaffa tape across my mouth to prevent me from screaming. I was picked up by two men, one on each side of me, and carried to a dirty looking transit van before being dumped on the road whilst they opened the doors. Usually, the Avenue had a steady stream of traffic passing through, but tonight when I needed it, there was nothing.

I was picked up again and thrown in the back onto a piece of old carpet. There was nothing else in the back of the van. The two men in the front of the Transit hadn't made any attempt to hide their faces from me, and that worried me; I tried to fight the fear and the temptation to vomit back down. The engine started on the second try and we pulled away from the kerb. We quickly took two left turns, putting us on Spring Bank and heading towards the city centre. I tried to follow the route we were taking but the darkness was disorientating. I felt the van increase speed and we drove over an incline. I could hear other vehicles, so it had to be Myton Bridge and the dual-carriageway which led out of the city towards Holderness, a largely desolate area only punctuated by the occasional village. As the transit continued its journey, the air changed, polluted with the smell of chemicals from BP Saltend, confirming we were heading in the direction I thought. The van slowed down several times, meaning we were passing through a series of villages before we turned off the main road. The way the van slowed and bounced up and down made me think we were heading down a private track. As the van came to a stop, I was thrown into the corner, ignoring the rising nausea in my stomach.

Roughly bundled out of the van, I fell face down into the mud. The two men picked me up, removed the gaffa tape and threw me forward so I landed on my knees. I looked up to see a freshly dug grave, lit up by portable lighting. I knew I was in the middle of nowhere and nobody would be disturbing us. Remembering what I'd been told about Salford's speciality, I turned to my side and threw up some bile. The two men walked towards the grave, laughing, and lent on the spades.

I wiped my mouth on my shoulder and spat on the floor.

'What can I do for you, then?'

Neither said a word and continued to inspect the grave.

'Mr Geraghty. Glad you could join us this evening' said a voice from behind me. I assumed it was Frank Salford but as he walked past me to join his men, I knew it wasn't. The man was in his late forties and was slightly built. He had a shaven head and a stud earring in his left ear which twinkled under the lighting.

'You've been a naughty boy, Mr Geraghty, haven't you?' He stared at me. 'Again.'

I continued to stare at him. 'Call me Joe if you like.'

'Very civil.'

'What shall I call you?' I asked.

'You can call me your worst nightmare.'

I laughed. 'If you like.' I'm not sure where the bravado came from, as given the situation, I wasn't feeling so brave.

'How about I call you Dave?'

He laughed. 'Very good, Joe. There's no flies on you, is there?'

Dave Johnson. Salford's lieutenant. It was an educated guess. I looked around. 'Where's the man who's in charge?'

Johnson laughed. 'You can deal with me.'

'I'd rather deal with the organ grinder than his monkey.'

Johnson stepped forward towards me and kicked me in the face. I collapsed backwards, tasting blood in my mouth. He grabbed my hair and pulled me back upright.

'Don't mess with me, cunt.' He was so close to my face, I could smell his breath. He let go of me and walked back to the grave. 'Mr Salford can't be with us this evening, but it seems like you're still not getting the message, Joe. The lads here have already paid you one visit, but you're still sticking your nose into our business.'

I looked at the hired help. They were every inch the thugs-for-hire I expected; big, dark clothes, no distinguishing features. I stayed still, saying nothing.

'To be honest, Joe, you're getting fucking tiresome' Johnson continued. 'I don't know what your game is, but did you really think it would be that easy talking to our barman? I watch them cunts like hawks, especially the ones who are leaving.' He walked back towards me. 'It's your fault he's ended up in that state, really. He was stupid to talk to you, as that's one of the house rules, but you should have left him alone. They're saying he might lose the sight in one of his eyes from the accident. These things happen, though, don't they, Joe? We both understand the way of the world.' He lent down and held his face inches from mine, smiling. 'Collateral damage.'

I said nothing but felt sick.

'My guess is you were asking about our friends the Murdochs, Joe. Is that right?'

I held his stare and remained quiet. He slapped me across the face but I didn't move. I didn't want to let him know it hurt, that my face was stinging.

Johnson laughed. 'I'll assume your silence means I'm on the right track. What's your interest, Joe? Why are you bothering us with your presence?'

I spat in Johnson's face. He screamed and punched me in the face and followed it up with a series of painful kicks to my body. I was carried to the open grave and thrown in. I looked up to see Johnson stood on edge.

'Listen up and listen good. We followed you tonight, Joe, and I have to say I'm surprised with you. I didn't think I'd have to tell you to leave the slags in the brothel alone, not considering how pretty your girlfriend is, but it's probably in your best interests. Speaking of your girlfriend, I was surprised to hear you had left her house and headed back to your own little cesspit for the night. If I was you, I wouldn't be leaving her alone, if you follow me. Still, I'll be sure to say hello for you when I pop round shortly. He nodded to his sidekicks, who had reappeared. The earth started falling onto me, increasing in velocity. I screamed out Sarah's name, but nobody heard me.

Eleven

Sarah pointed at my face. 'Not again, Joe.' She shook her head and pushed past me, heading up the stairs to my flat.

Johnson and his associates had covered me with earth, but not enough so I couldn't remove it with a bit of effort. They'd only wanted to scare me and they'd done a pretty good job of it. One of them had even pissed into the grave, but the mud had taken the brunt of it. I'd walked for what seemed like miles, thumb out, trying to catch a lift. Nobody stopped but eventually a taxi pulled over, heading back to the city after dropping off a fare. I'd had to offer him my new mobile phone as security, but it'd persuaded him to drive me to a cash-point. He'd also driven me past Sarah's house; all the lights were off and there was nobody hanging around, which confirmed my suspicion Johnson was all mouth. I'd called her as soon I was back in my flat; I needed to know she was alright. Her sister had kindly agreed to look after Lauren whilst Sarah was with me.

'Sit down' Sarah said, as I closed the door to my flat. She was filling a bowl with hot water and Dettol.

I glanced into the mirror; I had been too tired to clean myself up last night. My face was covered in dirt, as well as cuts and bruises.

'Just as the first beating was fading' I joked.

'It's not a joking matter, Joe. What happened?'

I explained events since I'd left her house the previous night. I decided not to mention the threats Johnson had made for fear of upsetting her. I couldn't see what purpose it would serve and I knew she was always careful enough to keep an eye on Lauren. There was no denying I was relieved to see her, though. She started to clean up a cut on my cheek and I instinctively grabbed her hand, as a reaction to the pain. We sat like that for a brief moment before she released herself to get back on with the job.

'How was your date?' I asked.

'It wasn't a date.'

'Fair enough. How was your night out, then?'

'Not too good. He was a bit boring. All he did was drone about his job. To be honest, I was glad to get home.'

I smiled, even though it hurt. 'Maybe next time.'

'Maybe. What do we know about this Dave Johnson?' she asked, changing the subject.

There wasn't much to tell. 'He's Salford's number two and runs the casino.' I explained he wasn't a popular figure at the massage parlour. Sarah looked at me in disbelief.

'You had a massage?'

'That's all I had.'

'Whatever. I can't believe you even went in the place.'

'It was necessary.'

'It must have been a right hardship for you.'

I tried to explain about Anastazja, but finding the right words was difficult.

Sarah stopped what she was doing. 'What do you want to do?'

I had no idea what I wanted to do. I wanted to help Anastazja and the best way to do that would be through Salford and Johnson. If I was really lucky, I might even find out something about Donna Platt, though I was beginning to think the investigation was a wild goose chase.

'Guess who I was talking to yesterday?' I said.

'Who?'

'That's not guessing.'

Sarah had finished patching me up. 'Who?'

'Coleman.'

110

She looked surprised.

'Let's say he pointed out we could all benefit from working together. We had a talk. I learnt some interesting stuff.'

'Such as?'

'Christopher Murdoch was under police surveillance. He reckons he doesn't know much about it, but there's been allegations of fraud and corruption.'

'Have you spoken to him?'

'Not yet. Hopefully I'll get the chance today.' I wasn't stupid enough to charge in and confront him, but I'd spent time brooding about the situation. I wasn't having him take the piss out of me like this and we'd certainly be having words in the near future. 'He also told me who the man Jennifer Murdoch was more than a bit friendly with at the casino is.'

'What did you have to tell him in exchange for all this?'

I slowly stood up and walked over to window, ignoring the pain from my ribs, thinking about how I was going to sell an evening in a swingers club to her.

I felt like death as I dragged myself out of bed. The cuts on my face stung and there was a constant, nagging pain around my upper body. Sarah had stayed the night, insisting she would sleep on the sofa. She'd taken the news about visiting the club remarkably well and even said it might be fun, before leaving for home. An hour later and with two strong coffees working their magic inside me, I parked as near as I could to the hospital's front entrance. I'd rung from my mobile, so I knew which ward to find Sam Carver on. I stopped short of the door and looked in through the large window. I could see two middle-aged people sat in plastic chairs at Carver's bedside and I assumed they were his parents. Before I took a step back, I could see Carver had a medical dressing covering his left eye, his face heavily bruised and cut.

I turned to look at the nurse stood next to me. She pointed to the bag of fruit I had in my hand. 'Who are they for?'

'Sam.'

She pointed to him. 'Nasty. Whoever did that wants locking up.'

I nodded my agreement.

'Are you his uncle?' she asked.

'A friend.'

'I'm sure he'll be pleased to see you then.'

I wasn't so sure. 'Is that his parents with him?'

'That's right. They've driven down from Newcastle. Hardly left his side.'

'Will his eye be alright?'

The nurse sighed. 'Too early to say, but we certainly hope so. He's getting the best treatment he can and he's keeping his spirits up.'

'Good.'

'Are you coming in, then?'

I passed her the fruit. 'I don't want to disturb him if his parents are here. Could you see he gets this, please?'

'I'm sure they won't mind.'

I shook my head. 'I'll come back another time.' I turned away and headed back towards the lift before she had chance to ask my name. Dave Johnson had done this, though I felt like I might as well have been at his side, handing out the kicking. Once I was outside the hospital, I made a call. I knew who could tell me all about Salford's right-hand man.

'Thanks for seeing me' I said to Julie Richardson.

'I was in town anyway and I want to help if I can.' She pointed to my face. 'Looks like you need some help. At least your reminder will fade.'

The office telephone rang but I ignored it, letting it click through to answer-phone. I'd left yet another message for Christopher Murdoch asking him to call me back on my mobile, but he still hadn't got in touch.

'Nice office you've got here' she continued. 'Quiet.'

We were one of many businesses based in the building. We shared the space with computer programmers, website designers and a design company. And that was only the people I recognised well enough to say hello to. We didn't shout about our work.

'Dave Johnson' I said to her.

She nodded, understanding. 'He did this to you?'

I told her what happened, from being bundled into the transit to thrown in the grave.

'Standard scare tactics from them' she explained. 'It was one of their favourite games.'

'Do you know Johnson?' I asked.

'He was Frank's best friend, no doubt still is. I saw far too much of him when I was with Frank. He was always the right-hand man, right from the word go. From what Frank told me, it goes all the way back to their school days. He used to find it hilarious talking about the trouble they got up to when they were kids, like he was sad they had to grow up. When I met Frank, Johnson was more than his assistant. If you wanted to get to Frank, you went through Johnson. He was trusted to do business, deal with people and problems as they arose.'

'What was he like as a person?'

'Horrible. I hated him. I'm not stupid; I knew what Frank was and how he made his money, but he was a different kettle of fish altogether. Frank was a violent man' she pointed to her scar, 'he was quite prepared to do this to me, but it was personal. Johnson was plain nasty. I can't think of another way to describe him. I think Frank was into the football violence because it started off as fun. It was a way to let off steam, I suppose. They used to get into some scrapes but most of the time it was just boys being boys, you know what I mean?'

I said nothing, remembering how it felt being caught up on the rugby terraces as a child with men fighting. It had stayed with me.

'It became more serious, though' she continued. 'Frank was always a schemer and a planner, and as he became more powerful, he dragged Johnson along with him. Frank was mainly about the money and soon cut out the fighting at the football, but Johnson couldn't stop. He liked it too much. He'd always be around, taking drugs, fighting and upsetting people. If you looked at him the wrong way, he'd lash out. He'd hit first, ask questions later.'

'If Johnson was an embarrassment, why didn't Frank do something about it?'

'I suppose it suited him to an extent. Frank stopped all the stupid behaviour but he still needed someone he trusted as an enforcer, to collect money and make sure people stayed in line.'

I nodded. 'Johnson fitted the bill.'

'Perfectly.'

'The problem was he became too violent. I remember Frank spent a lot of time mopping up the mess. There was one time when Frank had asked him to sort out another drug dealer. Their preferred method was intimidation around a freshly dug grave, like with you. Frank had meant give him a kicking, let him know who was in charge, but Johnson completely lost the plot and killed the man. The man who was working with Johnson told Frank he couldn't stop him. He'd gone totally mad and attacked the man with his spade, killing him.'

It tallied with what Don's former colleague had told us.

'What happened to the man he killed?'

She shrugged. 'I don't know. It wasn't spoken of. The body just disappeared. As far as I know, Frank sorted it. I remember Johnson feeling hard done by because, as usual, he needed help to clear his mess up.'

'What about the police? Didn't they investigate?'

She laughed. 'I doubt there would have been much in the way of forensics, and that's assuming anybody wanted to investigate Frank. He had all kinds of people on the payroll.'

'Didn't the police have a bite at Johnson, as a way to get to the main man?' I couldn't bring myself to refer to Salford by his first name.

'He was too important, so Frank had to protect him, which made him untouchable. It gave him licence to do as he wanted.'

I heard the door open and watched Don walk in. He headed towards his office, but seeing my face, stopped.

'It's a long story' I said, cutting him short. I thanked Richardson for her time. Johnson was the violent element of Salford's empire and although it wasn't good news, at least I knew more about the man and the danger he posed to me.

Don was surprisingly calm as I told him about Dave Johnson and what had happened the previous night. He thought I should tell Coleman about it but I wasn't prepared to look like an idiot in front of him. If I needed help, I'd ask. Sarah was chasing leads down on Donna Platt's disappearance and we needed a breakthrough, or something I could rattle Salford with. Christopher Murdoch was still very much in my thoughts. There was plenty he wasn't telling me. I tried his office again and got nowhere, so I decided to pay him a personal visit. His office was situated in the World Trade Centre, close to the marina. The receptionist pointed me in the direction of some chairs and asked me to wait. I glanced at the literature in the reception area, which grandly claimed the complex was the focal point for local and international business within the Hull and Humber area. Told I could go through, I put the leaflets down and thanked the receptionist. The walls in Murdoch's unit contained framed photographs of projects the company had worked on. The city was changing, but being in the centre of it, I didn't always notice. I glanced at the freestanding boards in the corner, detailing plans for regeneration work in the Newington Ward of the city, including the Hessle Road area. I pushed aside the memories I had of the area and hoped they had the nerve to create something really special.

'Can I help you?'

I turned around to look at the young woman who'd appeared in the room.

'I'd like to speak to Mr Murdoch, please.' She didn't look impressed with the state of my face. 'My name is Joe Geraghty, he knows who I am.' I smiled, hoping to relax her.

She walked over to the phone and mentioned my name. 'Mr Murdoch's not available all day.'

'All day?'

'I'm afraid so.'

'It's very important I speak to him. He's asked me to do some work for him.'

She looked embarrassed. 'There's really nothing I can do, I'm afraid.'

I smiled at her. It wasn't her fault. I was pretty certain Murdoch wasn't in the office but I didn't know where to look for him. His house was the next logical step. The phone rang again. I listened in, as she looked at me. She told the caller I was still here.

'Jane will see you' she said.

We sat down in the boardroom. On three walls there were more framed photographs and artists impressions of the company's ongoing projects. The centrepiece of the office was directly in front of me, with patio-doors opening onto to a balcony which gave a fantastic view of the moored yachts. Reluctantly, I turned away and sat down at the boardroom table opposite Jane.

'What happened to you?' she asked me.

'Long story.' I touched my face. 'You should see the other guy.' I got down to business. 'I need to speak to him.'

'I haven't seen him' she said. She looked upset.

'Since when?'

'Since he left the office the night before last. He said he was going home but I've not been able to get hold of him. I've been constantly trying his phone at home and his mobile. I've been round to the house and there's no sign of him, or his car. I don't know what to do for the best. I'm trying to hold it together here, so the clients and the staff don't know, but it's so hard. A lot of people depend on him for work and jobs and I can't handle it all by myself. I really need your help here, Joe. I've rung the police because I've no idea what to do.'

I was genuinely concerned for her. Murdoch had a lot on his plate. 'Have you tried anywhere else?'

'Such as?'

'Friends, family, favourite places.' I shrugged. 'That kind of thing.'

'I've told the police everything I know this morning. His parents are dead and I don't know how to contact his brother. He's never really mentioned him, so I can't imagine he'd go there.'

I'd not heard from Coleman. I wondered if he was aware Murdoch knew yet. 'I'll keep trying his phone as well' was the best I had to offer.

'I'm worried about him, Joe.' She wiped her nose and walked over to the window. I watched her compose herself and turn to me. 'I'm worried he's got involved with some bad people.'

'Any in particular?' I had at least one name I could suggest.

'No, just a feeling I've got. He's forever disappearing to meet people, but he won't say where he's going. It's like he's changed, acting differently. He's much more agitated and on edge. He's snappy at people here all the time, and that's not him at all. Before I'd help him to co-ordinate his diary, but I've been frozen out. He's not behaving how he normally does.'

I understood. 'Were you having an affair?'

She eventually nodded. 'It's not like you think.'

I waited for her to continue.

'I love him, Joe.'

'I'm sorry I have to ask you these questions, but did his wife know about you?'

She shook her head. 'Certainly not from me.' She turned to face me. 'I'm not stupid, Joe. I never asked him to leave his wife for me. I wouldn't have done that to him; I enjoyed what we had together. We had so much in common. I often wondered why he wouldn't leave her, but I wasn't going to force the issue. He'll do it when the time's right.'

'Did he ever say his marriage was unhappy?'

'Not in so many words, no. I think it suited them to stay together, it was easier for them. He has a reputation to maintain and he didn't want to rock the boat unnecessarily.'

'What about his alibi?'

'He said he was parked up in a lay-by on the M62, working.'

'Sounds about right. He's very dedicated to his work, and with laptops, you can work anywhere.'

'Are you sure he wasn't with you?'

'Fuck off, Joe.'

Seeing as I'd angered her and unsettled her, I asked anyway. 'What about you, Jane? Where were you?' Having an affair with Christopher Murdoch gave her more motive than most when it came to his wife's death.

For a moment, I thought she was going to attack me, but she sat back down and stared straight ahead. Eventually she sat up straight and nodded. 'You've got to ask. You're only doing your job.'

I smiled. 'Just doing my job.'

'I was out with a girlfriend. We had something to eat and then went to see a film.'

I believed her. Why lie when it can so easily be checked?

She showed me into Murdoch's office. It was pretty much like any other office. There were yet more framed photographs on the walls and although it looked tidy enough, when you looked closely it was obvious it had been done in a hurry. The only thing which differentiated it from other offices in the building was the executive sized chair.

'Have you got his diary?' I asked.

Jane disappeared to find it. I walked around the desk and opened his drawer. There was nothing unusual, just a collection of stationery and computer print-outs.

She passed me his diary. I flicked through the last couple of months. His volume of recorded meetings decreased steadily, with the gaps in the diary marked with a cross. I pointed this out to Jane. 'Any idea what it means?'

She shook her head. 'I can't say I've noticed any change in the number of meetings he's attended. He's always out of the office a lot.'

As an example, I turned to the previous week. 'Tuesday morning he had a meeting with a guy from the council, but there's nothing for the afternoon, just a cross at the top of the page.'

'I don't know. He doesn't always answer his phone, however much I ask him to.'

'You've no idea what he was doing that day?'

She sighed and shook her head. 'I was in the office trying to tie some meetings up but I couldn't find him. He wouldn't tell me where he'd been.'

I passed her the diary back. I suspected the crosses in the diary stood for meetings he didn't want others knowing about. 'I really need to know about his enemies, Jane' I said.

'He didn't have any, I've already told you.'

'Now's the time to have a hard think about it. It'll be a great help to us all if you can think of any names. Any at all.'

She sat down in Murdoch's chair. She looked completely drained. 'There's nothing. I can't think of any one he's upset or doesn't get along with.' She stood up and walked back towards me. 'He didn't kill his wife, Joe. I know he didn't.'

Twelve

Our office was only a ten minute walk from Murdoch's base, but my plans to use the walk as a chance to think over events so far were shattered by the vibration of my mobile in my pocket.

I looked at the caller ID. 'Detective Sergeant Coleman' I said, answering the call.

'How's it going, Joe?'

I said something about being better.

'Good news. The Murdochs' little group meet tonight and you're invited. I pretended to be you, so we're all set.'

I listened as he told me the address and the time Sarah and I were expected.

'I've given them your proper first names but said your surname is Smith and you run your own engineering company which you've recently set up. Our geeks have set a holding page up on the Internet for the company with a coming soon banner and a dead telephone number. It'll be enough to make you legitimate at first glance, and I can't imagine they'd look any deeper. If they do, you'll have to improvise. Tell them you've just moved back to the area and set the business up, something like that. Nobody's going to be bothered so long as you're well presented and behave yourselves.'

Coleman told me the plan. Or at least what he thought was the plan. He wanted to know who the Murdoch's were friendly with. I wasn't sure what I would share with him, assuming I learnt anything.

'At least we won't have to worry about your friend, Christopher Murdoch turning up' he said.

I pressed the button on the pedestrian crossing and waited for both the traffic on the busy dual carriage way to stop and for Coleman to continue.

'He's been reported missing.'

I said nothing.

'You'd best find him, Joe. The longer he's missing, the guiltier he looks.'

As I walked down Castle Street, several lorries thundered past me, so I told him I couldn't hear him very clearly and terminated the call, knowing he was right.

'Any word from Sarah?' Don asked, as I hung my coat behind the door. 'We've got a lead on Donna Platt.'

I sat down and started my laptop. 'A lead?'

Don pulled up a chair at my desk. 'An old friend of mine in Scarborough is into the club scene. He retired to the seaside but likes his club stuff. I had him ask around to see if anyone knew Donna and we got a hit. There's a woman singing in a club in Whitby who might fit the bill. She goes by the name of Donna Marie and she's apparently from Hull.' Don shrugged. 'I've had my friend check her out and apparently her back-story is somewhat vague. It might be something or nothing, but it's worth taking a look at.'

I agreed and Don said he'd set a meeting up. 'What's Sarah doing?' I asked.

'She's speaking to Lisa Day, trying to find out if the family had any links to Whitby. I didn't think it was a good idea to be speaking to Donna's mother in case it got her hopes up for nothing.' Don pointed at my face. 'Sarah said Dave Johnson did that to you?'

'No doubt under the orders of Salford. It seems Johnson is the enforcer but Salford is the brains behind the operation.'

'It's getting serious, Joe.'

'I know.'

'We should think about talking to the police.'

'Why?'

'Because Salford's not the kind of guy we want to mess with. We need to be careful.'

'We will be.'

'I mean it.'

'I know.'

I flicked through the day's post, trying to ignore Don staring at me.

He got the point. 'How's the guy from the casino you spoke to?' he asked.

'I went to see him earlier. His parents were there.' I looked away. 'I bottled it. I couldn't make myself go in and see him, not while they were there.'

Don shook his head. 'Poor bastard.'

I said nothing.

'It won't do any good beating yourself up over it.' Don said.

'Bottom-line is the kid knew what he was doing, didn't he?'

I nodded. Carver knew as well as I did that he worked for some unpleasant people. The knowledge didn't make me feel any better, though. 'Still makes me feel like shit, though.'

'Actions always have consequences. You've got to deal with it.'

I nodded and explained what Julie Richardson had told me about Johnson. I'd think about Sam Carver later.

'I know all about him' he told me. 'We crossed swords a few times when I was in the force. He was certainly known to us, as were his methods. The freshly dug grave was a regular tactic Salford used to scare people.'

'It worked for me.'

'I dare say. What was the message?'

'Take my nose out of their business.' It hung there until I continued. 'Jennifer Murdoch was a regular in the casino and she got special treatment. I don't know why yet, but it's obviously important and might be relevant in relation to her death.'

Don stood up and walked over to his desk. 'We're in this thing, aren't we?'

He was right. Things had turned much more sinister and dangerous.

'What does Mr Murdoch have to say for himself?'

'No idea.'

'No idea?'

'He's AWOL.'

Don sat back down. 'The police's main suspect is missing? And he's our client.'

I nodded. 'That's about the size of it.'

'Do the police know?'

'Coleman rang me earlier. We're all set for the Murdochs' club tonight. He mentioned it then; could barely contain his glee.'

'You'll be needing me to babysit tonight?'

I nodded. 'I'm sure Sarah would ask you nicely.'

'I'd love to.'

'Good.' That reminded me of last night. 'What happened to you last night? I had to look after Lauren. Sarah said you cancelled at the last minute?'

'I had some work to do. I had to speak to that friend about Donna Platt.'

I was sure it could have waited. I watched Don stare out of the window

'You shouldn't miss out on it.' I'd had fun reading stories with her. 'It's a granddad's privilege.'

He turned back to me. 'I might not be able to tell her what to do any more, but I can let her know when she's making a mistake.'

I wasn't needed for a couple of hours, so I headed for Salford's massage parlour. Johnson had warned me off Anastazja but I needed to make sure she was alright. I'd parked my car in the exact same place as I had on my last visit and walked straight into the reception.

'Nice to see you, Margaret. Who's working today?'

She was speechless. 'I know who you are' I said to her, 'and I know what you are.'

She took a step backwards and struggled to compose herself. I'd given it some thought on the drive across. There was no point beating about the bush. Salford and his team knew who I was, and what I was doing. They also knew I'd spoken to Anastazja.

'We've got Sky and Summer working at the moment.' She leered at me. 'Which of them would you like to fuck today?'

'I'd like to see Anastazja.'

'Anastazja?'

'That's right.'

'There's nobody of that name working here, I'm afraid.'

I took a deep breath. 'Don't piss me about.'

'Get to the point or I'll have you kicked out again.'

'Where is she?'

'Anastazja?'

'That's right.' I was starting to lose patience.

'She left our employment last night.'

I turned away. I'd have to find her. I knew which area she lived in. It wouldn't be too difficult.

She called me back. 'She's taken up a new position in London. When I say position, it'll be largely the same position she had here, lying on her back. One of our associates offered her the job and we were only too pleased to allow her the opportunity to further her career in our beautiful capital city.' She lent in closer to me. 'Of course, the work is much more demanding down there. Their overheads are that much higher, you see. They'll have her working much harder. She'll have her normal work, the bread and butter, but she'll have to entertain private parties. I understand some of the, shall we say, newcomers to the city go in for that kind of thing. The good news is though, if the work is too demanding, her new employers will be only too willing to help. Some drugs offer the user total oblivion. She probably won't even know what's happening to her.'

She enjoyed telling me this. I wasn't stupid, but I didn't want to hear it. She'd keep for another time. I took a deep breath and left.

I'd managed to hold it together throughout the evening, but all I could think about was Anastazja. I didn't know whether she really had been forcefully taken to London but her mobile constantly went straight to voicemail. Whatever the situation was, I was worried for her and angry with myself for not taking more precautions. I should have known Salford would be keeping an eye on me, but I'd been slack and now she was paying the penalty. I had to think of a way to make amends. I found Coleman sat in the corner of the bar. I'd agreed to meet him in what passed for his local; a bar and restaurant servicing a chain hotel. It suited me because the other drinkers would be passing through, waiting for tomorrow to roll around. Nobody would know who we were, or care.

'How did it go?' he asked.

I'd barely sat down. 'Interesting.'

'That's probably one way to describe a swingers party. What was it like?'

'What are you? Some sort of pervert?'

Coleman shrugged and laughed. 'It's interesting.'

'You wouldn't be saying that if you had to spend a couple of hours with them. I was alright, but they liked Sarah.'

'Don't blame them.'

I stared at him. He held his hands up and said he was a married man.

'Just an observation, Joe. That's all.'

I let it go. 'It was creepy, to tell the truth. We were treated like royalty when we arrived, or maybe fresh meat might be a better description. We got champagne as soon as were through the door. The couple who were clearly the top dogs introduced us to everyone, asking us questions and what have you. It was intense.'

'How far did you have to go?'

'A gentleman never tells.'

Coleman laughed. Don't be holding out on me.'

I took a slow mouthful of diet coke. 'Not too far. They were keen to make sure we were relaxed and comfortable with the set-up. Even when they started to pair off, they were happy for us to mingle and talk to people, get a feel for it.'

'Who did you speak to?' Coleman asked, switching back to business mode. 'Steve Taylor?'

I nodded. 'Nose.' He was a powerfully built man and clearly took good care of himself. 'We spoke to him and his wife.'

'What was he like?'

'Keen to talk to Sarah, as you can imagine. When I managed to corner him, we talked business.'

'Business?'

'I followed the script you gave me. I told him I'd just moved back to the city and was setting up a new company.'

'Did he buy it?'

'I think so.' What I didn't want to tell Coleman was that he'd given me his business card and offered to help me find suitable premises. I'd definitely be talking to him again. 'It seems to be as much about business networking as the obvious reason for being there.'

'What about your face? How did you explain that?'

'Nobody was that bothered. Maybe they thought I was piece of rough for them to look at. Besides, I wasn't the star attraction, as you've already noted.'

'How did you work the Murdoch's into the conversation?'

'We told him Sarah knew them from years ago and we'd bumped into them recently.'

'Did he believe you?'

I thought about it. 'I'm sure he did. He told us the Murdoch's were known to the gathering, though he stopped short of naming them as fellow members. We played the ghoulish tourist approach, asking what had happened.'

'Any theories?'

I shook my head. 'We spoke to a few people about it and they all said the same thing; they couldn't believe anybody would want to kill her.'

'Did he admit to sleeping with Murdoch?'

'Not in as many words, but it was pretty much a free for all as we left.'

'Literally?'

'They had the decency to head off in pairs to other rooms. It wasn't like one massive game of Twister.'

Coleman bought us more drinks. 'Did you find out who else the Murdoch's were friendly with?'

'So far as I could tell, no one in particular. Obviously, they were a little cagey with us, but it genuinely seemed to be an open house. They all seemed to know each other really well.'

'Did you get any details of the other members?'

I handed over a selection of business cards. I'd collected cards from accountants, solicitors, builders and even a minor reality TV celebrity star. I assumed they'd had them printed for such occasions. I passed them over to Coleman, as I'd already taken down the details. I watched him fan through them like a pack of cards.

'A right mixture' he said. 'I'll have them checked out.' He put them in his pocket. 'I was hoping for a bit more Joe.'

'They were hardly likely to tell us their darkest secrets on our first visit' I replied, not wanting to get into an argument.

'What did you find out about their involvement with the club?'

'What I've told you. They were regulars, and seemingly a popular pair.' I knew his game. He wanted a breakthrough to take to his superiors to claim the credit for. I knew he was looking to see if Christopher Murdoch stacked up, but he was also hedging his bets. And I wasn't prepared to go that far to help him. 'You've got a good selection of the other regulars with those business cards.'

'Fair enough.'

'Have you spoken to Sonia Bray yet?'

'This morning.'

'How is she?'

'Alright, I guess. A bit fragile, but she'll survive.'

I wondered if it was true. She'd been used by Jennifer Murdoch and left to pick up the pieces. 'Do you reckon Murdoch's financial state was behind her death?'

'I'm not going to discuss the investigation with you.'

'Worth a try.' I wondered about asking him for a favour in helping find Anastazja. He might know someone in London who could check out some likely places. I decided to leave it and wait. I'd keep an eye on Salford's brothel and see what happened.

'My DI has a hard-on for Christopher Murdoch, and frankly, Joe, I'm inclined to agree. We know he's got the motive.'

I cut in. 'But not the opportunity. He was on the M62, remember.'

'That's yet to be established.'

We both finished up our drinks and stood up.
'Find him, Joe. For both our sakes.'

Thirteen

I'd spent most of the night sat in my front room, music on low, watching the 24 hour news channels. I had Anastazja on my mind, or more likely, my conscience. I'd eventually fallen asleep on my couch but my alarm clock woke me a couple of hours later. I'd quickly thrown some bread in the toaster, jumped in the shower and made it to Sarah's house in time.

We drove north, through the market towns of Malton and Pickering before passing through the rugged countryside of Goathland. Turning onto Whitby's West Cliff area, where the majority of bed and breakfasts are found. I circled the long, straight streets until we spotted a family leaving the resort for the day and squeezed the car into the vacated space. We checked the map and quickly found the address we needed.

A man, similar age to Don answered the door. 'Jeremy?' I asked.

'That's right.'

I introduced us and we were invited in. His bed and breakfast was like any other. The long hallway had a room at the front for guests to use and passing through the dining room and kitchen, we headed towards the back of the building, where the private quarters were situated.

'Busy?' I asked him.

Jeremy sighed. 'Surviving. You name it, it's not helping us; food prices, heating costs, people going abroad on holiday.' He laughed. 'Tell the truth, if I knew it was going to be this difficult, I'd have stuck to catching criminals in Hull.'

Don had told us Jeremy's master-plan was to supplement his police pension with the earnings from the bed and breakfast. The early morning starts aren't great' he continued, 'but I'm used to them. The fresh air's good for me and I'm only ninety minutes from back home.'

'You'd recommend it?' I asked.

'I probably would.'

I had money in the bank and the thought of early morning walks on the beach was appealing. I couldn't see myself running a place like this, though.

'How's Don doing?' he asked us.

'He's good' said Sarah. 'As busy as ever.'

Jeremy pointed to some chairs at the table and we all sat down. 'He needs to slow down' he said. 'He always worked too hard; a perfectionist.'

'He won't change.'

'I suppose not, but I know he's made up to have you two working there now. He thinks you go together nicely.'

I changed the subject. 'Don said you think you've found our missing person.'

Jeremy put his glasses on and opened a file he'd placed on the table. 'It was a pleasure to be asked to help, truth be told. Keeps the old grey matter ticking over.' He produced some notes he'd typed up. I could see why he and Don had worked well together. 'Donna Platt hasn't been seen for ten years?'

Sarah and I both nodded.

'Which makes her 29 years old?'

'Right' I confirmed.

'That fits with the woman I've seen.'

'I assume she's not going under her own name?'

'Sort of. This one's stage name is Donna Marie.'

'What makes you think it's her?'

Jeremy laughed and shook his head. 'That's for you to decide. I don't know either way. I just did what Don asked and thought this woman might be worth a look. I know the local club scene anyway, so I knew who to talk to. They know she's from Hull, so it adds some credence to my thoughts. She's been in town for a few months, working the summer season in the clubs. The people I spoke to say she keeps herself to herself. Don said she hasn't had any contact with her family since she left?'

I explained some of the background to him.

'Strange carry on' Jeremy commented. 'I've seen her sing and I can tell you she's excellent, really excellent. A cut above the quality of the regular acts we get in this place. If it is her, I'm not surprised. She thought she was destined for great things.'

'Has she got any friends you know of?'

'You mean male friends?'

'Either.'

'Not that I know of. Like I said, nobody seems to know much about her. She's a bit of a mystery.'

'What's the club like?' Sarah asked.

'As you'd expect, really. It's on the edge of the town centre and caters for the tourists. It's seen better days but it's usually fairly busy. She sings there a couple of times a week and apparently does the odd night in the big hotels. In-house entertainment, that sort of thing.'

'Keeps her busy, then.'

'Seemingly so.'

He took his glasses off and tidied away the papers. He'd told us all he knew.

'We'll check out the club' I said to Sarah, standing.

Jeremy held out a piece of paper to me. 'You'll be wanting this before you go.'

I opened it up and looked at him.

'Her current address' he said.

'Where to?' I asked Sarah. We were stood outside Jeremy's bed and breakfast. He'd gone beyond the call of duty for us. We now had options.

'Her house?'

I shook my head and looked at my watch. 'I think we should go to the club first. They'll be open by now.'

'We might be able to corner her at the house, make less of a scene.'

'We need to make sure it's the right person first. If we make a mess of things, we might blow our only chance of speaking to her.' We had directions to the club, so I pulled rank and started walking.

The club was as I expected; run down and almost empty. Walking around Whitby, it was clear it was the kind of place the town was leaving behind. The old fish and chip restaurants were being replaced with trendy bars and bistros. We walked into the club and found an empty table. The walls displayed framed photographs of past performers, both semi-famous and unknown. In the far corner of the room was a small stage, with a drum-kit set up ready for use. On the table was a leaflet advertising the forthcoming attractions. We found Donna on the listings and looked at the small photograph. It was Donna Platt. Ten years older, but definitely her. I took the leaflet to the bar and ordered two diet cokes.

'What time's she on?' I asked. The leaflet didn't specify.

'Hopefully tonight, mate' the barman replied.

'Hopefully?'

'She was off sick last night.'

I handed over a five pound note. 'I've heard she's good.'

'She's excellent. Very popular with the regulars. She's been with us for a couple of months. Lucky to have her, really. We don't often get singers of her calibre offering themselves to us. She said she'd even sing for free to prove herself, and we snapped her up. She sings songs from the sixties right up to current chart-hits depending on who's in. She's got something to please everyone, which is pretty rare in these parts, I can tell you.'

'Reliable?'

He stopped and looked at me. 'What are you? Some sort of agent? If you are, you're wasting your time. We've got her booked up for the rest of the season and we've sorted something out for next year. She won't be interested in moving.'

I shook my head. 'No. I'm not an agent.' I accepted my change and headed back to Sarah, thinking Donna Platt was intending to put some roots down in this small seaside town.

I switched the engine off and looking at the address we had for Donna, counted the house numbers, looking for her address. The house was about a mile out of the town centre. It looked like the terraced houses had been converted into separate flats. I wasn't sure if the addition of 'A' on the end of the address meant Donna occupied the upper or lower accommodation. I locked the car and we walked across the road. The adrenaline was pumping. I smiled at Sarah, sure she was feeling it too. This was our moment of truth. Sarah pressed the buzzer and we waited. Neither of us said a word as we stood there. Nobody answered the door, so I pressed the buzzer again. Nothing happened. I took a step back and looked up at the window but there was no sign of movement, not even a twitching net curtain. I bent down and lifted the letterbox flap. There was nothing to see, just a takeaway leaflet on the floor and a table with a telephone sat on it. I straightened myself up, shook my head and told Sarah there was nobody home. We walked back down the path and almost reached the end before we heard the door open.

'Can I help you?' It wasn't Donna Platt. The woman stood at the door was in her seventies.

'We're looking for Donna' Sarah said. 'She lives in the top flat.'

'Debt collectors?'

'Not at all' I said. I offered the woman a business card and explained our situation. 'We're working on behalf of Donna's mother. She's lost touch with her.'

The old woman looked at the card. She shook her head.

'They've left.'

'Left?' said Sarah. 'When?'

'Last night. I saw them piling stuff into their car.'

'Might just be going away for a few days' suggested Sarah.

'They were putting everything in the car; bedding, pots and pans, books, you name it.'

'There was someone helping Donna?' I said, picking up on what she'd said.

'That's right. Chelsea, her daughter, was helping load the car up.'

We sat in the car, reflecting on what we'd learnt.

'She thinks Donna's daughter is about ten years old' I said to Sarah.

She nodded. 'Which means she was born around the time Donna left Hull.'

I nodded. 'Interesting.'

'And we know her father wouldn't have approved.'

I had to agree. From what we knew of Ron Platt, he probably wouldn't have been thrilled to become a grandfather. 'Would it be enough for her to leave the city, though?' I thought about Donna's boyfriend. It seemed like he was keen to settle down with her and had some sort of future. I was sure she could have turned to him for help. 'She's done a runner' I said. 'She was expecting us.'

Sarah nodded but didn't look at me. 'Lisa Day.'

We drove back to Hull without speaking. I dropped Sarah off at her house before heading to the office. I placed Don's sandwich onto the desk in front of him and watched him inspect it, checking I'd got the order he'd texted me right.

'She'll learn from this, Joe.'

'I know.' I didn't blame her. At one time or another, we'd all had to learn some harsh lessons. Lisa Day wasn't all she seemed to be and was obviously still in contact with Donna Platt. Why she was choosing not to share this information with us was something we didn't know. 'Assuming Lisa has told Donna about her mum dying, whatever caused her to leave home must have been serious if she's not got back in touch.'

Don nodded and continued chewing. 'The kid.'

'Donna's neighbour said the kid is about ten, which fits.'

'So we're saying she left because she was pregnant?'

I nodded. I'd turned it over in my mind as I'd driven back.

'Makes sense. I can't imagine her father would have approved.'

'It's a bit extreme in this day and age, isn't it?'

'Maybe, but everyone's different.'

'Was this neighbour able to tell you anything else?'

'Not really. Donna kept herself to herself and she didn't see much of the daughter, Chelsea.'

'Men friends?'

I laughed. 'Men friends?'

'What's wrong with that?'

I told Don he was old-fashioned. 'The neighbour didn't think so.'

'Did you go back to the club she was working at?'

'The barman was a little more forthcoming when we told him Donna had done a runner.'

'How did he take it?'

'Not best pleased. She was a good earner for him by all accounts. He was pleased to have her on his books. When we told him who we were, he mentioned there was one man who hung about with Donna on a regular basis.'

'Name?'

'Just a description.'

Don took a note of it. 'I'll ask Jeremy if he's interested in taking a look.' He stopped writing and looked at me. 'It's costing us a fortune.'

I knew Don was right, but it had gone too far now. We needed some answers. I changed the subject and told Don about last night.

'I assume you've heard nothing from Murdoch?'

I shook my head. I'd tried him again from Whitby but the calls had gone straight to voicemail. 'I did get to meet with Jennifer Murdoch's special friend, Nose. He's an estate agent called Steve Taylor.' I screwed up the sandwich wrapper.

'Speaking of which, I'm going to have a word with him. I'll leave you in peace.'

The office of Taylor & Co Estate Agents was as I expected; light, airy and very sleek. I closed the door behind me and glanced around at the boards on the wall. It appeared Taylor had a substantial portfolio of property to sell around the city, including several new commercial and private properties. I noted a young couple looking at the board displaying what they referred to as 'ideal starter homes.' The way prices had crashed, I'd sold my house at the right time. I couldn't complain; my money was sat in a low-interest, but safe account. It was security while I figured out what I wanted to do.

'Can I help?' I turned to look at the young woman stood next to me. She was wearing a stiff smile and the staff uniform blouse and jacket. I was glad I was self-employed. She closed her laptop down and walked across the room to me. 'My name's Melanie and I deal with all our commercial property.'

I nodded, offered my hand and told her the false name I'd been supplied with by Coleman the previous day. 'I actually met Mr Taylor at a function last night. I was hoping to speak to him if at all possible.'

'I'm afraid Mr Taylor's tied up at the moment. I'm sure I can assist you in his absence.'

I tried not to laugh at the mental picture it conjured up. 'He did say to ask for him personally.'

I watched her walk back to her desk and make a call. Her eyes didn't leave mine. I'd put her nose out of joint but it couldn't be helped. She said he'd be with me in a minute and left me to browse the property boards.

I was looking at a property on Sutton Fields, close to where Briggs's premises where situated. I turned around when I heard Taylor call my name. It took a second for me to remember I was Mr Smith, but I fixed a smile on my face and turned to greet him. He shook my hand and showed me through to his office, stopping only to ask his assistant to bring us a fresh pot of coffee. His office was small but perfectly formed, with the sleek office furniture complementing his wafer-thin laptop. I guessed he was in his late thirties, but he was wearing it well. It was dangerous to judge people on appearance, but if you'd asked me to guess his profession, estate agent would have been near the top of the list.

We exchanged pleasantries until the woman returned with coffee. He asked her to close the door on her way out.

'My daughter' he said by way of explanation. 'Thankfully I'm divorced from her mother.'

'Keeping it in the family, I see.'

He laughed and wagged a jokey finger at me. 'Don't be getting any ideas.'

I held my hands up to concede the point. 'Never crossed my mind.'

He lent back in his chair and smiled at me. 'Great night, wasn't it.'

I shrugged, trying to play it cool. 'We certainly enjoyed ourselves. It was our first time, so we'll get into it, I'm sure.'

'I hope so. That wife of yours is a bit special.'

I resisted the urge to hit the man and fixed a smile back on my face. 'She's certainly that.'

'I hope I'm afforded the opportunity to find out.'

'All in good time.'

He poured me a coffee in a Taylor & Co Estate Agents mug. 'Nice touch.'

'Thanks. We like to try.' He put my business card on his desk. 'I assume you've come for some help in finding premises?'

I took one of my real business cards out of my wallet. 'Not quite.'

Taylor looked like he was going to be sick before composing himself. 'If it's money you're after, you've come to the wrong place. Besides, I've done nothing I'm ashamed of.'

I didn't say anything. The idea he was skint was interesting, as I knew he'd been throwing money about in Salford's casino.

'What do you want?' he repeated.

'Jennifer Murdoch.'

'Don't know her.'

He turned away from me. A sure sign he was lying.

'I think you do know her. I'm investigating her murder.'

'I knew you weren't all you made out to be.' He lent forward. 'I bet she isn't even your wife. A woman like that wouldn't look twice at you.'

'Jennifer Murdoch.' I took a deep breath and ignored his attempts to wind me up. 'She was murdered.'

'Like I said, I don't know the woman.'

'Cut the shit. The Murdoch's were members of your little club.'

Taylor shrugged and sighed. 'I barely knew her. We aren't there to talk.'

'What about her husband?'

'What about him?'

'Do you know him better?'

'We're essentially in the same line of business. It gave us something in common and yes, we've done some work together in the past.'

'What kind of work?'

'None of your business.'

I didn't push it. It was probable they were acquainted but I'd find out more when I spoke to Murdoch.

'So you were friendlier with him?'

'That's correct. I'm not denying she was an attractive woman, but she wasn't really my cup of tea.'

'Why did you socialise with her so much, then?'

'I don't follow you.'

'You were regulars at Rischio, the casino.'

'I don't know where you're getting your information from, but you're totally wrong.'

I laughed. 'I don't think so.' I waited for him to continue. Don had taught me silence was oppressive. Someone always broke it and it wasn't going to be me.

He slumped back in his chair and appeared to be thinking. 'So what if I was friendly with the woman? It doesn't mean anything.'

'You were having an affair with her' I said, more a statement than a question. Taylor said nothing, so I continued. 'If you don't talk to me, it'll be the police knocking on your door, not just me.' I leant forward. 'And I don't give a shit about the amount of drugs you're doing.'

Taylor looked beaten. I hammered the point home. 'It's all on the casino's CCTV and the barmen have told me all about it. Your reputation precedes you.'

'I wanted her to leave her husband' he said. 'He had no idea what he had. She was special.'

It seemed like I'd finally found someone who did have a good word for her. 'How long had the affair been going on for?'

Taylor sat back in his chair, looking like I'd relieved him of a large burden. 'A few months. I met her through her husband, at some function or other and it went from there.

The chance to join their club made it easier for us, I suppose.'

'And you didn't mind that?'

'I hated it.'

I nodded. I wouldn't feel comfortable with that situation either. 'How were you funding your spending at the casino? You said you've got no money.'

'Jennifer paid.' He shrugged. 'I didn't like it, but she said she had the money.'

'Where did she get it from?'

'No idea.'

'You didn't ask?'

'Why would I? She had a good job, her husband is well off. I assumed she was alright for money.'

'She owed a lot of money.'

'I had no idea.'

'What about her husband?' I asked. 'What was their marriage like?'

'We never spoke about it. It was off-limits.'

Changing the subject, I asked who bought the drugs.

'She did. In the club.'

'Sure?'

He nodded. I had no idea if he was telling the truth or not.

'What about Frank Salford?'

'Who?'

'Frank Salford.' I didn't tell him who he was.

'Never heard of him.'

He looked genuinely confused. 'Never heard of him.' He looked like he was on the verge of tears, the confident facade long gone. 'Look, I didn't kill her.'

Fourteen

'**Can** I come in?' I asked.

Lisa Day lent on the open door. She wasn't surprised to see me. I followed her into the house and sat down in the front-room.

I got to the point. 'Why did you lie to us, Lisa?' She didn't respond. I watched her hunt around the room for her cigarettes. Finding them, she lit one up. 'Why did you tell Donna we were coming to see her?'

'She's my friend' Lisa eventually said.

'And you've always been in touch with her?'

She nodded.

'Look, I've not come here to have a go at you. I'm trying to do my job, which is to find her for her mother. That's all.'

'I can't help you.'

I looked her in the eye. 'Yes you can. I know you can help me. All I want to do is talk to her.'

'If you can't give me an address, a phone number will do.'

She shook her head.

'Could you pass my number on to her, then?' I asked. 'Tell her who I am and why I want to speak to her?'

'Donna said she doesn't want to talk to you.'

'Have you told her that her mother's dying?'

She wiped her nose and nodded. 'She knows.'

'Does she want to talk to her?'

'No.'

Lisa was upset, so I went back to the beginning. 'Why did Donna leave Hull? Was it because she was pregnant?' She said nothing, so I continued. 'You've got to help me here, Lisa, because I don't understand it. I know her kid is the right age to tie in with her leaving. So what if she was pregnant? She was old enough to have a kid, wasn't she? It can't have been the end of the world?'

'She had to leave' Lisa eventually told me. 'The pressure was too much for her.'

I thought about Donna's boyfriend. 'Tim wanted her to settle down?'

'He would have married her and bought them a house, but it wasn't for Donna. She didn't want all that.'

'Does he know he's got a daughter?'

She shook her head. 'No.'

What a mess. 'Did her parents know?'

'No. Her dad would have hit the roof.'

'They didn't see eye to eye, did they?'

'Not really.'

'Surely they'd have helped with the baby?'

'Her father wouldn't have allowed it. He was quite strict on what she could do.'

'Did she tell them she was pregnant?'

'She wouldn't.'

'What happened after she left?'

'What do you mean?'

'It was a long time ago. What's happened since?'

'She's moved about a bit but hasn't really settled anywhere. I don't really know. We don't talk about it.'

'Maybe she wants to come home?'

'Maybe.'

'She can come home, you know. Nobody's angry with her.'

'I know.' Her voice was a whisper. 'I've told her loads of times.'

'Her father is long gone. She's got no reason to be angry with her mother, has she?'

Lisa looked away and shook her head, but I wasn't convinced. I knew her father dominated the household but she had no reason I knew of to harbour any bitterness towards her mother. It didn't make sense. I could understand her parents feeling disappointed she was having a child so young. It was natural for them to want a better life for their children. 'There's more to this, isn't there, Lisa? Something you're not telling me. It might not have been ideal, but she was old enough to have a child if she wanted. I stood up.

'Why did her father really disown her?'

She composed herself and nodded. 'Jimmy' she eventually said to me.

'Jimmy?'

'Donna's brother.'

The only brother I knew of was Gary, and we'd already spoken to him.

'He died. Drugs.'

'When?'

'Years ago. Me and Donna were only kids ourselves. We didn't really understand what was happening.'

It was starting to make some sense. I finally felt like I was beginning to get a grip on the Platt family.

'You won't tell Donna's mum about this, will you?' she asked me.

I looked around the bar and found Derek sat in the same corner we'd shared on my previous visit. I'd struck lucky, though I suspected this was where he spent a lot of his time. Walking towards him, I paid no attention this time to the Hull FC photographs. I saw him, sat with a man, draining the last of his drink. I gave the man a five pound note and told him I needed a private word with Derek. Reluctantly, he disappeared to the bar and didn't come back.

'Why didn't you tell me about Jimmy?' I asked him.

Derek looked shocked and took his time before asking me how I knew about his nephew's death.

'Doesn't matter.'

'Matters to me.'

'It's my job to find things out. I'm asking you to save your sister the bother.' I repeated the question. 'Why didn't you tell me about Jimmy?'

'Because it's none of your business.'

'Wrong, Derek. If you want me to find to Donna, I need to know everything about her life, and I'd say her brother dying was pretty important.'

He looked up. 'Why don't you buy us a drink, toast his memory.'

I wasn't in the mood for messing around. 'Tell me about it.'

'Drugs, Joe. The drugs killed him.'

'Overdose?'

Derek nodded. 'June 1986. He was eighteen years old. That's all; eighteen years old. It's no age to die.'

I agreed. 'What happened?'

'Jimmy wasn't a bad lad really. He never got the opportunities. Truth to be told, he wasn't too good at school, no shame in it, some people just aren't. He was always in trouble, disrupting the class and then it became fighting and bullying. He was thrown out at fifteen without sitting any exams.'

'What did he do?'

'Nothing. There wasn't much doing for the likes of Jimmy. At least in my day you could go to sea and you had a chance of making some sort of life for yourself.' He shook his head. 'Jimmy never stood a chance.'

'How did he get into the drugs?'

'Started hanging around with the wrong crowd. Simple as that. He had far too much time on his hands and he started bothering people. His gang would hang around the shops, causing trouble and then the drugs started. First off it was smoking stuff in his bedroom and then it got out of control. It didn't take long for him to move into some cesspit or other with his friends and before we knew it, it was heroin.'

'How did you find out?'

'He wasn't the first youngster we knew to get into it. We knew the signs when we saw them.'

'How did Ron and Maria react?'

'How do you think? It destroyed them to watch him slowly kill himself, but there was nothing they could for him.'

'What did they try?'

'They didn't know what to do for the best. Neither did I, to tell you the truth. They tried stopping his money, giving him money, keeping him locked in the house, but none of it worked.'

'Wasn't there people they could ask for help, professionals?'

'Not really in those days. Nobody wanted to know people like Jimmy back then. He was an embarrassment.'

'Did he try to clean up?'

'No. Not at all. I think the thing was, he liked it. He had nothing else to live for, so he learnt to enjoy what he had. Like we all do, I suppose.'

'But he didn't make it.'

Derek shook his head. 'He died in what you'd call a squat, a few streets away from his proper home. He overdosed and his so called friends didn't even tell anyone for nearly two days. It was only when Maria went looking for him, they did something about it.'

'Did Maria see him?'

'No. She knew what'd happened but it was Ron and me who went into the place and found him.'

I felt terrible for dredging up the bad memories, but I had to continue. 'How did Donna react?'

'She was still a kid, so I don't think she really understood what had happened to her brother.'

'What about Gary?'

'He's a bit older than Donna, so he understood it all a bit better. He used to worship Jimmy and it broke his heart to see him acting like he was. I think he learnt from what happened to his brother, especially as he got older, but he was always angry with his dad for not doing more. It was unfair, but how do you tell a teenager that? Ron could never do well enough in his eyes. You could say Ron lost both his sons at that point.'

I understood why he'd retreated further into himself as time passed. 'How about Donna? I assume it changed his relationship with her?'

'I suppose it explains why he behaved like he did with her.'

He was probably right. I had nothing more to ask, so I stood up, ready to leave but turned back to him. 'You went to the casino because you know Salford?'

'I can't just sit here, doing nothing. I'm not scared of Frank Salford. I've known him for years. He's always thought he could rule by fear, but he's not frightening me off. I didn't like Donna singing in his clubs and if he knows anything that might help us find her, I want him to tell me.'

'Did you know he managed her band?'

'Not as such.'

'What does that mean?'

'I didn't really ask any questions about it. Donna wouldn't have listened to me, anyway.'

I pointed to the bruises on my face. "It's best you leave him alone. The police are well aware of him. Leave it to them.'

Derek shook his head. 'Somebody's got to do something.'

I could tell Sarah had been crying. Her eyes were red and she had a tissue in her hand. I smiled and held the bottle of wine aloft. 'Can I come in?'

She stood aside and let me in. I walked into the kitchen and found the corkscrew and two clean glasses. She was sat on the couch in the front room, legs tucked under her chin. I passed her a glass. 'It wasn't your fault' I said.

'Yes it was.'

I took a sip of wine and shook my head. 'Really, it's not.'

'Whose fault was it, then?'

'Nobody's fault. I had no idea Lisa Day was still in touch with Donna, either. Nobody knew.'

She blew her nose. 'It doesn't make it any easier.'

'You live and learn.' I knew how true that statement was after investigating my wife's death. I had no experience and didn't know what I was getting into. You've got to learn the rules of the game. I told Sarah what I'd learnt about Donna's brother, Jimmy.

'A drug addict' she said. 'It certainly explains why she was wrapped in cotton wool.'

I felt bad for Jimmy. It seemed like he had never stood a chance. We were a similar age and we'd both grown up in a decaying city which offered little. I had been fortunate and lost myself in rugby, and for all the pain it caused me, I'd also got some priceless moments to look back on. I'd never known the despair of drug addiction or experienced the knowledge life wasn't going to offer you anything. I poured us another glass of wine. 'Are you working tomorrow?' I asked.

'If Dad'll have me.'

'Course he will. You've got to remember she played all of us, not just you.'

'I suppose.'

Sarah leant across and squeezed my hand. 'Thanks, Joe.'

I turned to face her and smiled. 'All part of the service.'

She kissed me gently on the lips.

I picked up my glass and found an empty corner of the pub. I didn't know how I was supposed to react when Sarah had kissed me. I wasn't sure if I was overreacting and reading too much into it, but I needed to get out of her house and have a think about what had happened. I swallowed a mouthful of lager and wondered if it meant anything. I knew there was more to consider than simply kissing her back. There was our professional relationship to think about. There was also our friendship to consider, and Don. More importantly, there was Debbie to think about. Would she be happy for me? I finished my pint and went back to the bar for another. I listened to the acoustic artist the pub had performing in the corner. Normally, his unusual songs about doomed World War One soldiers and life's drifters would have interested me, but not tonight. I put a flyer in my pocket and decided I'd look him up another time. It was time to go home.

Alcohol wasn't what I needed. It had been tempting to stay in the pub all night, listening to the music, but going home was the right thing to do. I could close the curtains, darken the room and put some music on low. Then I could think rationally about what I should do. It was a ten minute walk to the flat from the pub and the fresh air felt like it was doing me some good. I fumbled in my pocket for the door key and became aware of a presence behind me. I took a deep breath and turned around, ready for the worst.

'Now then, Joe.'

I took a step back, so I could see who it was. 'The wanderer returns,' I said to Christopher Murdoch.

He waved a bottle of Jack Daniels at me. 'Can I come up?'

I stood my ground, not really in the mood to deal with him. 'What do you want?'

'I want to talk you.'

I closed the door to my flat and rinsed out two glasses. Murdoch passed me the bottle and I poured us both generous measures. We took them into the front room and sat down.

'Where have you been? I asked.

'Here and there.'

I put my glass down and told him not to fuck with me. I was beyond the point of caring.

'Amsterdam. I jumped on the ferry and had a couple of nights away. I needed to get my head together.'

I laughed. I didn't mean to, but the situation was so ridiculous. 'You're the chief suspect in your wife's murder.'

Murdoch shrugged. 'I thought you could handle it for me.'

'You thought I could handle it for you?' I was shouting. 'What made you think that? You've told me nothing, given me no help.' I calmed myself down. 'You're taking the piss out of me.' I swallowed the drink and put my glass down. 'Why should I work for you?'

'Because you understand me, Joe. You know what it's like to be accused of something you didn't do. I didn't kill my wife. It maybe doesn't look good, but it's the truth. I needed to get away, clear my head and come back ready to sort this mess out.' He was silent until I looked at him. 'I'm sorry for running away, but I didn't kill her. You've got to trust me on that.' He took his cheque book out. 'How much do you want?'

I snorted and waved away the cheque. 'Trust you? I haven't heard from you for days and I've got the police breathing down my neck. Do you understand how your disappearing act makes you look?'

'I know.' He poured us another drink. 'It doesn't look great.'

'Have you told the police you're back?'

Murdoch shook his head.

'Jane?'

'No.'

Nobody knew he was back in Hull. It was a chance for me to ask my questions. I asked him if he knew Dave Johnson.

'Name doesn't ring a bell.'

'Don't bullshit me. He works for Frank Salford at the casino.' I described Johnson to him.

Murdoch admitted he knew who I was talking about. 'I'm not on first name terms with him, though.'

He picked up a handful of my CDs. 'What is this stuff?'

I ignored him. 'What's going on at the casino?'

'How do you mean?'

'Why was your wife allowed to run up large debts in the place?'

'I don't know. It wasn't any of my business. She wasn't the kind of person who would ask for help. She was independent.'

'But she asked for your help?'

'Eventually she did, but I wasn't much good to her, I'm afraid.'

'Why not?'

'She wanted money and I didn't have any to give her.'

'No money?' I thought back to my visit to his office. It was state of the art. He certainly looked like a successful businessman on paper. 'You're skint?'

'I don't have access to the kind of money she wanted.'

'What happened?'

'What do you mean?'

'I assume Salford wants his money back?'

'I would assume so, but I couldn't really tell you. Jennifer dealt with him and kept it to herself.'

'I warned you, don't bullshit me.' I could feel the anger rising again. 'I was dragged out of Hull to a field with a freshly dug grave and told quite clearly to mind my own business.' I was specifically told you and your wife were off-limits and I want to know why.'

'I've no idea. She owed them some money, that's all.'

'I don't think so.' I leant forward. 'I don't mind telling you, I was shitting myself. These aren't people you mess with. Do you know about Frank Salford?' I asked, but didn't give him time to answer. 'His speciality is to bury alive those who cross him.'

Murdoch was silent. I took another big slug of bourbon. 'Johnson is his right hand man, and if anything, he's even more violent. These kind of people don't play games. If they're warning me off, they've got good reason to.'

'I don't know what my wife was involved in' he whispered.

'I don't believe you. Jane said you've been acting strangely at work. I was on a roll and I wasn't letting him off the hook.

'I've just lost my wife.'

'Before then. She said you weren't acting normally; disappearing all the time and not telling anyone where you were going.' I poured another drink. 'What changed?'

'It's a stressful job. I have a lot of responsibilities to a lot of different people. You wouldn't understand.'

I laughed. 'Try me.'

Murdoch shook his head. 'It's nothing really, the normal stresses of the job, that's all.'

I nodded, but I didn't believe him. I pressed on. 'You like the massage parlours, don't you.'

'What?'

'Massage parlours, paying women for sex. That's your kind of thing, isn't it?'

Murdoch laughed and put his glass down. 'I don't know what you're talking about.'

'I saw you.'

Murdoch looked crestfallen. 'It's just a massage. What's wrong with that?'

'Massage?'

'It's all perfectly above board.'

'I said don't fuck me about.'

Murdoch drained his glass and laughed. 'So what? I like to have sex. It's hardly a crime, is it?'

It wasn't a crime, but I knew the city had countless massage parlours, and he'd chosen Frank Salford's place. He still wasn't telling me the whole truth. I passed him the Jack Daniel's back and told him to get out of my flat. I'd had enough of the man. 'I don't act for you anymore.'

Fifteen

I hadn't slept well after Murdoch had left my flat. I'd eventually given up and sat in the front room with a pot of coffee and a book. As usual, I'd started to fall sleep just as it was time for my alarm to go off. Arriving at the office early, I threw the newspaper onto my desk and sat down to catch up on the police's progress in finding Jennifer Murdoch's killer. The lead story amounted to little more than a thinly disguised attack on her husband, but I wasn't too bothered. There was little which was new.

I said hello to Sarah when she arrived and busied myself on my computer. I could hear her making coffee and contemplated what I should do.

She passed me my mug and smiled. 'Get home okay last night?'

'Murdoch was waiting for me on my doorstep.'

'Really?'

'Said he'd been away for a couple of days, needed to get his head sorted.'

'Doesn't look good though, does it?'

'Not really.'

Don arrived, poured himself a drink and joined us. I told him about Murdoch's visit.

'I don't think we're acting for him now' I explained. 'He's still holding back on me. He's still claiming he knows nothing about Frank Salford.'

'If he won't co-operate with us, it's pointless' said Don. 'We can't help him. It's as simple as that.'

Don had never been keen on me taking the case, but he could have tried to hide his glee a little better.

'I'll send him his money back' I said.

'Don't be sending it all back, though. We've spent legitimate time on him.' He passed me the electricity bill which had arrived in the morning's post.

I nodded. 'Right.'

The phone rang and Sarah gave us the thumbs up. I watched her start to take the caller's details down. Don lent forward and lowered his voice. 'Sarah told me about Lisa Day.'

I shrugged. 'Wasn't her fault. She wasn't to know we were being taken for a ride.'

'I think she's embarrassed.'

'I've already told her she shouldn't be. It's helped us get closer to the truth, which is what we all want. Did she tell you about Donna's brother?'

Don nodded. 'Terrible business.'

I looked at my watch. It was time to see Maria Platt.

Sarah offered to put the kettle on. I knew she was still embarrassed over what had happened in Whitby, but mentioning it would only make things worse. Maria Platt sat in front of me, close to her fireplace. She was pale and still in her dressing gown. She looked worse than the last time I'd seen her.

'I assume you know why we're here' I said, once Sarah returned to the room.

Maria Platt nodded. 'My brother told me.'

Derek Jones had beaten me there. His nephew was on the agenda, so I ran with it. 'Why didn't you tell us about Jimmy?' I asked.

'I was ashamed' she eventually replied. 'My son was a junkie and he died. I don't like talking to people about it.'

I got the message and let Sarah continue with the questions.

'We know it's difficult for you' Sarah said. 'But we need to talk about it. The death of her brother must have hit her hard.'

'It did hit her hard. Jimmy was her hero; she'd follow him around everywhere, even though there was a few years between them. He loved looking after her, too. He was great with his brother and sister.'

'But then Jimmy got into drugs?'

'It changed him. The Jimmy I knew died the first time he took that muck. We tried to help, we really did. We even locked him in a bedroom and stood guard over him in an attempt to get him to kick the stuff. It didn't work, though. He got out through a window. There was nothing we could do. He didn't want to help himself.'

'How did your husband react?' I asked her.

'Ron was angry, like I was' she said. 'But he was our son. We loved him and tried to help him best we could, but it wasn't easy.'

'I assume it scarred you both?'

'We lost a child. What do you think?'

I stood up and walked across to the mantelpiece to look at photographs of Jimmy. I found one at the back, probably in his early teens, looking smart in his school uniform. Nearer the front were photographs of Ron with various ships and crews. I bent down to read the names and noted several of them reoccurred over the years. Long lasting ties, I assumed. I bet they could tell some stories. One of the names was Briggs, and looking closer I could tell it was a brother of Terrence Briggs. Remembering he had photographs of trawlers on his walls, I asked if I could borrow it to take a copy. I knew if my uncle was alive, he'd be interested at looking at the faces. I must be softening, because I thought Briggs would be the same.

I sat back down and thanked her. I tried to sound conciliatory. 'We all lose people we love, but we deal with it in different ways, don't we? I don't mean to upset you, but I want to know how your husband reacted. Did it change his relationship with Donna?'

'How do you mean?'

'Did he become more protective towards her as she grew up?'

'It was only natural.'

'Perfectly understandable.' I put my mug down. 'How did he react to Donna's pregnancy?' It was a question she wasn't expecting.

'How do you know?' she asked.

'It doesn't matter.'

She sighed, accepting the point. 'Nothing really matters to me now other than seeing Donna again.'

'We're trying out best' Sarah said. We'd agreed not to mention Whitby yet in case we got her hopes up.

'Donna was fifteen when she was pregnant. It took her months to tell me, her own mother. She was scared and didn't know what to do. I found out eventually and she broke down in tears when I confronted her. She thought I'd be ashamed of her, but I couldn't be ashamed of my own daughter. Truth be told, I was angry at first, but it was only because I wanted the best for her. I didn't want her to make the same mistakes as I had.'

'What happened?' Sarah asked. I was doing the maths. We weren't talking about Donna's daughter, Chelsea.

'She had an abortion.'

I looked away as Maria Platt started to cry. Sarah sat next to her and comforted her.

'I promised Donna I wouldn't tell her dad, but I broke my word. He had a right to know.'

'How did he react?' I asked.

'He went mad, saying she'd let us down. He couldn't believe it. Donna wouldn't tell him who the father was, which just made it worse. She eventually told me it was a boy in her class at school, but it wouldn't have done Ron any good knowing. I took Donna to the clinic for the abortion but Ron wouldn't come. Things weren't the same after that.'

'Was that the last of it?' I asked. We weren't talking about Donna's daughter, Chelsea, but I didn't really want to make any trouble for Lisa Day.

Maria Platt shook her head. 'No. Donna fell pregnant again.'

'When?'

'Just before she left.'

'How did her father react?'

'Badly.'

I waited for her to compose herself.

'He hit the roof, saying she was ruining her life and not learning from her mistakes.'

'I would have thought he'd have been pleased. It would have stopped her singing in the clubs?'

'I think Ron thought he could stop her doing it. He was worried we'd have another mouth to feed and no money. He wanted Donna to have another abortion. He reckoned she'd only attract losers if she had a kid to be thinking of.' I glanced at Sarah. 'I'm sure that's not true.'

'That's how he felt. I tried to persuade him, but he wouldn't budge. He couldn't accept she was pregnant. She told him she was keeping the baby.'

'Wouldn't Tim have stood by her? I would have thought Ron would have been happy for that to happen?'

'Donna said she didn't want anything more to do with Tim. She said he was too boring for her. They had a massive row and he told her she couldn't stay in our house with the kid.'

'So she left?'

Maria Platt gave me the slightest of nods and turned away from me.

I sat at my desk, staring at the photograph Maria Platt had lent to me. I knew I still needed to tell Briggs about his auditor and the photograph was giving me the kick-start I needed. I also still had questions for him and couldn't leave it alone. I finished my coffee and stared at my laptop. The initial excitement of locating Donna Platt had evaporated. We were back to square one. All we could hope was that she made her way back to Whitby and our man heard about it. Sarah would keep chasing and pushing where she could.

'Joe Geraghty?'

I looked at the man asking the question; cheap suit, clean shaven and short hair. His side-kick was almost identical in appearance, just twenty years younger.

'Who's asking?' I immediately knew who they were. They flashed identity cards at me and sat down. The titles they gave me were pompous and overblown. Fraud Squad Officers.

'You know why we're here.'

'I don't even know who you are.'

'You can ring DS Coleman if you like' said the older man. 'He gave us your details.'

He was clearly in charge, but I wasn't in the mood for them. 'What do you want?'

'Christopher Murdoch.'

'There's a surprise.'

'We need to talk to him.'

I sat back in my chair and stared at him. Murdoch still hadn't been in touch with them. 'I can't help you.'

'We think you can.'

I laughed. 'Why would you think that?'

'He's your client.'

'I don't know where he is.' It was partially true, at least.

'Let's not go down that road, Joe.'

I shrugged. 'I know nothing more than you. He rang to say he'd be back any day.'

'Well, that's good news, isn't it? I believe Richard is also very keen to talk to him.'

'I'm sure he is.' We sat in silence until I broke the golden rule and continued. 'What's your interest in Mr Murdoch?'

'There's been a development.'

'What kind of development?'

'We've got some new information we'd like to discuss with him. I assume he's been completely frank and open with you about his business activities?'

They knew the answer as well as I did. 'If you've got something to say, spit it out.'

'Tell him' the older man said to his colleague.

'You're familiar with the Newington Ward of the city?'

I nodded. I'd spent a lot of time there lately and knew of Murdoch's involvement.

'Mr Murdoch's company is in charge of delivering the planned regeneration of the area' he continued. 'It's a big project because as I'm sure you appreciate, the area is a shithole. The plan is to demolish a load of the old houses and buildings and pretty much start again.'

The older man turned to me. 'Which means there's a lot of money floating around in the system. Compulsory house purchases, nice new ones to build. Accountants, architects, they've all got their grubby fingers in the pie.'

I said nothing but I'd got the point.

'And given our economic times, people are desperate to be involved. It's highly profitable work, as I'm sure I don't need to tell you. Pay lip-service to creating jobs and preserving the area's heritage, and you're on the gravy train. Simple as that.'

'So what's the problem?' I asked. I knew what was coming, but felt I had no option but to play along.

'Mr Murdoch is driving the train' said the older man, taking over. 'He's in charge of the budget and he's the one dishing the work out.'

I shrugged. 'It's his area of expertise. I'm sure he knows what he's doing. I wouldn't worry about it, if I was you.'

'But we do worry. Let's say he has some business associates who are of interest to us.'

'Of interest to you?'

'Come on, Joe. I don't need to spell it out to you, do I? Your client is corrupt. I'm sure he started off with good intentions, you know how it is, but he's involved with some very bad people.'

'How do you know this?'

They both laughed. 'We're the police.'

'And we were having a chat with a mutual acquaintance.'

The younger man made a show of flicking through his notes, looking for the name. 'Mr Taylor. A local estate agent.'

'We've met.'

The older man was back in charge. 'So he told us. He said he was in a relationship with Mrs Murdoch.'

'I think calling it a relationship might be over the top' I said.

'Don't care. Either way, he was very keen to talk to us about Mr Murdoch's business practices. He even coughed to a few indiscretions himself, which we might see our way to turning a blind eye to.'

'Is that so?'

'Indeed. He's proving to be very forthcoming.'

'Good for you.'

The older man lent forward. 'It is good news for us, make no mistake about that. Your client is involved with some very naughty people. I can think of one property developer who's making an absolute killing from compulsory purchases.'

'Name?'

He laughed and shook his head. 'I think we're done here.'

'I'll find out' I said.

He nodded to his colleague and they stood up. 'Which would be your prerogative.' They towered above me. 'You need to choose your friends more carefully, Joe.'

Briggs was as rude as I remembered. As I sat in the reception area waiting for him to see me, I wondered why I was bothering. I leafed through the trade magazines in an attempt to distract myself before he beckoned me through to his office. I passed Briggs the photograph.

'What's this?'

'I borrowed it' I explained. 'I had an uncle who went to sea. He'd have loved to see this, so I thought you might be the same.' Leaning forwards, I pointed to the face I thought he'd be interested in. 'I assume he's a relative.'

Briggs examined it before placing it on his desk. 'My brother.'

'I thought you might want to show him.'

'He's dead.'

'Sorry.'

'Don't be. Happened years back.' He picked the photograph back up and looked at it. He sat back in his chair, saying nothing. It was the first time he'd looked lost for words.

'Are you from Hessle Road?' I asked him.

'Born there and hated the place. Couldn't wait to get away. My dad couldn't always find work. The thing was, if the trawler owners didn't like you for whatever reason, they could stop you from working for months. I used to hate it when the trawlers came back in. The blokes on them would have loads of money on them and they thought it made them royalty around the area. If you were different, or wanted to do something different, you were

158

marginalised. Nobody wanted to know you. Everything was geared towards the trawlers. If you're part of the community, you're fine. If you're not, you might as well not exist.'

The venom in his voice surprised me.

'I had no intention of following my dad and brother to sea' he continued. 'It was a horrible life. My mum never knew what money she'd have, or more likely not have. My dad hated it, too, but never managed to get out. He was dead set against my brother joining him, but a job was a job, even in those days.'

I changed the subject. 'Lot of building work going on in the area now, though.'

'Not before time. The house we lived in was a shithole; always damp and cold. We couldn't afford any better, so we were stuck. I don't mind telling you it'll be a pleasure to knock some of those buildings down.'

'I don't suppose it's to be sniffed at.'

'Not at the moment.'

'Did Jennifer get you the contracts?'

Briggs shook his head. 'She introduced me to her husband, but that's all.'

'Handy, though?'

'Of course it was useful. It's how the world goes around.'

'How's he to work for?'

'What's it to you?'

'I'm looking into his wife's death.'

'I told you I don't need your help anymore.'

He stood up but I pressed on. I wasn't finished. 'Mr Murdoch has asked me to investigate his wife's death.'

'Keeps you in a job, I suppose.'

'I assume the police have spoken to you?'

'A couple of days ago. I've got nothing to hide. I've accounted for my movements and they're happy with that.' Briggs sat back. 'Are you sure you're on the right side?'

'How do you mean?'

'I've heard about how he does business.'

'You said you worked for him.'

'I work with him, not for him, but I wasn't born yesterday. I've seen it all down the years. He's nothing new. All mouth with little to back it up. Typical of the people involved with the local council.'

'Are you saying he's corrupt?'

'I'm saying he knows how to play the game.'

'Does it bother you?'

'Not really. I know how it works and I just get on with it and mind my own business.'

The talk of corruption made me uneasy. 'Have the police spoke to you about his business affairs?'

'They've asked me all kinds of questions. If you ask me, they don't like your client very much.'

I couldn't disagree. 'What have they said about him?'

'Nothing specific, but then it's not going to be, is it? They wanted to know what kind of relationship we had, what he was like. I didn't really have much to tell them. I was busy with running my own business, and besides, I barely know him. We've worked together, but that's it. Been at the same charity nights and what have you, but we've never really socialised together.'

He called his PA and asked for coffee. He didn't offer me one.

'What's the crack with Jennifer?' he asked.

'The police investigation is ongoing.'

His eyes narrowed. 'And you don't think your client did it?'

My client – There was no backing out now. 'No.'

'They seemed pretty certain to me.'

I shrugged. 'He tells me he didn't do it. It's good enough for me.'

'I suppose if he's paying, it would be.'

I watched him pour himself a coffee.

'If he didn't kill her, who did?' said Briggs.

It was a good question. 'I'm looking at a few things.' I didn't want to tell him how little I had to go on, though I'd certainly be talking to Taylor again in the near future.

He placed his mug down and looked at me. 'She was my employee, and for all I've said about her, I do want her killer caught.'

'It's what we all want.' I told him what I knew about Sonia Bray and his auditors.

Briggs considered the information. 'I'm not surprised.'

'No?'

He shook his head. 'Sonia was a dependable employee, the kind you could rely on. I never really bought the fact she was stealing from me.'

'Why sack her, then?'

'Because it was easier.' For once, Briggs looked ruffled and I knew I'd embarrassed him. 'If I lost Jennifer, I might have lost the work her husband put my way.'

It wasn't embarrassment. It was shame. He'd willingly sacked an employee who'd done nothing wrong. 'You just let it drift?'

'I did my best to stop it without saying anything. I took an interest in my books, made sure I wasn't signing cheques without good reason, that kind of thing. I had the auditors come in more regularly, too.'

'The auditor was involved with Jennifer.'

'I didn't know that.'

'What are you going to do about Sonia?'

'What do you mean?'

'You accused her of theft and sacked her.'

'She's got another job now.'

'That's not the point.'

Briggs shrugged. 'What do you expect me to do?'

I stood up. I'd had enough of listening to him for one day. I put my coat on and turned back to him. 'I'll tell you what you're going to do. You're going to send her and a friend on a nice holiday. They'll travel first class and have plenty of spending money on them. How's that for starters?'

Briggs nodded. 'I'll think on it.'

'Make sure you do.' I walked to the door, thinking Briggs must really need the work Christopher Murdoch put his way, if he was prepared to accept the thieving. He called my name and I turned around.

'Can I keep that photograph, please?'

I threw it towards him. It was only a copy.

SIXTEEN

I nodded a greeting to Don as I walked into the office. He stopped what he was doing and removed his glasses.

'I've been trying to find you' he said.

I took my mobile out of my pocket. 'No battery.'

'Where have you been?'

'Seeing Briggs.'

'Briggs?'

I put the paperwork I'd gone through with him on my desk. I showed Don the original of the photograph I'd shown to Briggs. 'I'd borrowed this from Maria Platt and I needed to see him.'

'Briggs?' asked Don, pointing at the photograph.

'His brother.'

'Right.'

He passed me it back and I pinned it onto the wall behind my desk. That way I wouldn't forget to return it.

'I told Briggs about his auditor' I explained.

'What did he say?'

'I don't think he cared, to be honest.'

'Why not?'

I explained how he got some of his work.

Don shook his head. 'At least it's done. I didn't particularly fancy talking to him about it.'

I laughed. 'I told him about Sonia Bray as well. Told him he had to make it up to her.'

'So far as you can make it up to her.'

'Pretty much.' Don asked what else I'd been doing.

I took a deep breath. 'Christopher Murdoch.'

'Murdoch?'

'What?'

'I thought you'd had your fill of him?'

'Things change.'

Don stopped working. 'Like?'

'I want to finish this thing.'

'Good.'

'What?'

'I said, good.'

'I didn't think you approved?'

'I don't approve of you throwing the towel in.'

I smiled and tried to not to show my pleasure. The attitude of the two Fraud Squad officers had convinced me to help Murdoch. Their attitude annoyed me. If they were prepared to talk to me in such a condescending manner, I was going to kick back and make things as awkward as possible for them. Debbie always said my pigheadedness was my worst trait.

'So what's new?' he asked.

I told him about the two officers.

'Anybody I know?'

'Don't know, but I'll find out when I talk to Coleman later. They wanted to know where Murdoch is but I wasn't really in the mood to help them. They reckon they've got some new information on his activities.'

'What kind of information?'

'Steve Taylor, the estate agent guy. Sounds like he's getting worried.'

'What's his story?'

'Murdoch is leading some regeneration in the Hessle Road area and there are plenty of people who want a piece of the action. The police reckon Murdoch's corrupt and involved over his head.'

'Any proof?'

'Don't know.'

'Kick backs?'

I nodded. 'Compulsory purchases of buildings; that kind of thing.'

'Talking about a lot of money. Can we find out what the project entails?'

I said I'd do my best. Google - the investigator's best friend would be a good start.

He passed me a print-out. 'In the meantime, take a look at this. Steve Taylor knocked his first wife about.'

'Married more than once?'

'Onto his second wife but that seems to be all but finished. Off the record, it sounds like he's up to his old tricks. Police have been called to his address on a couple of occasions for disturbances of the peace, but no charges have ever been brought.'

It was interesting stuff. I didn't trust or like the man.

'Who do the police reckon have got their claws into Murdoch?' Don asked.

'They wouldn't say. All they'd tell me was that there was a property dealer who was making some serious money from it all. He's the man we need to talk to.'

'You think this property developer might be involved in Jennifer Murdoch's death?'

It was a big leap. 'I bet they know something.'

'Name?'

'They wouldn't tell me.'

Don made a note. 'I'm sure we can find out.' He stood up, walked over to my desk and picked up a piece of paper. 'Let's get things straight, then.'

Ten minutes later we had most of the pertinent issues surrounding Jennifer Murdoch's death written down. It was a tangled web, with Christopher Murdoch at its centre. We knew Terrence Briggs was involved with the building work on Murdoch's projects and was now struggling for work. Although I'd made a note to take a closer look at his finances. I wanted to know how much work Jennifer Murdoch got him through her husband. Beyond that we knew Steve Taylor was involved, as the police said they were prepared to overlook some of his indiscretions. I assumed his involvement came about when the properties were sold. He was also having an affair with Jennifer Murdoch and wanted more from her. A large question mark remained against Christopher Murdoch. His alibi was flimsy and he had financial difficulties his wife's death would resolve. I only had his word he hadn't killed her. On top of which, we needed to know the identity of the property developer.

I pinned the sheet of paper on the wall, next to the photograph and made us both a cup of coffee. As I drank, I thought about what I needed to do. I had to speak to Murdoch and I wanted to see what Taylor had to say for himself. I weighed up what leverage I could use to make him talk.

'Where's Sarah?' I asked.
'Working from home.'
'Since when?'
'Since today.'

The Internet filled the blanks in. Murdoch's company, FutureVision Limited had a temporary exhibition space on The Boulevard, the former jewel of Hessle Road. The houses which lined the street were once home to the city's rich and influential. Now, the area was dilapidated, packed with self-contained flats and shared houses. If any part of the city needed a shot in the arm, this was it.

After my visit from the police, I wanted to know more about the work Murdoch was doing here and take something back to Don. I hated myself for it, but I couldn't walk away. Murdoch had involved me in something, and I was going to get to the bottom of it. Looking around, the exhibition was impressive; large blow-ups of artist's impressions lined the walls. The thrust of the project was the building of new, eco-friendly housing, complimented by the refurbishment of the older houses in the immediate area.

'Help you, love?'
I turned to face the woman asking me the question. She wasn't wearing a name-badge. 'Just looking, really' I said.

'It's very impressive, isn't it' she said, pointing to the plans for new housing. 'The area has been crying out for this kind of thing for years.'

I nodded my agreement. 'It all looks very interesting.'
'Live round her?'
'Not really. I know people in the area. Thought I'd have a look.' It wasn't really a lie.

She stood next to me. 'It'll certainly change for them.'

'Do you work here?' I asked. We both laughed at the how stupid the question sounded.

'Volunteer' she said. 'We get the locals come in to see what's going on and I think they prefer a familiar face.'

'It's a private project, right?'

'The council are involved, but they contract a lot of the work out to specialists, especially the design and management kind of stuff.' She pointed across the office to more exhibition boards. 'It's not only housing we're working on. There's going to be programmes to cut anti-social behaviour from the youngsters. We're consulting with them to see what facilities they'd like in the area. There's plans in place with the heritage team to restore some of the fountains you'll have probably walked past to get here back to their former glory. This area has had its share of bad luck over the years and it's still tough going for a lot of people but it's going to be a much nicer place to live when it's finished.'

I smiled back at her. 'I'm sure it will be.'

'It's a start. Give people some hope and maybe it'll kick-start getting some jobs back into the area. We're even hoping to get an education resource, which will focus on the area's fishing history. If it comes off, it'll be great for the kids and provide a real link to the past for them. It'll bring the community together.'

'Is all this definitely going to happen?' I asked.

'This is the consultation stage. Nothing's set in stone yet, so you need to have a look around and see what you like and don't like about the suggestions. That way, we can put suggestions forward to the powers that be.'

'The council?'

'And their partners.'

I nodded. The plans were certainly impressive.

'How much money are we talking about?' I asked the woman, wondering how much the work was worth to Murdoch.

'We're talking tens of millions over the long-term. We're not messing around here, love.'

I was hungry, but I wanted to see Murdoch before I called it a day. His house was situated at the bottom of a quiet suburb in North Ferriby, a small village hidden away on the outskirts of Hull. I parked at the top of the street and paused for a moment to admire the view of the Humber Bridge. As evening was starting to draw in, the bridge lit up like a beacon. As you approached the city you drove underneath the bridge and you knew you were almost home. I loved the feeling it gave me. Murdoch's house was an imposing detached building, set well apart from its neighbouring properties, the well-tended garden suggesting the services of a gardener were used. I walked down the side of the property, to get a closer look at where the police thought Jennifer Murdoch's killer had accessed the house. A couple more steps and the security light burst into action and flooded the front of the house. I quickly retraced my steps and rang the front door bell. Christopher Murdoch opened the door.

I nodded a greeting. 'Can I come in, please?'

'Why?'

'We need to talk.'

From the television and the hi-fi to the furnishing and decor, everything was top of the range. Murdoch offered me a drink, so I settled on water. I was driving and didn't want to spend the night on the sofa, like he'd done at my flat.

'I thought we'd reached the end of the road' he said to me.

I shook my head. 'Unfinished business.'

'Good. I'm glad you came.'

'Have you spoken to the police?' I asked him, wanting to side-step the matey chat.

Murdoch swallowed his Jack Daniels and nodded. 'I spoke to DS Coleman.'

'Pleased to see you?'

'Delighted, I'd say. He was that happy to see me, he wanted to record our chat and everything.'

'Don't worry. Standard procedure.'

'Didn't feel like it.'

I leant forward. 'I can only help you if I know the truth, so I'm only going to ask once more. All I want is the truth. Did you kill your wife?'

Murdoch stared at me. I'd given him an out. I'd offered to help, whatever the situation. I held his stare. We were going to do this eye to eye. He shook his head and eventually said he hadn't murdered his wife.

I nodded. 'Good. So what did the police have to say?'

'What?'

'The police.'

'You accuse me of killing my wife and then change the subject?'

'That's pretty much how it works.'

Murdoch stood up and paced the room. 'I can't believe I'm hearing this.'

'Believe it.'

'I didn't kill her. I loved her.'

'You loved her so much you were having an affair?'

'What affair?'

'I've spoken to Jane.'

Murdoch sat back down in his chair and poured himself another drink. 'It's not important.'

'You're having an affair, your alibi is worthless and you're financially better off with your wife dead. I'd say it was important.' It sounded worse than I'd meant it to.

'My wife is better off dead?'

'I believe you' I said. He looked shaken and lost for words. Something in the way he'd looked at me, totally stripped of everything, convinced me. I asked him again about Coleman.

'He wanted to know where I'd been' he explained. 'Why I'd run away, as he put it.'

'What did you tell him?'

'Same as I told you; I needed to get away for a few days, clear my head.'

'Did he believe you?'

'He said it made me look guilty and told me to confess, that I'd feel a lot better for it if I told him what'd happened. The usual rubbish but I'm ready for him now.'

'I hear you're corrupt.'

'Corrupt?'

'You're under investigation.'

Murdoch finished his drink and poured himself another. 'I know.'

'Want to tell me about it?'

'It's not what you think.'

I drank a mouthful of water and put the glass on the table which separated us. 'Tell me about it.'

'My wife had a gambling problem and it got us into a financial hole. You know how it is, debts start to mount and we were in trouble. Jennifer's job wasn't particularly secure and my line of work isn't what it was a couple of years ago. Things started to get on top of us.'

'What did you do?'

'Nothing at first. Jennifer was out of control, gambling more and more, and I couldn't reach her. She didn't want my help to start with.'

'What did you offer to do?'

'I offered to help. I wanted to support her but she made it very difficult for me. There was nobody to ask for help, so I had to let her decide what to do. She'd met someone in the casino she went to; they knew who I was and what I did. It was suggested her debts could be taken care of if I worked certain things into my regeneration plans.'

'For the Hessle Road area?'

'Right.'

'When was this?'

'About a year ago.'

'How did it make you feel?'

'I felt fucking angry. I wanted to help Jennifer but she'd put me in a difficult position. She was asking an awful lot from me. She was asking me to jeopardise everything I'd worked for.'

'What did you do?'

'I stalled the matter and held some meetings with these people; see if there was a way forward I could work out, but it wasn't so simple.'

That explained the mysterious meetings, I thought. 'We're talking about the compulsory purchases?'

'For the scheme to work, they wanted the houses they owned knocking down, but it didn't fit the scheme I'd designed. I had no choice, I had to go back to the drawing board and make changes. I can't even begin to tell you how it's destroyed me. I've worked for years to get a shot at a project this big and important. I believe in what I do. It's important and this was my chance to make a real difference.'

The woman I'd spoken to earlier in the day was so full of enthusiasm and belief in the project. I couldn't believe what I was hearing. I didn't particularly like the man but I thought he had some integrity.

'Everybody knew it was wrong' he continued. 'The plans I'd redrawn were wrong, but it seemed like the only option at the time. They're undergoing a consultation process at the moment, but they'll pass. They always do.'

'Change the plans back.'

He laughed. 'I'm too far in. As well as settling Jennifer's debts, they sorted us out financially.'

I couldn't believe what I was hearing. 'How much are these compulsory purchases we're talking about worth?'

'Hundreds of thousands.' Murdoch shrugged. 'I'm not keeping score.'

'And you went along with this?'

Murdoch nodded.

'Fuck's sake. And now the police know about it?'

'Evidently.'

'How?'

'No idea.'

The amendments to the plans would have drawn attention. The fact they knew was what was important.

'Maybe Taylor blabbed?'

It was getting worse. 'Why would he have blabbed?'

'He's involved.'

'And he was having an affair with your wife?'

'She said we could count on him. She didn't enjoy it, but it was the only way.'

'And this is what Jennifer wanted you to do? This was your part of the deal?' He eventually nodded. 'Who did she owe the money to?' I wanted to hear him say the name.

Murdoch composed himself. 'Frank Salford.'

'Can I come in?' I gave Sarah my best smile. 'I'm starving.'

She shook her head, smiled and let me in.

'I've got some Bolognese left if you're interested?'

'Definitely.'

I sat at the table and waited. I watched her, stood at the hob, warming the food up.

'Wine?' she asked.

'Twist my arm.'

I was so hungry I could have eaten a horse, but it was genuinely fantastic. The alcohol was also helping me to calm down. 'Lauren with her dad?'

Sarah nodded. 'Back tomorrow.'

'Are they doing anything good?'

'I hope not on a school night.'

Not unreasonable. 'What do you know?'

'I spoke to Donna Platt's landlord today.'

'Anything?'

'He's not heard from her, but she's paid up for another month.'

'I bet she can't afford to lose the money, either.'

'That's what I thought, so I rang the club, see if they've heard from her.'

'And?'

'They've got word through a friend that's she coming back next week. Told them she had to get away for a few days, get this, for family reasons.'

I laughed. Donna had a sense of humour. 'At least we don't have to go chasing around looking for her.'

'I'd still like to speak to her.'

After all this work, I didn't blame her. We couldn't make her speak to her mother, but I felt we had a right to know the full story now.

'What have you been up to?' Sarah asked.

I smiled. 'We need a proper drink. It's a long story.'

Zest was a ten minute walk from Sarah's house and her favourite bar. In the corner, a literature event was underway, with a guest speaker holding court. We ordered our drinks and found a quiet table away from the crowd.

'Spill the beans' she said.

I sat back and smiled.

She playfully hit me on the arm. 'Spill.'

'I'm acting for Murdoch again.'

'Dad said you'd given him up.'

'I got a visit from the Fraud Squad today, wanting to know all about him. Let's say it aroused my curiosity again.'

She shook her head. 'Doesn't sound great.'

'You know about the Hessle Road regeneration stuff he's working on?'

'The house building and stuff?'

'Right. It turns out he's got his hand in the till.'

'Why are we acting for him, then?'

It was a good point and I thought about it for a moment before eventually answering. 'Because it's not important at the moment. The police are on to him.'

'What good is our involvement going to do? What's the point?'

'The point is he's got what you might call an unwanted sleeping partner in the project. It's a lucrative business, lots of money swilling about.'

'Who?'

'Someone's blackmailing him.'

'Who?'

'A property developer. There's a lot of compulsory purchases going on in the area and this property dealer wants it to be his properties which get bought.'

'And receives compensation well above their market value?'

'Spot on.'

'Anybody we know?'

I nodded. 'Frank Salford.'

'Salford?' Sarah put our refilled drinks on the table. 'That's why he's doesn't like you sticking your nose into his business?'

'Sounds about right.'

'This is serious, Joe. We're talking about a lot of money. He isn't going to back down.'

I nodded and agreed. I was more worried than I was letting on.

'This links back to Murdoch's wife at the casino, doesn't it?'

'She'd been allowed to run up large debts' I explained. 'In exchange, she'd applied pressure to her husband. If he cut Salford into the plan, the debts would go away and there'd be a bit extra for his trouble.'

'And he went along with it?'

'Said he had no choice. The debts were mounting and it was the only way out. Once you even dabble a toe in that kind of business, you can't back away. You're not allowed to do that.'

'He's got no one to blame but himself, Joe. You shouldn't be acting for him out of pity. It's a dangerous game he's sucking you into.'

'I know.' I tried to explain how the project had been Murdoch's big chance; the opportunity to leave a legacy. Not many people had the vision or the ability to deliver it in this city. It made me sad and angry that he probably wouldn't get the chance to finish it now.

'That's not your problem, though. He's got to face the consequences of what he's done. And he was having an affair. Not a very nice man, is he?'

'There's more.'

'More?'

Murdoch had broken down and told me the full story before I'd left his house. 'He didn't want to play with Salford anymore and told him he was going to go to the police.'

'He should do.'

I shook my head. 'He can't.'

'Why not?'

'Salford threatened to kill his wife if he did.'

We finished our drinks and headed back towards Sarah's house. It'd started to rain whilst we were in the bar, so I huddled next to her underneath the umbrella. She was a little tipsy, so I steadied her with a hand around the waist. We dodged the groups of students heading home and turned into her street. As we approached her door, she fumbled in her bag for the house keys.

'Are we alright?' I asked her.

'What do you mean?'

'This working from home business.'

She sighed. 'I'm sorry, Joe. I didn't feel like coming into the office today.'

'Because it'd be embarrassing?'

'No.'

'No?'

'Yes. I was embarrassed about the kiss. It was stupid of me. I was feeling a bit emotional, like I'd let you down over Lisa Day.'

I smiled. 'It wasn't stupid. Not at all. And you didn't let me down.'

We both stood there, in the rain, saying nothing, before she stepped into the house. 'Goodnight, Joe.'

I threw my wet clothes in the washer and put on an old tracksuit. I found a single bottle of beer in my fridge and took it through to the front-room. Flicking through my CDs, I wanted something loud and raucous. Inserting The Hold Steady into the player, the vocals beat down on me like vicious jabs. I smiled at the irony of the album's title, 'Stay Positive.' I now knew for certain Frank Salford was a major threat and I'd stuck my nose into his lucrative business plan. He'd also issued threats to kill Murdoch's wife if he refused to play ball, which had to make him a prime suspect in her death. I drained the bottle and put it down on the floor. If I was to prove Murdoch's innocence, I was going to have to go looking for Salford.

SEVENTEEN

I woke with a renewed sense of purpose. First thing, I called Murdoch, but his mobile was switched off. No sooner had I put the phone down, Don had called to make sure I wasn't going to do anything stupid. He'd obviously spoken to Sarah. I wasn't in the mood for a lecture, but I was mindful of his advice. Just because Salford had established himself as a credible suspect, it didn't mean I could discount all others. With this in mind, I'd telephoned Steve Taylor's estate agency in an attempt to set up a meeting with him. His receptionist told me he'd called in sick, so fingering the business card he'd given me, I'd decided to pay him a visit. I'm sure the address he'd scribbled on it wasn't intended for me, but I wasn't going to turn away the opportunity.

I pressed the buzzer to his flat in the BBC building, where he occupied a penthouse suite. The intercom crackled into life and I told him I needed a word. Reluctantly, he'd allowed me access. Stepping out of the lift and seeing him stood at his door, I could see why. 'Probably walked into the same door as me' I said, as I walked past him and into the room. His face was almost as bad as mine, covered in cuts and bruises. The view of the city centre was spectacular. Below me Queens Gardens sprawled out, the people passing through looking like ants as they went about their business. Extending the view, I could see past the Princes Quay shopping centre and out towards the Humber. 'Nice view.' Taylor said nothing. I assumed it suited his image. This was the kind of place that screamed money, or at least a veneer of it. I pointed to his face. 'Want to talk about it?'

Taylor was drinking a generous measure of whiskey. It was a bit early for me.

'Murdoch's told me you have a business arrangement.'

He was shaking his head. 'I haven't spoken to him since Jennifer's death.'

'I doubt you're on his Christmas card list. You were sleeping with his wife.'

'I'm scared.'

I reluctantly turned away from the view and sat down opposite him. 'And so you should be.'

He laughed. 'You're telling me.'

'Frank Salford?'

Taylor nodded.

'Why?'

'I told his sidekick I was thinking of getting out.'

'Dave Johnson?'

'That's the one. I've had enough. I didn't want to get involved in the first place, but Jennifer was very persuasive.'

I asked him about Jennifer Murdoch. 'What did she do?'

'She introduced me to her husband, told me what they were doing.'

'Did she tell you why they were doing it?'

'No. Just that it was easy money. I didn't ask, and I suppose I didn't want to know.'

'And you went along with it?'

'I need the money. Business is tough at the moment.'

'What did you do?'

He put his drink down and looked at me. 'Didn't Murdoch tell you?'

'I want to hear it from you.'

'He needed valuations for the properties Salford owned. He told me how much I needed to make them worth.'

'And you got some sort of kick-back on that?'

Taylor nodded. 'Based on the valuations I gave the houses. He also promised I'd be the chosen party to market the new properties once they were built.'

'What changed?'

'I know the police have been asking around and Johnson wanted the valuations increasing to levels I couldn't justify. I told Murdoch I didn't want to be a part of it anymore. I told him he had to get me out of it, because it was his wife's fault I was in this mess in the first place.'

I shook my head. The man was naive in the extreme. You don't walk away from people like Salford. 'What did he say?'

'That it'd gone too far.'

'He's probably right.' You roll the dice, you take your chances.

'I tried to reason with Johnson' he continued. 'I went to the casino last night to discuss it. I told him I didn't want to be involved, he could even have the money I'd made, but I wanted to be left alone.'

'He didn't take it well?'

'You could say that.'

'What happened?'

'I thought he was at least going to have a think about it. It was a business proposition. I was jumped outside the casino. I don't know who they were, I'd never seen them before, but they said Johnson would be in touch.'

'Why did you use the casino with Jennifer?'

'They pretty much let us have free reign, so long as were discrete.'

'Didn't you find it strange?'

Taylor shrugged. 'I didn't think about it.'

'What about her debts?'

'I didn't know about them. I assumed her husband was taking care of them, maybe as part of the deal with Salford.' He put his empty glass down. 'Did you know they were after sleeping with her?'

I shook my head. 'They?' It was news to me.

'Salford and Johnson. They were desperate, behaving like teenagers. They were pressurising her. It wasn't nice to watch.'

'Didn't you say anything to them?'

'To them?' He laughed.

'I think we know they won't listen to me. I told Jennifer to be careful.'

'Did you tell her husband about their interest?'
'No.'
I wasn't really surprised. She was probably off-limits, as topics go.
'Can you help me?' he asked.
'With what?'
'Salford.' I watched him pour another drink.
'Why would I want to help you?'
'Because Jennifer meant everything to me. I really wanted to make a go of things with her and told her how we'd set up home together. I know she didn't love her husband; not like she loved me. I'll pay you.'

I stood up and headed towards the door. His actions hadn't matched his words - not by a long distance. I didn't like the man and remembered the information Don had given me about his liking for using his fists. 'I can't help you.'
Taylor followed me. 'Should I go to the police, then?'
I stared at him, wondering how much trouble he'd got himself into already. I wasn't going to validate a decision he'd already made. 'That's up to you.'

'DS Coleman, please.' I smiled to the officer manning the reception desk of the station. I'd called Murdoch as I'd walked to the station, but his mobile was switched off. I needed to speak to him about Steve Taylor.
The officer turned away from me and picked up a telephone. 'Take a seat' he told me.
I paced the room. The uniformly grey walls were decorated with crime prevention posters. The only other person waiting was a teenager, dressed in the standard issue tracksuit and baseball cap. He stared at me, so I smiled back. 'DS Coleman is unavailable' the officer shouted across to me.
I walked across to the desk. 'Try him again. Tell him if he's unavailable, I'm sure a journalist at the paper will be able to help me with my questions.'
He picked up the phone again but never took his eyes off me. I'd made another friend.

Five minutes later, I was sat with Coleman in an interview room. It was even less welcoming than the reception area, but I suppose that was the point.

'What's so important you had to drag me out of my meeting, Joe?'

'I thought you'd be happy to escape a meeting.'

'Get to the point.'

I sighed. 'I thought we had a relationship. Any chance of a coffee?'

He sat down opposite me. 'No.'

I was enjoying getting under his skin. 'I received a visit from a couple of your friends yesterday.'

'Which friends?'

'Fraud Squad or whatever you call it nowadays.'

'So?'

'It'd have been nice to have known they were coming.'

Coleman shrugged. 'Nothing to do with me.'

I nodded and let it go. 'You didn't tell me Murdoch was in Frank Salford's pocket.'

'There's lots of things I don't tell you.'

I understood. There was plenty I wasn't telling him. 'It throws a different light on things, though.'

'Not for us. We're continuing to investigate his wife's murder and we'll consider all the avenues open to us.'

'Checked Salford out?'

'None of your business.'

'My client is under suspicion for a crime he didn't commit, and you're telling me you're not interested in another potential suspect?'

'Why would we be interested in Salford?'

'Because he controls Murdoch.'

'It doesn't mean anything, does it? Murdoch'll be punished for what he's done in due course. That's not my concern.'

I didn't want to mention Salford's threats to kill Jennifer Murdoch yet. 'Have you asked Salford for an alibi?'

'He has one.'

I nodded. Of course he'd have an alibi. 'What about his staff?'

'Nothing doing there.'

'It's your client who has the motive for his wife's death as well the opportunity' Coleman continued. 'She was battered to death. He was more than capable.'

'Bullshit' I said. It was the best I could do. 'He gave you an alibi. He was sat in a motorway lay-by, working on his laptop before he went to the casino.'

Coleman sighed, looked like he was bored by our conversation. 'The casino is irrelevant. Time of death makes it so, and that's being generous to him. We've plotted out the routes he could have taken from the house and it fits.'

'What about CCTV in the lay-by?'

'Nothing on it. He wasn't there, Joe.'

I held his stare, not wanting to look surprised. I felt sick. Murdoch still wasn't giving me the whole story. 'Maybe he parked off camera?'

'We couldn't pick him up on the motorway, either.'

'There's some mistake, then. Why would he give you an alibi which doesn't check out?' I knew it sounded weak.

'People do strange things when they're under pressure.'

'Have you spoken to Steve Taylor?' I asked, changing the subject.

'The guy Jennifer Murdoch was sleeping with?'

I nodded. 'He wanted her to leave her husband.'

Coleman shrugged. 'So why would he kill her?'

I didn't want to reveal what I knew - not without some return. 'It wouldn't be the first time we've seen a crime of passion.'

Coleman laughed. 'That's not the impression I got from talking to Mr Murdoch.'

He glanced at his watch. Hardly subtle. 'Look, Salford's alibi has been checked out; it's rock-solid. He didn't kill her. You're barking up the wrong tree, Joe. You need to be taking a closer look at your client.'

I shook my head. 'Don't forget we went into the swingers club for you. I've tried to help you. Don't treat me like an idiot.' I thought about the state Steve Taylor had been left in and stood up, ready to leave. 'You might not want to leave it too long before you talk to Taylor again.'

'Yes, please' I said to Sarah, seeing her cup of coffee. I picked up the small pile of letters on the corner of my desk and glanced through them.

'Make your own.'

Putting the letters back, I threw my coat into the corner and sat down. 'Please?'

'What's up with you?'

'I've been talking to Coleman.'

She nodded and made me a coffee.

'What did he want?' she shouted to me from the kitchen.

'It was more what I wanted from him.'

She wheeled her chair around to my desk. 'I don't follow.'

'I went to see him about Murdoch.' I put my mug down. I checked my mobile. He hadn't returned my call. 'He didn't kill his wife.'

Sarah shook her head.

'What? I can't just let things drift. It's not right.'

'Why didn't he kill his wife?'

The directness of the question took me by surprise. 'I just know he didn't.' It was the best I could manage, even though the evidence against him was mounting.

'He had the motive, didn't he? And he needed the money?'

I shrugged. 'Everybody has life insurance. It's not a motive by itself.' I hadn't taken any life insurance on Debbie, but decided not to mention it.

'They were both having affairs. He was being blackmailed by Salford. He's a desperate man' said Sarah. 'And his alibi isn't standing up, is it? He's not the kind of man you should be trying to help.'

I thought about how we'd both lost our wives, but kept it to myself, deciding not to mention what Coleman had told me. Instead I told her she was worse than Coleman. 'He didn't do it, Sarah.'

'Fine.' She picked up a writing pad. 'Who did kill her, then?'

I told her about Steve Taylor.

'And why would he have killed her?'

'He wanted her to leave Murdoch, but she wasn't keen.'

'Says who?'

'Murdoch.'

She pulled a face.

'He said it was a convenience thing' I continued, ignoring her protests. 'He needed to keep Taylor sweet as part of the regeneration deal. It was his wife's way of helping.'

'And you believe that?'

'Why not?'

'You've got a lot to learn, Joe. Maybe she did want to leave her husband? Maybe he killed her because she wanted to leave?'

'Maybe Taylor killed her because she wouldn't leave Murdoch?' I countered.

Sarah sighed. 'What about an alibi?'

'Coleman reckons he has one. He wasn't telling me the truth but he was bored just listening to me. He'd have told me anything to get me out of the station.'

'Can we check it out?'

'We can try.' I scribbled a note to follow it up. 'He was beaten up outside Salford's casino last night.'

'Don't go there, Joe.'

'He was told to keep his mouth shut.'

'About what's going on with Murdoch?'

I nodded. 'He's vulnerable. Salford doesn't want him talking to the police about it.'

'And Salford had threatened to kill Jennifer Murdoch.'

I nodded again, pleased Sarah was starting to take my concerns more seriously. She wrote his name on the pad.

'Why would Salford kill her?'

'Murdoch wanted out of the whole thing. This project is what he's been working towards his entire career; his chance to leave a legacy behind. Salford's come along and hijacked it.'

'I'd hardly say hijacked.'

I waved away her words. 'Either way, Murdoch's in over his head and he hasn't got an out.'

'So why would Salford kill her?'

'Take your pick. He wanted to control Murdoch and keep him in line. He couldn't afford him pulling the plug on the deal.'

'But killing his wife?'

'Taylor said Salford and Johnson wanted to sleep with her.'

'Maybe she didn't fall for their charms?'

'It's not cut and dried, is it? I can't believe Coleman is only looking at Murdoch for this.'

'It won't be Coleman's decision, though, will it? Whatever he's doing will be done on orders from higher up.'

'It's still wrong, though. We went out of our way to help him at the swingers club. He was the one giving it all the co-operation bullshit.'

'He's not going to help us.'

I knew she was right; it's his job but it didn't make the way he'd dealt with me taste any less bitter. I finished my drink and switched on my laptop.

'Where's your dad?' I asked.

'Don't know. Said he had a few jobs to do before he came in.'

I nodded. I'd speak to him later.

'I've been thinking about Donna Platt' Sarah said. 'Do you think we should tell her mother we've found her?'

'We haven't really found her yet.'

'We know she's alive. She'll want to know.'

Sarah was right. We probably should let the family know we'd made some progress. 'I'll give Derek a call, see what he thinks.' He also knew Salford. It'd be a chance to find out more.

'Leave it with me. If she's not well, we don't want to charge straight in. Do you think we should mention Lisa Day has been in contact with her?'

'It'll cause more harm than good.'

Sarah cleared away our mugs and busied herself at her desk. I logged into my email account and quickly scanned through them. 'Any plans for tonight?' I asked, starting to formulate a plan.

'I've got a date.'

'A date?'

'With the guy from the other night.'

'I thought you didn't particularly like him?'

'A girl can change her mind, can't she?'

I clicked on my unopened messages and started to read them.

I didn't want to know the details of Sarah's date, so I set off to find Derek. Choosing the pub, I struck lucky first time.

'Now then' I said, placing the drinks in front of us.

'Now then.' He picked his glass up. 'Cheers.'

'Cheers.'

'You're taking a chance, aren't you?'

'What do you mean?'

'This is a black and white pub.'

Rugby. I smiled. 'You've been checking me out.'

'Do you blame me?'

'Not really.'

'How's the knee?'

'Painful.' The cold weather today didn't help.

'I did my knee at sea. Bloody painful.'

'Tell me about it.'

He folded his newspaper up. 'What can I do for you? I assume we're not going to talk rugby?'

'I need to know about Frank Salford.'

'What makes you think I can help?'

I sighed and shrugged. Derek was my best bet. 'I just thought you might be able to.'

'He's seriously bad news' Derek explained. 'Always has been, always will be; ever since he got involved around these parts.'

'He ran clubs around here, didn't he?'

'That's right. Proper clubs, not the rubbish kids go in for nowadays; more variety clubs, I suppose. The thing is it's no lie to say they were the best clubs in the city. People would come from miles around. He always had the best bands, the best comperes, everything.'

'Bit weird, though, wasn't it? Salford would have been around thirty when he started the clubs? Bit young for that kind of thing?'

Derek nodded. 'Sounds about right. You'd have to ask him. I think he just liked the entertainment. And it was somewhere quiet to drink, where he'd get no bother or hassle.'

It made sense. Salford was the kind of man who didn't like attracting attention, so working mens clubs were a safe bet.

'It was his father's influence, I reckon. His dad had owned a pub in the area. The young Salford used to hang around with his mates. A right bunch of tearaways, they were; always in trouble.'

'They used his dad's pub as a base?'

Derek nodded. 'We're sat in it.'

Small world, I thought. 'Did you have any dealings with him?'

'Not at first. He was just a young lad, making his way in the world. Once he had some power, I avoided him best I could.'

'What were his clubs like?'

'He ran a tight ship. Nobody stepped out of line, because you knew what happened if you did. But for all of that, you knew you'd get a good night from him. There was never any funny business when he was there.'

'Ever see anything with your own eyes?'

'Once or twice. It was always him and his side-kick.'

'Dave Johnson?'

'That's him.'

'Did they run their businesses from the clubs?'

Derek nodded. 'Drugs.'

'Drugs.' I nodded and thought about his nephew but didn't ask. 'What did you think about it?'

'I hate drugs, but what can you do? Salford controlled the area and the people. If you had a problem, you went to Salford and he sorted it out. He was more effective than the police. Things only changed when he got too big for his own good. Before that you knew if you kept your nose clean and didn't cause any trouble, you'd be alright. Once he lost interest and the kids started running wild, the area was done for.'

'Ever had any dealings with him?' I asked. 'Other than the other night.'

'One or two. Years ago, now.' He turned away from me.

'I want to take him down' I said.

Derek turned to me. 'Don't be stupid.'

'Why not?'

'Because you don't take people like Salford down.'

'I think he's killed someone.'

Derek laughed. 'Wouldn't surprise me.'

'Have you been reading about Jennifer Murdoch? She was murdered in her house.'

'I've been following it in the paper.'

'I think Salford killed her.'

'Why would he kill her?'

I explained his involvement in the area's regeneration and how it tied in to her husband, the man I was acting for.

Derek put his drink down and paused.

'What's the matter?' I asked.

Derek composed himself and smiled. 'It's starting to make some sense to me.'

'What is?'

He stared at me. 'Some of the things which have been happening around here.'

I took the hint he wanted another drink.

The pub was all but empty and I took the liberty of signalling to the barman we wanted a refill.

'Go on' I said to Derek.

'I run the Neighbourhood Watch and a while back I had people coming to me, telling me they'd received offers on their houses.' He turned to face me. 'The area's run-down and crime's high, so those who accepted offers sold up and got out, and fair play to them. It used to be a great place to live. The houses were tightly packed in together, in sort of mazes, I suppose, but it was fine. Everyone knew each other and kept an eye out. We were a community within the city because, one way or the other, we all worked in the fishing industry. Those were the good old days and no mistake.' He picked his drink up. 'Times change, I suppose.'

I agreed with him. 'What happened to those who turned down offers to buy their houses?'

'Some of them were attacked until they agreed to leave. Their lives were made a misery, and once one house goes to ruin, it doesn't take the rest of the street long to follow. It's a vicious circle.'

'You think Salford was behind it?'

'If you're telling me he's been busy buying up houses in the area, it makes sense. This area used to be bursting with pride, but now there's nothing left. I've got no problems with the rebuilding. In fact I welcome it; anything to make the place better. But what I can't stomach is people taking advantage. We need all the help we can get. We don't need them ripping off their own.'

'No proof though?'

Derek shook his head. 'None at all.'

I was starting to get a bad feeling and I knew it wasn't going to go away this time. I needed another drink, but I pushed the urge aside.

'Spit it out.'

'Spit what out?' I asked.

'Whatever's on your mind.'

I had to tell him. 'If we'd found out something about Donna, would you want to know?'

Derek put his drink down and nodded. 'I don't know if Maria's strong enough. All she's got left in her life is hope, and I don't want to take it away from her.'

I nodded. I understood what he was saying.

'What do you know?' he asked me.

'I know Donna's alive.'

EIGHTEEN

'**I** want to see him' I said to Jane. 'It can't wait.'

'It'll have to. He's in a meeting with the council.'

I paced around Murdoch's office. 'He's not returned my calls.'

'He's very busy today.'

I stood still. 'Glad to hear it. Has he forgotten why I'm working for him?'

'Joe.' Jane stopped what she was doing. 'I'm sure he appreciates all you're doing for us.'

'What?'

'He appreciates your hard work.' She looked flustered.

I shook my head. 'In the boardroom, is he?' I set off in that direction.

Jane followed me. 'You can't go in there.'

I walked straight in. Murdoch was at the head of the table. Next to him were three middle-aged men in suits. I didn't care who they were or what they did.

'Joe' Murdoch said, as he stood up. 'I'm a little busy at the moment. Perhaps Jane could look after you in the reception area until we're finished.'

Jane stood next to me, looking embarrassed. 'I did tell him you were unavailable.'

He switched on the politician's smile. 'I'm sure you did, Jane. Perhaps if you could escort him out of here, please?'

I shook my head. 'Meeting's over, gentlemen. I'm sure Mr Murdoch will be in touch with you all in the very near future.'

'What the fuck are you playing at, Joe?' The room had been cleared and Murdoch was in my face.

'That was a very important meeting. You can't charge in and make me look like an idiot in front of my clients.'

He was a man in denial and had seemingly forgotten the police were closing in on him. 'You won't have any clients soon.'

Murdoch paused before sitting down. 'Thanks for that.'

'Why did you lie to me?'

'What about?'

I laughed. It summed the man up. 'Your alibi for starters.'

Murdoch said nothing. I walked around the room and sat down next to him. 'Why did you lie to me?'

'I was working for most of the night, like I told the police.'

'That's not what they say.'

'I know.'

'So why the fuck are you lying to me?' I stood up and walked over to the window, this time not looking at the amazing view of the marina. 'I thought I'd made it perfectly clear to you about my position.'

'You have.'

'So what's the problem?'

'I was with Jane.'

I turned around and shrugged. 'I know about the affair.'

'Her husband doesn't.'

I sat back down and processed the information. 'You lied to me about your alibi because of Jane?'

Murdoch said nothing and looked away. I stood up and walked to the door. 'Fuck you.' I'd had enough this time. Don had been right. It was a waste of time.

'Sit down, Joe.'

I turned back. 'I was told I shouldn't be working for you, but I wouldn't listen.'

'I need your help.'

'I can't help you anymore.'

'Yes you can.'

I sat back down. 'Have you any idea of the trouble you're in? I spoke to Coleman yesterday. They're looking at you. You've got motive and now they think you had the opportunity. I tried to tell them about Salford and Taylor, but they didn't want to know. It's you they've got a hard-on for.'

'Taylor?'

'I went to his flat and he'd been given a good kicking. He'd gone to the casino to tell Salford he wanted out of your scheme.'

Murdoch looked like he was going to be sick. 'And he was beaten?'

'He's thinking of going to the police.'

'You've got to tell him he can't do it.'

'I'm not going to tell him anything. Coleman's your problem.'

Murdoch shook his head. 'He can't touch me. I didn't kill my wife.'

'He's not going to be looking anywhere else in a hurry.'

'He's going to have to.'

'Tell him about Jane.'

'I can't. I promised Jane.'

'It's gone too far for that.'

'Her partner is a policeman. It'd embarrass him.'

I shrugged, scarcely believing the reason he'd lied. 'Not your problem. You've got to clear your name. It's gone too far. If you don't co-operate with the police, Salford is going to come looking for you, and he won't be just talking.'

'I can't go to the police.'

I told Murdoch about Sam Carver, the casino worker. Doctors were still hopeful the surgery on his eye was successful and no permanent damage had been done. Either way, he had a lot of recuperation ahead of him, and that was before you considered the impact it would have on his life. 'You've got to speak to Coleman.'

'I can't.'

I stood up. 'We're done, then. I can't help you.' Don had been right all along.

'I need your help, Joe. I can't do it by myself.'

Ignoring him, I opened the door, ready to leave.
'Joe.'
I turned back and told him to spit out what he had to say.
'Frank Salford killed your wife, Joe.'

'Hiya, Louise. How it's going?' I was stood on my sister-in-laws's doorstep.
She sighed and stared at me. 'Joe. You're drunk.'
I shook my head. I'd had a drink, but I wasn't drunk. 'Can I come in, please? It's important.'
She leant on the door frame. 'I'm busy.'
'Please.' I'd headed for the pub after I'd left Murdoch's office. A double-whiskey had calmed me down, but I still was having difficulty processing the information. I'd tried to think it through, to find some logic in what I'd been told, but I was too emotional to think straight. All I could think about was Debbie.
Louise relented and let me in. I walked through the hallway and popped my head into the living room. It was empty and tidy, no sign of the children; children I'd barely seen in the last eighteen months. Her house was well maintained, in contrast with Lisa Day's house, which was less than a five minute walk away. I remembered how Debbie had urged her to move out the area. They could afford to, but it was where her husband grew up and felt comfortable.
'Kitchen' she said to me.
We went into the kitchen and I pulled out a chair from under the table. Louise filled the kettle, sat down next to me and asked me how I was doing.
Quite a question. 'Some days are better than others.'
'I know.' She brought the pot of coffee over and poured the drinks.
'Where's Neil?' I asked.
'At work.'
I nodded. 'The kids?'
'With my mum.'
I didn't know where to start. Turning up on her doorstep had unsettled her. We'd agreed I'd call before I visited but it couldn't wait.

'Busy at work?' she asked.

'A couple of things on. Busier than we've been for a while.'

'That's good.'

I sipped my coffee and agreed with her.

'It doesn't get any easier, does it?' she eventually said.

'It doesn't.' I glanced at the photographs on the sideboard; happy faces and memories.

Louise turned away from me and started crying. 'I'm sorry.'

'It wasn't your fault.' That much was true, but every decision we make has consequences.

'It's all my fault' she said. 'All my fault.'

I shook my head and put my mug down. 'We need to talk about what happened.'

'Not again, Joe.'

I knew it was difficult for her. 'It's important. Tell me again what happened, please.'

'You already know what happened.'

'From the start.'

Louise shrugged. 'Debbie offered to babysit, so me and Neil could celebrate our anniversary.'

I nodded. I was working, so Debbie had gone there by herself. She was going to stay the night.

'We'd gone for a meal and then the theatre before coming home about midnight.'

I held her hand. 'It's alright.'

She shook her head. 'The first we knew about the fire was when the taxi couldn't get down the street for all the fire-engines and ambulances. I can still remember how noisy it was and how much smoke there was. We paid the taxi driver and hurried towards what was going on. You don't think it's going to be your house, do you?'

I nodded and encouraged her to continue.

'The neighbours were all stood outside, trying to see what was going on. Once I realised it was ours, I remember screaming and trying to run to the house. The fire brigade and police had roped it off, so we couldn't get close. I shouted and shouted and eventually someone took me aside. They told me the kids were alright; Debbie and the neighbours had got them both out.'

Debbie hadn't made it, though. The fire brigade had done their best, but the fire had taken hold. The smoke had overwhelmed her and by the time they got in, she'd died.

'I'll never forget what she did for me and my family. Or forgive myself.'

I nodded. Time had started to give me some perspective and I was proud of what she'd done that night. 'It wasn't your fault. She made sure the kids were safe. You'd have done exactly the same thing if the situation was reversed.'

'I should have been there.'

'You can't think like that.'

'She never had the chance to have kids.'

'I know' I said, pushing the thought aside.

Louise stood up and found us both some tissues. 'I live with it every day.'

'I know you do' I said, before changing the subject. 'What did the police do?'

'Neil dealt with them. I didn't have the strength for them.'

'I know.'

'They investigated but didn't get anywhere.'

Coleman, I thought. He'd been part of it and we'd fallen out. The police established the fire was started deliberately, but they never made any real progress. It was the kind of area where nobody talked to the police. The investigation had been quickly scaled back. If there was no likely arrest, they couldn't afford the resources. It was still officially open, but it had been made clear new evidence would be needed for them to think again.

'Have they been in touch recently?'

'No.'

I smiled. Of course they hadn't. Following the fire, I'd done my best. I'd investigated it to the best of my ability, but I hadn't made any real progress. Coleman and his colleagues had been little help, officially or off the record. They'd told me to leave it to them, the implication being I should mind my own business.

I took a deep breath and sat upright in my chair. The coffee and our talk had cleared my head. 'This is important, Louise. Were you ever threatened?'

She looked confused. 'Threatened?'

I nodded. 'Did anything unusual happen before the fire? Anything you told the police?'

'We'd had a few problems. Some kids were harassing Neil a bit. We'd had some dog mess pushed the letterbox?'

'Did you tell the police?'

'It was just kids messing about.'

'Why would they do that?'

'Neil had told them off. They'd been bothering some of the older people in the area.'

I nodded and thought about what Derek had told me earlier about the area. 'Did anyone ever offer to buy your house?'

'How did you know about that?'

After leaving Louise's house, I walked to Salford's casino, only stopping in a near-by pub for a drink to settle my nerves. I now knew Salford was behind my wife's death, and that I had to do something about it. The only thing that made any sense was seeing Salford. The casino was quiet; only a handful of people stood around the game tables and at the bar. The credit crunch was taking its toll. I ordered a whiskey and waited. I tried to make small talk with the barman, but he ignored me. Word had probably spread about being seen with me. It didn't take long for my presence to be noted, with Dave Johnson appearing behind me.

'What do you want?' he asked.

'Salford.'

'You're drunk.'

'I've never been more sober.'

He lent in to me, so no one could hear. 'Walk out.'

I sipped my whiskey and shook my head. 'Not until I've seen him.'

'I suggest you walk out while you can.' The smile fixed on his face.

'I won't be leaving quietly.'

Johnson stared at me. I smiled, enjoying the balance of power swinging in my direction. 'I'll shout the place down' I added.

'Follow me' he eventually said.

We walked down several dark corridors, past various closed rooms before we sat down in his office. There was nothing personal on his desk, just a small stack of CCTV monitors. I could see the one covering the bar area. He'd probably tracked my every move. Shelves lined the walls, all containing labelled folders. Despite myself, I was impressed. The operation seemed more professional than I expected.

He selected a file and sat down, ignoring me.

'You don't understand that at all, do you?' I said, watching him study a spreadsheet print-out.

Johnson put his pen down and looked up at me. 'Don't take the piss out of me.'

'Why not?' I knew I was treading a fine line, but I didn't care. 'The money isn't your department.'

Johnson walked to the door and told the two shadowy figures who were lurking to wait outside. He closed the door and sat back down. 'I thought we understood each other.'

I shook my head.

'You were going to keep your nose out of our business' he said to me.

I said nothing.

'You're really starting to fucking annoy me.'

'I want to see Salford.'

'You're dealing with me.'

I laughed.

Johnson lent forward, pointing. 'You're dealing with me.'

'He killed my wife.'

Johnson laughed. 'Fuck off, Joe. We don't go around killing people. We're businessmen; all above board. Take a look round, or have your accountant come down. We've got nothing to hide.'

'She died in a house fire.'

Johnson relaxed back into his chair. 'Accidents happen' he said.

'It wasn't an accident.'

'You're not going to thank me for this but people are careless, accidents happen.'

'It wasn't an accident. It was started deliberately.'

Johnson laughed again. 'It sounds like you go around pissing people off.'

'Accelerant was used.'

'Like I said, you should stop sticking your nose into other people's business.' Johnson was leaning forwards again, angry. His temper was a like a tightly sprung coil, ready to go off at any moment.

'My wife was babysitting her sister's children.'

'Like I say - accidents happen.'

'She'd also received an offer for her house.'

Johnson shrugged. 'It happens when people really like the house. My wife was the same. She gave me some shit about falling in love with the house. I had to buy her it; she'd got that feeling, know what I mean?'

I told him where the house was and how generous the offer was. He had a good poker face, giving nothing away.

'I spoke to Steve Taylor earlier today' I continued. 'He told me how the scheme worked. Salford's been buying up cheap housing, whether the owner wants to sell or not, and making them available when the compulsory orders from the council came rolling in. Having Taylor value the properties probably didn't hurt, either.'

Johnson stood up and paced his office, saying nothing.

'How much money has Salford made from this?' I was stood up, shouting at Johnson. 'Enough to justify my wife's death?' We were toe to toe, neither of us blinking.

Johnson was the first to back down, taking a step away from me. 'I suggest you get the fuck out of my office. You're on very, very dangerous ground here, Joe. So far, I've managed to persuade Mr Salford you're not worth bothering with.' He laughed. 'I've convinced him you're a joke. But now you come in here, into my office, making accusations you can't back up.' I could see the spit around his mouth, his anger erupting. 'I'm fucking sick of you.' He gestured to shadowy figures who had returned. 'Show this cunt the door.'

'We're not finished' I shouted, as I was dragged out of the room.

'Been upsetting people again?'

I handed over the right money to the barman and shook my head. 'Nothing to worry about.'

He nodded back and walked off to serve the other waiting customers. I found a quiet corner and sat down. Johnson's men had literally thrown me off the premises, leaving me face down on the pavement, cuts all over my face. One of them had kicked me in the stomach as I got to my feet, but I hadn't fought back. The other guy had eventually dragged him away and I was left in peace. After getting my breath back, I limped to the nearest taxi-rank and asked to be taken to Queens, hoping to find some solace in a familiar setting. I drank the first half of my pint quickly and thought things through. I had to get close to Frank Salford. I didn't know what I'd do or say when I got the chance, but I had to see the whites of his eyes and hear the truth, however hard it might be. If my wife died because Salford wanted her sister's house to sell as part of the regeneration plan, I needed to know.

I thought back to the night of the fire and remembered Debbie being transferred to the hospital. I was taken there by the police and kept a vigil at her bed for almost 24 hours before she died, never regaining consciousness. What hurt the most was not saying all the important things I should have said to her. How she was my life, how I'd be nothing without her. Drying my eyes and wiping my face on the back of my hand, I quickly left the pub before people noticed. Remembering how I'd woken Lauren the last time I'd visited, I rang Sarah's mobile, hoping she was still awake. She didn't answer, so I left a message. By the time she'd called me back, I was sat on her doorstep.

She looked down at me. 'What's going on, Joe?' she asked.

I smiled and stood up. 'I had some bad news.'

After I'd washed my face, we sat down in the front room with hot drinks. This time the cat was nowhere to be seen.

'How did your date go?' I asked.

'It was alright. We had some food and saw a film.'

'Very nice.'

'He was the perfect gentleman.'

'You've not got him hidden away upstairs, then?'

'Piss off.'

I wondered how to tell her the news about Debbie.

'Are you going to tell me what's going on, Joe?'

'I tried to talk to Salford.' I told her the reason I'd tried to speak to him. Saying it aloud meant I couldn't hold the tears back. Sarah sat next to me and held me until I'd finished.

'I'm so fucking angry' I said.

'Don't swear, please.' She passed me a tissue.

I smiled and apologised. 'What should I do?'

'Have you spoken to Coleman?'

I shook my head. 'I'd tried his mobile from the pub but it was switched off. 'He did nothing for me at the time. He won't do anything now.'

'You can't think like that. If you've got new evidence, he'll have to re-open it.'

'I don't have any new evidence.'

Sarah took my empty mug out of my hand. 'He'll have to listen to you. He has to.'

I shook my head. 'He had the nerve to question me over the fire. Tried to imply I'd started it.' I thought back to the investigation. The inquiry had been quietly scaled back until it was classified as inactive. I was put under considerable pressure at the start, as most crimes are committed by individuals known to the victim, but after some heated exchanges between us, he'd backed away, seemingly accepting I hadn't been involved.

'I'm sure he was only doing his job.'

'Not very thoroughly. He eventually decided it was kids messing around. Messing around? My wife died. That's not messing around, is it?'

Sarah held my hand and told me to calm down.

'I need a drink.'

'You've just had one.'

'A proper drink.'

'It's the last thing you need.'

'My wife died. Two kids nearly died, and yet the police did nothing.'

'It's not always that easy.'

'They backed away because they knew the truth. Coleman knew what was going on in that area. He knew Salford was behind it, but chose to turn a blind-eye.'

'You don't know that.'

'I do.'

'Joe.'

I turned away from Sarah. She was probably right, but I couldn't think straight.

'Do you want to stay here tonight?' she asked.

I wiped my face and nodded. 'If you don't mind.'

'Not at all.'

She walked out of the room and came back with a duvet and pillow and made me a bed up.

'Goodnight, Joe.'

I smiled at her. 'Thanks.'

And then the brick came through the window.

I'd cleaned most of the glass up within ten minutes. Sarah had sat with Lauren until they'd both calmed down. I didn't want to, but I'd called Don to tell him what had happened. We sat there and waited for him to arrive. The cat was intrigued by the cold air blowing in, so I passed the time trying to push her back into the kitchen, well away from the open window.

Don walked in, looked at the smashed window and then at me. I said nothing.

'Uncle Joe said some silly people did it.'

I smiled at Lauren. 'That's right.'

Sarah made her give Don a kiss and took her back to bed, closing the living room door behind her. 'Well?' Don said.

'What?'

'What's going on?'

'I'm not sure.'

Don was in my face. 'We're talking about my daughter and her kid. If anybody hurts them, I'm holding you responsible.'

I sat down and nodded. I didn't like being threatened, but his anger was understandable. I'd brought trouble to his door. 'I'm sorry.'

He sat down next to me. 'Who did this?'

It could have been kids, or even students; just bad luck. The odds on it were probably incalculable. 'I tried to speak to Salford earlier tonight.'

Don sighed and rubbed his face. 'This has to stop. We'll have to go to the police.'

'I can't.'

'Can't?'

'He's involved in Jennifer Murdoch's death and I know why now. I spoke to Steve Taylor earlier. He's involved in the valuations of the compulsory purchases and he's had enough. He told Salford he wants out and he ended up taking a hiding. We're talking about a lot of money.' I looked at Don.   'It's enough to kill over.'

'You need to let the police deal with it.'

'I can't' I repeated.

Don raised his voice. 'So my family have to put up with this?'

I told him to be quiet. 'You'll scare Lauren.'

'You don't think you've done a good enough job of it?'

'Salford killed my wife.'

That stopped Don in his tracks. He stared at me, unable to say anything. He stood up and walked across to the broken window before turning back. 'Salford killed Debbie?'

'That's right.'

'I don't understand.'

'Salford wanted Debbie's sister's house so he could sell it on as a compulsory purchase. He'd already tried to force them out. Starting a fire was the next step.'

'That's some accusation to make, Joe.'

I shrugged. 'It makes sense.' Whether or not he meant to kill her was irrelevant. It'd happened.

Don sat down. 'Have you got any proof?'

'Murdoch told me.'

Don laughed and shook his head. 'And you believe him?'

'Why would he lie?'

'Because his back is against the wall. Because he's the main suspect in his wife's death. Because he thinks you can help him in some way. Any number of reasons, Joe.'

I couldn't see it. I'd looked into Murdoch's eyes and saw a man who'd also lost his wife. The pain he was feeling wasn't false. I recognised it.

'Have you spoken to the police about it?' he eventually asked me.

'No.' I was getting a bit sick of Don's stock answer to all our problems. We were investigators. We could conduct our own investigation. The police weren't going to be any help to us.

'You should speak to Coleman' he said.

'No point.'

Don stood up. 'You've got to do what you've got to do, right?'

I nodded.

'You'd best do it quickly and not drag my family into it, then.'

He turned towards Sarah, who had walked back into the room. 'Pack yourself a bag. You and Lauren can come and stay with me. Joe can wait here until they come to fix the repair.'

Don was right. They shouldn't stay here. Not if Salford was gunning for me.

Sarah packed quickly and five minutes later they were ready to go. She gave me a key and they headed out to Don's car. He waited for them to leave the house before returning to speak to me. 'Think about what I said.'

I said I would.

'We'll speak tomorrow.'

NINETEEN

The light shone in through my curtains, hurting my eyes. I shuffled up the bed, feeling terrible. Looking at my alarm clock, I knew I was going to have to get up and face Don and Sarah. A hot shower and pot of coffee later and I was feeling ready to face the world. The anger I'd felt the previous day was turning into resolve. Anger was no good; it wouldn't help me. I wanted justice for my wife and I needed to press on and get the answers. Grief would have to wait for now.

Sitting down in my front room with my breakfast, I opened my wedding photos album. Neither of us were religious, so we'd married at Hull Registry Office; Debbie wearing a new dress, me wearing my only suit. It had been the best day of my life. The ceremony was quick, simple and just right. Leaving the building as man and wife, we'd headed to the pub for a low-key celebration before heading off on honeymoon. My mobile rang and I put the album to one side.

'Are you coming in this morning?' Sarah asked me.

I mumbled something about running late and asked how she was doing.

'Fine.'

'Really?'

'Really. We're going to stay with Dad for a few days. It's not a problem, really.'

'How's Lauren?"

'At school.'

I smiled. They were tough cookies. 'How's Don?'

'Mad at you.'

'Thought so.'

'Is he there?'

'He's out and about today, so it's safe for you to come in.'

I laughed. 'Good.'

'Besides, I've got someone here asking for you. You need to come in now.'

'Who is it?'

'Says she's called Anastazja.'

I made it to the office in less than thirty minutes. Anastazja was sat at my desk, drinking from my mug.

She smiled at me. 'Hello, Joe.'

She looked terrible. Her clothes were dirty and her face bruised. I sat down opposite her and pointed to the damage. 'Who did this to you?'

'It does not matter.'

'It does. Who did it?'

'Mr Johnson.'

I sighed and nodded. Of course he did. I explained how I'd been looking for her, but I'd gotten nowhere with it. Sarah stood up and left the room.

'Why would you look for me?' Anastazja asked me.

'I wanted to make sure you were alright.' I didn't add that I felt responsible for her situation. I was also relieved to learn she hadn't been sent to London.

'Thank you, Joe.'

I smiled. 'What happened to you?'

'Mr Johnson did not like me talking to you and told me it had to stop. I said to him, why does it have to stop? We are not doing anything wrong, we are friends. Then he hit me and told me it had to stop. I was not to speak to you again. I was kept in my house and he said I was not to leave. He took my keys off me and sent people around to check on me. He said if I left, he would find me and hurt me.'

I nodded. 'He's not going to hurt you. Not now.'

'I hope not.'

'How did you find me?'

'You gave me a business card when we first met. I put it in a safe place in my room. They did not think to look for such a thing. The door of the house was left open this morning, so I left. Nobody was watching, so nobody stopped me. I walked into the city centre and found a street map. Then I found you.'

'I should give you a job.'

'Maybe you should.'

I made more coffee and sat back down. 'Did I tell you my wife died?'

She shook her head. 'You did not.'

'In a fire. She was looking after her sister's children and the house burnt down. She saved the kids but didn't get out of the house fast enough herself.'

'I am sorry, Joe.'

'The fire was started deliberately.'

Anastazja looked shocked and touched my arm. 'I do not know what to say.'

'There's nothing you can say.' Talking about it and finding some purpose was renewing me. 'I can't bring her back but I know who started the fire.'

'Who?'

'Frank Salford.'

She was shocked. 'Why would he do that? I do not understand.'

I explained it the best I could.

'Money' she said, summing it up in a single word. 'How do you know Mr Salford did it?'

'Christopher Murdoch told me.'

'You believe him? He is not a nice man.'

I nodded, taking her point. 'He's not a bad man, though; at least I don't think so. He got involved in something he didn't understand and couldn't control. It got his wife killed and now he's alone like me. I believe him, Anastazja.'

'I think I understand.'

'Did you ever hear any talk of the fire when you were working?'

She shook her head. 'It was mainly Mr Johnson who visited me. Mr Salford stopped coming as much about one year ago.'

'But he never spoke about the fire?'

'Neither of them did.'

'Did any of the other girls talk about it?'

'No.'

I tried not to show my frustration. It wasn't Anastazja's fault. I knew my anger should be directed at Salford and Coleman.

'If I knew, I would tell you' she said. 'Mr Salford and Mr Johnson are not nice men. I would like them to be punished. You have been very kind to me, Joe. If I could repay you by helping you, I would do it.'

I smiled. 'I'm sorry. I know you would.'

Sarah walked into the room and I introduced her properly to Anastazja, and explained how she'd helped me. Anastazja excused herself.

'You can't save her' Sarah said to me.

'I'm not trying to.'

'You are.'

I put my mug down and said nothing.

'If she can't go back to her house because of Salford and Johnson, where's she staying?'

I watched Anastazja walk back into the room. 'She can stay at my flat.' I owed her that much. I gave Anastazja the keys to my flat and put her in a taxi with instructions to lock herself in. I couldn't be sure whether Johnson knew where I lived, but I was working on the principle that he wouldn't look in the most obvious places. Besides, there were no other options. If Sarah wasn't staying with Don, I'd have asked her for the favour, but she'd made her objection to Anastazja's appearance loud and clear. I didn't have the time or inclination to discuss it, or try to figure out what she was thinking, so I left the office and headed to see Coleman.

The same officer from my previous visit was manning the duty desk and didn't look pleased to see me again.

'DC Coleman, please' I said, smiling at him.

'He's in a meeting.'

I laughed. 'You've not even tried him.'

'He's on my list.'

'He'll want to talk to me.'

'I doubt it.' He turned away from me. 'Pleasure speaking to you, though.'

'It's about my wife.' We were the only two people in the reception area. 'I'm not messing' I explained. 'If he won't talk to me, I know people who will.'

'Sit down.' He pointed to the seats behind me and picked up his phone.

'I thought we understood each other?'

I stood up and walked over to Coleman, who was leant on the frame of the reception door. I didn't care how pissed off he was. 'I want to talk to you.'

'It's not a good time, Joe. Can't it wait?'

'No.'

'It'll have to.'

'Fine.' I started to back away. He looked like he hadn't slept properly for days. 'I'll have to speak to the press, then. I'm sure they'll be interested.'

Coleman looked at me like he really didn't need the hassle. I wasn't letting him off the hook so easily. He relented and we went into an interview room.

'Why did you drop the investigation?' I took a deep breath and calmed down. I was shouting.

'It's not like that' Coleman replied.

I wondered if we were being recorded, but I didn't care. 'It was exactly like that.'

'We've been through this before.'

'Tell me again.'

'What's the point?'

'My wife is dead.' I was shouting again.

Coleman shook his head. 'We've been over and over it. There's nothing I can do.'

'Unless there's new evidence?'

'That's right.'

I looked him in the eye. He looked nervous. 'Frank Salford was behind the fire.'

'You've got to do better than that' he said, shaking his head.

I saw red. The smile on his face as he shook his head, like he thought I was stupid. I flew across the room and pinned him to the wall. I had hold of him by his tie. I was close enough to smell his coffee breath. 'She was my wife' I said quietly, 'and she died.' I slowly released him from my grasp, knowing I'd overstepped the mark. I sat down and said nothing, waiting for him to do likewise.

He straightened his tie. 'What new evidence?' he eventually asked me.

'Murdoch told me about the fire.'

'Murdoch?'

I nodded.

'He'd tell you anything you wanted to hear. You're all he's got.'

Coleman had a point but I was still convinced Murdoch was telling me the truth. 'He knows you'll be arresting him soon' I said. 'The fraud he's involved in is unwinding. He knows it and has nothing to lose by telling me the truth. In fact, it'd probably help him.'

'What proof does he have of Salford's involvement?'

'He's involved with them.'

'Was he there?'

'Don't be ridiculous.'

Coleman shook his head. 'I need more than his word. You can't come charging in here, taking me away from my work, assault me, and all because you've got a hunch.'

'It's not a hunch.'

'It is unless you've got some evidence of his involvement.'

I leant across the table. 'What was his alibi?'

'It's not your concern.'

'I'll look into it for you. Prove it's a lie.'

Coleman shook his head. 'You can't do that for me.'

'I can.'

'I don't want you to.'

I sat back. 'Why not?'

'It's not how we work.' Coleman stood up and paced the room. 'You've got to trust me. We're looking at Salford and if he's involved, it'll come out in the wash.'

'My wife died in an arson attack. That kind of thing doesn't come out in the wash. It was murder; it should be your priority.'

'And it is.'

'That's not how it looks sat here.'

'The investigation was very thorough. Speak to Don, he'll tell you that.'

'It's nothing to do with Don.'

'Right.'

'Did you ever question Salford?'

'I can't tell you things like that.'

'You'd tell Don.'

'I wouldn't.'

'Did you question him?' I repeated.

Coleman sighed. 'Not under caution.'

I nodded. 'And?'

'What do you expect me to say? He denied any involvement and gave us his alibi.'

'And that was it?'

'There was nothing more we could do.'

'So what did you do?'

'We followed up all lines of inquiry.'

'Which were?'

'Other lines of inquiry.'

He was exasperated, but I didn't care. I asked him about the lines of inquiry.

'I'm not going to give you the nuts and bolts of the investigation, but you'll be the first to be informed if there was a development.'

'Not good enough.'

'What do you want from me, Joe?'

'I want you to re-open the investigation properly.'

'I can't do that. You know that.'

'You can take what Murdoch's told me seriously.'

'I am doing.'

'And speak to your superiors.'

Coleman shook his head. 'They won't be interested. I can tell you that much.'

'Unless there's new evidence?'

'That's right.'

It was my turn to stand up and pace the room. 'I need your help.'

'I can't help you.'

'More than your job's worth?'

Neither of us spoke for a few moments. It was below the belt and I should have apologised, but I wasn't in the mood. I wanted Coleman to feel uncomfortable. I wanted to hurt him.

'Look, I can speak to DI McCormack about it' Coleman offered. 'See what he says. We might be able to tag it into the other stuff.'

I stopped my pacing. 'Tag it in? Have you not heard a word I said? I'm not asking you to look into a theft from my garden shed. My wife was murdered by Frank Salford.' I shook my head, knowing I'd wasted my time. Coleman wasn't prepared to help me. I was on my own.

'Did Anastazja get off ok?' I asked Sarah. Having nothing further to say to Coleman, I left before I said something stupid.

She nodded. 'The taxi came straight away.'

'Good.' I sat down, ready to think over what Coleman had said.

She looked like she had something to say about the situation, so I cut her off and asked about the note she'd left on my desk. 'A new client?'

'They want to see you urgently.'

'What about Don?'

'They asked for you.'

'Personally?'

'Your must have a reputation.'

I looked at the note again. 'I must do.'

Sarah passed me a piece of paper. 'They've booked a table. At least you'll get lunch.'

I looked at my watch; an hour to kill. 'What's your dad doing?'

'Keeping out of your way, I think.'

'What are you doing?'

'Trying to do the same.'

I nodded. 'Right.' I thought about calling Anastazja's mobile and even got as far as punching in the first three digits before stopping and replacing the handset. I could talk to her later. I closed my eyes.

The restaurant was one of Hull's finest and the kind of place which made me uncomfortable. From the look on the waiter's face, he knew I was in the wrong place, too. He seated me and left me with a menu. Twenty minutes later, I had ordered a mineral water and was losing patience fast.

'Mr Geraghty. How pleasant to see you again.'

I stood up and turned around. Dave Johnson.

He laughed and pointed at me. 'Surprise.'

'Hardly.' I tried to push past him, but his two burly assistants closed the gap.

'Sit down and eat with me' he said, all smiles.

'I don't think so.'

Johnson turned to his assistants and shrugged. 'What can you do?' He jabbed a finger in my chest. 'Shut the fuck up and sit down.'

'Or you'll throw me in a freshly dug grave again?'

The smile hadn't left his face. The section of the restaurant we were in was dark, secluded and most importantly, empty. He'd chosen well. I sat back down.

'What do you want to eat?' he asked me.

'I'm not hungry.'

'Order something.'

'I'm not hungry.'

Johnson shook his head before shouting for the waiter. The speed at which he sprinted over confirmed Johnson had some clout in the place. He pointed at something on the menu and told them to bring the same for me.

'After I left Salford's casino last night, my colleague had a brick thrown through her window' I said.

'Really?'

'Her kid was in the house.'

'I had a problem like that. Teenagers.' He shrugged. 'I had a word, though, and it got straightened out. Sometimes you just need to talk to people, take the time to understand each other.'

'How much did you pay them to throw the brick through the window?'

Johnson shook his head. 'I'm offended you'd even say that to me, Joe.'

I held his stare. 'Leave her alone. This is nothing to do with her.'

Johnson drummed his fingers on the table. 'I'll have a word. Sometimes you just have to do what you're told, even though you don't agree with them.'

'Salford?'

'He's the boss.'

'It goes back to your football hooligan days.'

'Very good. You've done your research. I like a man who's prepared.' Johnson sat back in his chair. 'They were the fun days, alright. Heading off to some shithole on a double-decker bus, not knowing what you'd walk into. Great stuff. It's in our blood, you see. We're a city of drinkers and fishermen. We were born to fight. Even the rugby was great. The police would never turn up and because you were usually heading for some tip of a mining town, there was plenty of handy lads with nothing else to do. They'd be up for it.'

It was a chance to find out some more about Salford. 'And it gave you the opportunity to build an empire.'

'   Where there's large groups of young men and testosterone flying about they'll want drugs. It's a fact of life. What they needed was someone who could bring it altogether for them. The biggest problem was the rugby. Having the two clubs in the city was great for some rucks, especially in the weeks leading up to the derbies, but it made it difficult at the football. There were too many knobheads worried about the east and west divide of the city which the rugby divided itself up on. If they could have put that to one side, even just on match days, we'd have been one of the top firms in the country.'

I stood up. Johnson was deluded, still living in the past. 'You can tell your boss I'm not scared of him.'

Johnson also stood up. 'Sit down.'

'We've got nothing to talk about.'

'We've got plenty to talk about. Now, sit the fuck down or I'll have you strapped down in the chair until I'm finished.'

I reluctantly sat down.

'Good. Let's be adult about this.'

'You what?'

'We're both businessmen. Shouldn't we able to help each other out over a pleasant lunch?'

I couldn't believe what I was hearing. I was being forced against my will to eat with a known local gangster, and he thought it was a legitimate business meeting.

'Why are you shaking your head, Joe?'

'Why would I want to help you out?'

'Because you can. It's called a mutual exchange. We're all professional people here.'

I laughed, unable to stop myself. This man had threatened to bury me alive not too long ago.

'The brick was a mistake. We both know that. It's not how things get done, is it?

'Get to the point.'

He laughed at me. 'I like your attitude. You want to know who killed your wife, right?'

I put my drink down. 'I know who killed my wife.'

'My employer?'

'Got it in one.'

Johnson smiled. 'Are you seriously telling me he goes around starting fires?'

'He's the one giving the orders.'

'Can you prove it?'

It was like speaking to Coleman again.

'It's a serious accusation to make it' he said.

'It's a serious business when you go around killing people. I know you've forced people out of their houses, just so you can sell them on as compulsory purchases. Profitable, I assume?'

'I'd hardly say we forced people out. We made homeowners offers and they decided if they wanted to sell to us. We can't control council policy.'

I pressed on. 'My wife died and I'll make whoever did it pay.'

Johnson sat back in his chair and looked at me, like he was weighing me up. 'I appreciate that, Joe, I really do, and I think we can help each other out. I need you to lay off whatever you think you're doing. Yes, Christopher Murdoch was someone we were using as a consultant on a few projects, but that particular relationship has now been terminated. It's finished.'

'Are you threatening me?'

He laughed again. 'Hardly. We both know Murdoch is finished. If he stepped outside the law, that's not our problem. He'll have to answer to the police. Assuming he gets that far.'

'I'll take that as a threat against my client.'

'Take it however you want to take it.'

The waiter served our food and left.

'The point is Joe, it's a hassle we don't want and you can make it go away for us.'

'I can't make it just disappear, even if I wanted to. It's gone too far' I said.

Johnson pointed at me. 'You'll drop your investigation and tell Murdoch to keep his mouth shut.'

'Why would I want to do that for you?'

Johnson smiled and sat back in chair, staring at me. 'Because we can give you the scrotes who started the fire.'

TWENTY

I'd felt sick after leaving the restaurant and headed to Queens to reflect. What it seemed to boil down to was how far I was prepared to go for the truth. Coleman had made it clear he wasn't prepared to help, even though I'd given him a heads-up. After walking out of the police station, I thought I would do anything to get some closure on my wife's death. Speaking to Johnson had put doubt in my mind. Johnson had told me he could deliver the people responsible for the fire to my doorstep, but what good would it do? His offer confirmed Salford was behind the fire, so meeting the toe-rags who started it seemed pointless. I could beat them until my hands bled and the tears stopped, but it wouldn't change anything. They weren't the ones my anger should be directed at. They were probably told the house would be empty that night and bunged £50 for their troubles. I knew getting into bed with Johnson on this was a bad idea, but I wanted justice.

My mobile vibrated on the pub table and I thought about ignoring the call. I looked at the caller ID - Sarah. I put my glass down and listened to her excited message. Donna Platt had been in touch, offering to meet us. Thirty minutes later and we were on the road, Sarah driving. I wasn't keen on being driven but I was probably over the limit. As we drove out of Hull, towards the coast I'd called Anastazja and confirmed she hadn't left my flat all day. She told me she was bored, which wasn't surprising, but was cooking me a meal using the ingredients found in my cupboard. I couldn't begin to think what she could do with them, but said I looked forward to finding out. I closed my eyes and slept for the duration of the journey; I needed the break.

An hour later, we'd parked and found the place we were looking for. The pub was yards from Scarborough's seafront and like most British resorts, it'd seen better days. Being out of season, the town centre was quiet, the cafes and souvenir shops in hibernation. Only the odd amusement arcade was open, entertaining the local teenagers, who ran past us. The only people in the pub looked like regulars. There was a stage in the corner but no act was performing tonight. I bought the drinks and Sarah directed us over to the corner. There was no mistaking the woman sat there – Donna Platt. The permed hair on the photograph had given way to a more modern style and the make-up had been toned down, but it was definitely her. Seeing her in the flesh brought the ageing process to mind and I wondered how I was faring in comparison. Did the teenager who looked set for a career in professional sport remain? I pushed the thought aside and sat down.

'Hello' Sarah said to Donna. 'We meet at last.'

She said hello.

'Thanks for agreeing to meet us.'

Donna shrugged. 'I wanted to check this place out.' She took a deep breath and waited until she had our attention. 'And I wanted to make my position clear to you. I've no interest in seeing my mum again.'

I nodded. 'We're not here to make you do anything you don't want to do. Your mother asked us to look for you because she wanted to make contact before it was too late. You understand what I'm saying, don't you?'

Donna nodded and said she also understood. 'It's none of my business.'

'I've spoken to your mum' Sarah said 'and she's really sorry about what happened.'

'About what happened? She doesn't know anything.'

'She regrets listening to your father' Sarah explained. 'She really does. I'm not trying to justify what she did, but she knows it was wrong. All she wants is one more chance.'

'She can't have one.'

'She's dying.'

'I know.'

I said nothing, but weighed her up. There was no doubting she was cold; her mother's imminent death didn't bother her in the slightest.

'Your brother would love to see you' I said.

Donna looked away. 'I can't see him.'

'Why not?'

She composed herself. 'How's he doing?'

'Good. He's got a job, seems to be doing well for himself.'

'I was worried about him.'

'After Jimmy?' I asked.

'How do you know about him?'

'Your uncle told us.'

'He had no right.'

'He was trying to help us.'

'Did he tell you how the family treated Jimmy?'

I said he'd told us.

'They practically disowned him' she continued. 'Jimmy needed their help and they didn't give him any. Dad was too busy sitting on his arse watching TV, gambling what money we had away and my mum let him. She didn't say a thing. I was probably too young to understand at the time, but I know now. Jimmy was crying out for their help and they didn't offer any.'

It wasn't how Derek and Maria had told the story, but that wasn't important. 'I know your mother regrets it.'

Donna laughed and shook her head. 'But she did nothing about it. I can't even begin telling you how horrible growing up in that house was. Dad thought he could tell everybody what to do, but yet sit in his armchair doing nothing. Once Jimmy died, I could barely breathe in that house. Whenever I went out, I had to tell him where I was going and who I was out with. It was horrible, yet Gary could do as he pleased, just because he was bigger than my dad. I hated living there.'

It didn't sound any worse than the house I grew up in, but it wasn't my place to comment. 'It got worse when you started the band?'

'A lot worse. He didn't like me performing in the clubs he drunk in because he said it was embarrassing for him. He didn't like my friends, he didn't like the way I looked. Never mind I was doing something positive about my future.'

'He wanted you to settle down with Tim?'

Donna nodded. 'Tim was a lovely bloke; probably still is, but we were too different. He was keen to buy a house and all that kind of stuff. I wasn't ready for the commitment. My dad thought I should snap Tim's hand off; damaged goods like me don't always get a second chance.'

'The abortion?'

She nodded. 'I was a kid. I didn't know what to do, so I did what I assume most teenage girls do and turned to my mother. The one thing I asked of her was she didn't tell my dad. Of course, she told him and he went mental. He called me all sorts of names and made me feel worthless. He even refused to come to the clinic with me, can you believe it?'

Sarah reached across the table and offered her a tissue. I felt terrible for bringing the bad memories back. I took a deep breath. 'And you fell pregnant again?'

Donna wiped her tears away and stared at me. 'You say it like it's bad.'

' I didn't mean to' I apologised. I appealed to Sarah, but she ignored me. 'Chelsea?'

'She's the best thing that ever happened to me. I thought I wanted to be a famous singer.' She laughed. 'But all I want is to be a mother, if that makes sense?'

'It does' said Sarah, explaining about Lauren. 'How old is she?'

'Nearly ten.'

I asked her about the factory job and explained I'd spoken to her ex-boyfriend.

Donna thought about it before answering. 'I don't know what I was doing, to be honest. I missed home, so I moved back for a while and got a job.' She put her glass down and looked at us. 'I wasn't sure how I felt about my mum, so I wanted to be a bit closer to see if I could figure things out.'

'But you didn't make contact?'

She shook her head and picked up her glass. 'No. I knew almost as soon as I was back. It wasn't what I wanted, but I'd started to see Simon, and it was just nice to have someone who was interested in me. Chelsea liked the school she went to, so it was easier to stay.'

'Weren't you worried you'd see people?'

'I lived on the other side of the city and I never really went out.'

I nodded. Hull could be a big city when you wanted it to be. It was a weird situation, but it seemed to make sense to her. I asked her what had happened with the band.

'It just didn't work out' she told us. 'We started out by singing in clubs and pubs in Hull, but I thought we were better than that. I wanted us to be a proper band, write our own songs and play with musicians, not backing tapes.'

I nodded and leant forwards. 'Frank Salford offered to help, didn't he?'

'How do you know about Frank?'

'Lisa told us about him managing the band.'

'Frank knew what he was doing. He was in the business. He was the best person in the city for us. He put is in a studio to record a demo and asked around in London on our behalf. I like Lisa, I really do, and it's all in the past now, but if she'd had the drive, we'd have succeeded. I know we would have. We were good.'

'What was the problem with Salford?'

'Who said there was a problem?'

'He's not a popular man.'

'He was nothing but professional when dealing with the band.'

'Away from the band?'

'I don't know what you mean' she said, turning away from me.

She understood perfectly well what I meant. I waited for her to continue.

'We had an affair' she eventually offered.

'Did it get you special favours?'

Donna laughed and looked at me like I was an idiot. 'Quite the opposite.'

'What do you mean?'

She put her drink down and stared straight at me. 'Do you want to know why I left Hull?'

I nodded, wanting her to say it.

'Chelsea.'

I nodded. We'd done the maths. Donna had left around the time of falling pregnant.

'Tim's not the father, is he?' I said. 'She's Salford's.'

I went to the bar and bought more drinks. Returning, I noticed the addition to the table. Donna introduced him as her boyfriend. He'd been sat elsewhere in the pub whilst we'd talked. She said he knew everything.

'I told my mother when I fell pregnant again' she explained. 'I have no idea why, but who else could I turn to? I told her not to tell Dad this time, but of course, she did.'

'What happened?' I asked.

'He went mad. Said I had to get an abortion, but I couldn't go through with another one.'

'But you let your parents think Tim was the father?'

'That was wrong of me.'

'But it was easier?'

Donna nodded, the coldness returning. 'I suppose. I just didn't want to tell them the truth. It wouldn't have done any good.'

I supposed that much was true. 'Did you tell Salford?'

She nodded but said nothing.

'He didn't take the news well?'

' He told me to get rid of it. Offered me money.'

The golden question. 'Does he know he has a daughter?'

She shook her head. 'No.'

We drove home in silence after agreeing to talk about Donna Platt in the morning. Anastazja had fulfilled her promise and prepared a meal for me. Looking around, it felt like my flat was no longer my own. It had been cleaned, tidied and a makeshift bed was in the process of being made on the sofa.

'I will sleep on here' said Anastazja, pointing to it.

I removed my coat and shoes and told her it was fine. She could take the bed and I'd sleep on the sofa. I'd spent half my life sleeping on them; it wasn't a problem.

'I have food' she said.

It smelt good. I hadn't eaten since lunchtime. 'I'm surprised you found something in this place.'

'You are not trying hard enough.'

'Clearly.' The food was good. 'Have you been alright today?' I asked.

Anastazja nodded. 'Yes. No problem. I have just watched the television. I hope you do not mind?'

I shook my head and wondered what I was going to do with her. I didn't mind her staying in my flat, but it was a situation which needed resolving.

'What have you been doing today?' she asked me.

I told her about Donna Platt.

'So she will not talk to her family? That is incredible.'

'Her father didn't treat her particularly well.'

'It sounds like he was concerned for her. As any father would be.'

I wanted to ask her about her family, but it wasn't any of my business. I tried to explain about Ron Platt. 'He had his own troubles. He worked on the trawlers, bringing fish in from the North Sea. It was a hard life.' I tried to explain how hard it had been for him, but I doubt I did it justice. I also didn't want to sound like I was apologising for his behaviour. 'When the industry was wiped out, he couldn't get another job. It's the story of the area he lived in, really.'

'I understand, but if you lose a job, you get another one? You start again?'

'He couldn't adapt to it, or find one.' I shook my head. 'I don't really know.'

'He could have been a better father, though?'

I couldn't disagree with that. His teenage daughter falling pregnant must have been a shock, but it was something lots of families get through. I tried to put myself in his shoes in an attempt to work out how I'd feel if my daughter formed a band. It seemed harmless enough in itself, and the fact Donna had some focus and ambition had to be a good thing. I wondered if it was Salford's involvement he objected to? Derek knew all about Salford, so it was a fair assumption Ron also knew the man. In that context, his behaviour was understandable. It also made Donna's decision to leave Hull, carrying Salford's baby sensible. Her father wasn't going to offer any support and I couldn't see Salford welcoming the news. It left Donna's mother, now dying, powerless. There wasn't going to be a happy ending for her.

'What does your girlfriend think?'

'Girlfriend?'

'The lady you work with.'

'Sarah's not my girlfriend.'

'I see.' Anastazja looked embarrassed.

'Why would you think she was my girlfriend?'

'I thought she was. She is very fond of you, I can tell that much.' She laughed. 'I am a woman.'

I didn't know what to say, or think, but was saved by my mobile phone ringing. It was Coleman and he wanted to meet me. I put my plate in the sink and told Anastazja I wouldn't be long.

I walked back into Queens and found Coleman in a quiet corner, away from the regulars. He'd already got me a drink. I said thanks and sat down opposite him.

'Thanks for coming' he said.

'Did I have a choice?'

'I'm here as a favour to you, Joe. Off the record.'

I nodded. 'Why would you want to do that?'

Coleman sat back, staring at me. 'You're not making this easy for me.'

'Should I be?'

He put his drank down. 'I don't think we did enough for you when your wife died, and I want to give you a heads-up.'

'You didn't do enough?'

He lowered his voice. 'I don't think we followed up on the fire investigation when the going got tough. We both know it wasn't an accident, and we both know the kids who did it were acting under orders. I tried to speak to my DI earlier today and his response was the same; he doesn't want to dig any further.'

'Why not?'

'Because it's part of something bigger.'

'Salford.'

Coleman nodded. 'He's a long-standing target and we expect to get to the truth about the fire when we arrest him.'

'If you arrest him.'

'Fair point, but we're closer than ever. The net is closing in on him and Christopher Murdoch.'

'Murdoch didn't kill his wife.'

'We'll have to agree to disagree on that, but he's up to his neck in shit, Joe. I'm not here to go over the whole alibi and motive stuff with you. If you can bring me something, I'm telling you I'll make sure it's looked at.' He shrugged. 'Truth will out.'

'I'm glad you're so confident.'

'I'm here in my own time and out of choice. Do you think the fire didn't affect me? I was there, at the scene, Joe. I saw things nobody should have to see. I know it was your wife who died, but that doesn't mean you're the only one who wants to see some results.'

I held his stare. 'What are you telling me?'

'I'm telling you I want to see justice done, and the best way to do that is to let me do my job.'

'Not good enough.'

'It has to be.'

'You said your boss isn't interested.'

'He's been told not to be interested. Other people are looking at Salford. We know what's going on. He can't run from us.'

'I want justice for my wife.'

'You'll get it.'

'I don't trust you.' It was the truth. If you want a job doing, do it yourself, I thought.

'You have to trust me.'

'No I don't.'

Coleman sighed. 'Leave it alone, Joe.'

'No chance.'

'Dave Johnson isn't going to help you.'

I paused. 'What do you mean?'

Coleman laughed. 'Come on, Joe. We know you had lunch with him today.'

'You're watching him?'

He nodded. 'I told you, the net's closing. He's not your man.'

'Who sent you here?'

'I'm here because I thought I should be, and that's the truth. No one sent me. I know you better than you know yourself, Joe and I know what you're thinking and I'm telling you it's a bad idea.'

'What am I thinking?'

'Johnson is the man with the answers; he can give you whoever started the fire. Whatever deal he's offering you, it's not worth it.'

'Who says he's offering me a deal?'

'I am. If he wants your silence in exchange for some names, it's not worth it.'

'They killed my wife.' I understood the point and knew my argument was weak. I looked away from him.

Coleman took his time. 'He might be able to give the people who lit the fire but they're not the ones you want. It's not the answer.'

'The answer works for me.'

'No it doesn't.' Coleman finished his drink and stood up. 'Stay away from Johnson.'

TWENTY ONE

'**The** net's closing in on me, Joe. I need to get my affairs in order, make sure I know things are going to be okay.'

I paid attention to Murdoch. I hadn't been expecting him to be waiting for me at the office first thing this morning, but it wasn't a problem. It seemed I always had more questions for him.

'I'm sorry I had to be the one who told you about your wife.'

I shrugged his words aside because he'd only told me when he had been backed into a corner. I knew where I'd find the answers and my talk with Coleman confirmed I was on the right track. He didn't want me causing trouble, but his warning didn't bother me. My initial anger had turned into a desire to see things through. It felt like all I needed to do was ask the right question to unlock the door; I was willing to do whatever it took for Debbie. I watched Murdoch pick up the photograph Maria Platt had lent to me.

'Jennifer's brother's into this kind of thing. He's been collecting them, trying to put together their father's life story.' He put it back down and laughed. 'I wish I had the time for that kind of thing. They used to call him Lucky, because he was some sort of Jonah out at sea.'

Sarah walked into the room and stared at Murdoch before asking if I was alright. I told her I was fine and waited for her to leave.

'She thinks it's a bit weird that I'm still giving you the time of day' I explained once she'd gone.

'Understandable, I suppose. I'm still the police's chief suspect, despite everything I've told them. I really appreciate all your doing for me, Joe.'

'What can I do for you?' I looked at my watch. I had more important things to be doing.

'The police will be coming for me today but I want you to carry on. I've told Jane to sort the money out for you. You'll only have to ask her. I've made sure there's enough in the bank account.'

I picked up my coffee and waited for him to continue.

'It's important, Joe.'

'I know.'

'I didn't kill Jennifer.'

'I know.'

'It's important you believe me.' I'm guilty of what the police are going to arrest me for and I deserve everything I'm going to get for it, but I'm going to pay for it. I know that. I'm finished, totally finished. Nobody is going to work with me now.' He lent forward, agitated. 'But I'm not a murderer. I'm not going to prison for that.'

I hadn't changed my opinion of the man; I still didn't think he'd killed his wife, but I wanted more. I didn't trust him. 'Why didn't you tell me about my wife sooner?'

He put his mug down. 'It wasn't my place.'

'You were using me.'

He said nothing.

'You used me to try to get Salford off your back? You think Salford killed your wife, and if you got me to prove it, he'd be off your case. The whole mess you've made of the regeneration work might go away?'

'It wasn't like that.'

'What was it like, then?' I was starting to see things more clearly. 'We've both lost our wives, and that gives us some sort of strange bond other people can't understand. I know how it feels, how helpless you are, how much anger and bitterness you've got inside you? My wife was killed because she was in the wrong place at the wrong time and because of Salford's greed.'

'He killed my wife, too.'

'We don't know that.'

'Who else would it be?'

I shrugged. I felt like I was slowly starting to see things more clearly, but I wasn't ready to share it yet. 'I don't know, what about Taylor?'

'He's nothing.'

'He's got motive.'

'You're my only hope, Joe.' Murdoch was visibly upset.

'You used me.'

He shook his head.

'You used me and when you thought I was going to walk away, you used the only card you had – my wife.'

I wasn't sure if I felt pity or revulsion. 'My friend had a brick thrown through her window, just because I was investigating your wife's death. It was a warning. Can you imagine how scared she was? Can you imagine how her young daughter felt?'

'I'm sorry.'

I shook my head. 'I don't think you are.'

He blew his nose and wiped his face before looking at me. 'I'm sorrier than you could ever imagine.'

'I thought when we first met we were both looking for the same thing – justice.'

'We still are.'

'We have different ways of trying to get it, then.'

Murdoch exhaled and sat back. 'I wanted Salford and Johnson off my back. They were trying to ruin me. I didn't know what to do and I thought you could sort it out for me. I thought if you put Salford in the frame, he'd leave me alone.'

'And you expected that would work?'

'I wasn't thinking straight. Above all, though, I want the truth about what happened.'

We were going round in circles. Despite the way he'd behaved and misled me, I still wanted to get to the truth behind Jennifer Murdoch's death. I wrote a note for Sarah, asking her to check something out for me, before showing Murdoch out of the office. I promised to stay in touch and continue looking into his wife's murder, but it felt like a final goodbye.

If the net was closing in on Murdoch, the same would apply to Salford, and if Don's old colleague, Gerard Branning was anything to go by, the police would most likely be rubbing their hands at the prospect of taking him in. It was now or never. I was planning on driving to the casino, but noticing my hands were shaking, I parked up at Queens for a shot of whiskey to settle the nerves. An hour later, and I handed over a ten pound note to the taxi driver and told him to keep the change. Looking up, the casino looked dull and lifeless in the daytime. The area was deserted and quiet. The only vehicle I could see parked in the car park was Salford's Jaguar. I pulled the mints from my coat pocket and threw two into my mouth. I didn't want Salford smelling the alcohol, thinking I was scared of him.

The entrance was unlocked and the only person who challenged me as I walked into the building was a cleaner. She told me to sit down and wait, she'd see if Salford was available.

'Mr Geraghty?'

I turned to see a man staring straight at me. Salford was older and frailer than I imagined he would be from the photographs I'd seen.

I nodded. 'That's me.'

'I understand you want to see me?'

'That's right.'

He nodded to the cleaner. 'We'll be in my office.'

Salford's office was far more impressive than Johnson's. Rather than a cheap, self-assembly table and a bank of CCTV monitors, the office's centrepiece was a solid cherry oak table. I glanced around the room, the same CCTV monitors were discretely stacked in the far corner, but a flat-screen plasma television dominated the wall. He switched it off.

'It's about time we had a talk, Joe.' Salford poured two generous whiskeys and passed me one. 'Are we on first name terms?'

I nodded, unsure how I should react. I thought when we met I'd be angry and full of hate for the man. Instead, I was stood in the middle of his office, frozen, not knowing what I should be doing.

'I know you've been asking around my businesses.' He gestured to the chair opposite him. 'Sit down. I hear you were a bit handy at rugby in your younger days. More of a football man myself, but I admire any sportsman. I wish I'd had the talent.'

He'd done his homework, but I ignored him. 'I work for Christopher Murdoch' I said, sitting down. 'His wife was murdered.'

'I know.'

'She was a regular in this place.'

'So are a lot of people.'

Salford was all smiles and joviality. It was unnerving. 'She was murdered.'

'So you said. I don't see how I can help you?'

I laughed. 'I think you can.'

His mood darkened. 'I don't think I follow you.'

I held his stare. 'I think you do.'

Salford sat back in his chair and laughed. 'Maybe you should be looking closer to home.'

'He didn't kill his wife.'

'How can you be so sure?'

'I'm sure.'

Salford nodded and put his drink down. 'Decisiveness - I like that in a man. I could probably use you in my organisation.'

'Did you kill her?' I asked, getting to the point.

Salford laughed, stood up and paced the room before standing behind me. I couldn't see him, but I knew he was inches away from me. I didn't move, staring straight ahead.

'I didn't kill her.'

'Convince me.'

He lent closer. 'Why would I need to do that' he whispered in my ear.

'You were jealous. You wanted her, but she didn't want to know.'

'Don't be ridiculous.'

'She was an attractive woman.' I shrugged. 'Who wouldn't fancy her?'

'Not me.'

'She wouldn't be the first, would she?'

'Excuse me?'

'I've spoken to Julie Richardson.'

He stepped away and sat back down behind his desk. 'You have been doing your homework.'

'I've seen her face.'

Salford turned away from me. 'It was a long time ago.'

'Not to her. It's like it was yesterday.'

He turned back to me. 'Decisions have consequences.'

I nodded. He wasn't wrong, though I doubt it was any consolation to her.

'You don't like it if you don't get your own way?' I said.

'Who does?'

'So you killed Jennifer Murdoch because she couldn't pay the money she owed you? Because you couldn't get your own way?'

'Come on, Joe. You can do better than that. One minute it's I fancied her, the next it's I killed her because of money. Make your mind up.'

'She owed you money.'

'She owed me a lot of money.'

'Why didn't you stop her credit?'

'Let's put it down to wider business interests.'

'Her husband is an influential businessman.'

'So I understand.'

'Why did you threaten to kill her?'

Salford laughed. 'Who said that?'

'Her husband.'

He shook his head. 'Wasn't me.'

I drank my whiskey, feeling it burn down my throat. 'Johnson did the threatening?'

'If he did, I didn't know about it. He always had a temper, even when we used to go to the football as lads. Thinking's not his strongest attribute.'

It was my turn to laugh. 'Of course you knew.'

Salford shook his head. 'I didn't know and that's the truth. I know the Murdoch's, and I know what his job is. Truth is, though, he's a bullshitter. I listened to his plans, and what he wanted to do, but it's pie in the sky. This is Hull, Joe; we don't go in for the kind of change he was proposing.'

'Why not?'

'On Hessle Road?'

I nodded.

'I was brought up there and I can tell you, it was a rough place to be a kid; survival of the fittest. We had nothing; no money and no way of getting out. And from where I'm sat, the area hasn't changed that much apart from the dossers and Eastern Europeans who live there.'

'Like Anastazja?'

'Who?'

I let it go. 'It was a chance to make things better' I said. 'For everyone.'

'Murdoch is a dreamer' he continued. 'He had nothing to offer me or my business. I didn't want to have any involvement with his project. There's too many obstacles, too much bureaucracy when you're dealing with the council.' He smiled at me. 'There wasn't going to be enough fun for me to get involved. You've got to like and trust the people you're working with, and I didn't.'

'The money's good, though. The project's worth millions, so a cut of that's hardly loose change' Salford said nothing, so I continued. 'Compulsory purchase orders. You remember Derek Jones? He told me how it worked, how you forced people out of their homes because you wanted to tell sell them to the council for a large profit.'

Salford looked baffled. 'Derek Jones?' He laughed. 'Why are you wasting your time talking to that loser?'

'He didn't have much good to say about you, either. Do you remember his nephew, Jimmy? Died from a drugs overdose?'

Salford said he couldn't remember. 'Derek's always had an overactive imagination. He's probably spun you a fairytale.'

My anger was rising. 'What about the people you forced out of their homes? You made them derisory offers, but they were hardly free to choose whether or not to accept, were they? I think the catch was, if they didn't accept, they'd be forced out. How about burning their houses down? How does that sound?' I slammed my glass down onto his desk, not giving him chance to answer. I was too angry. 'We all lose things we love, don't we.' I pointed at him. 'It cost you your daughter.'

230

Salford looked like he was going to hit me before standing up, walking around the desk and pouring me another whiskey.

He sat back down. 'You think you're bringing me news?'

I watched him slowly sit back down. 'You know about her?' I asked.

Salford shook his head. 'Suspected.'

'Because Donna left?'

'It doesn't take a genius, does it?'

He was genuinely upset so I waited for him to compose himself. 'Chelsea's nearly ten years old now.'

I shrugged.

'Have you seen her?' he asked me.

'No.'

'But you've spoke to Donna and I'm definitely the father?'

I nodded again.

'I knew it.'

'You scared her off by making her have an abortion. She wasn't going to have another.'

'She told you that?'

I said nothing, waiting for him to continue.

He picked up his telephone and told whoever answered it he wasn't to be disturbed. Turning back to me, he told me it hadn't been so simple. 'I had my wife to think of. I couldn't tell her I'd got Donna pregnant.'

'And you'd already put Donna through one abortion.'

'I'm not proud of that, but what could I do? I had my business to think about, and so did Donna. She wanted to be a singer and I was managing her band. They weren't up to much, but in those days my dick ruled my head. I wanted to have some fun with her, and she was willing. I had the money and influence to throw around and she liked it that way. It was convenient for both of us.'

'Like with Julie?'

'That was different.'

'How?'

'I would have left my wife for her.'

I laughed.

Salford lent forward, pointing at me.

'Show me some respect, or I'll start to get fucking annoyed. I'm letting you sit in my office and talk to me like this, so watch your mouth.'

I held his stare, saying nothing, waiting for him to continue. 'Julie was everything my wife wasn't. In many ways, we were perfect together. But at the end of the day, I stayed with my wife for the kids and because it's easier.'
I thought back to Richardson's small flat and the situation she found herself in. 'But you had to cut her face to shreds?' She wanted revenge.

'Sometimes you have to do things you don't like. I work in a difficult industry, as I'm sure you appreciate. If I let people take advantage of me, I'm finished. And when she grassed on me, I had no choice. I couldn't have it.'

'Couldn't you have told her to disappear?'

Salford laughed and shook his head. 'She had to pay for what she'd done. It was expected.'

'How did you find her if she was in a safe house?' I asked, remembering what Branning hold told me.

'You pay the right people. Nothing more difficult than that.'

The case had haunted Branning. He'd wasted his life chasing a ghost. People like Salford are always one step ahead of the police. 'Don't you feel any remorse?'

'For Julie?'

'Or Donna.'

He poured himself another drink and thought about the question.

'However I reckon it up, Julie got what was coming to her. She was a big girl and happy enough to take the money and all the trimmings when it suited her. If you do that, you have responsibilities. Number one on the list is to keep your mouth shut.'

I felt ill sat in his office. The air seemed to be warmer, the room smaller. I had to press on. 'What about Donna? She hadn't done anything wrong.'

He slugged back his whiskey. 'You're probably about right. I paid for her abortion and I thought she'd learn the lesson. She couldn't have the baby. I didn't want it, and knowing her family, I bet they didn't, either. After a bit, things got back to normal and I thought that was it. Before she disappeared, she started to make noises to others that she might be pregnant, but I never got chance to talk to her. She left.'

'Did you pay her off?'

'Didn't get the chance. She just went. Everybody assumed she'd gone to London, like she'd always threatened to.'

'And you didn't care?'

'Not at the time, no. I didn't want a baby and it saved me a headache. Besides, I didn't know for certain she was pregnant.'

'You knew.' I could see how it would have unfolded. Salford was used to rampaging around the city, doing as he pleased. A pregnant teenager causing trouble for him with his wife didn't appeal very much. Having forced Donna into one abortion, he'd have no problems with her having another, however much persuading she needed. The room was silent other than for the clock on his desk. 'What's the situation with Chelsea?'

'What?' I couldn't believe he was even asking the question.

'Do you think I could see her?'

'Shouldn't think so.'

Salford sighed. 'I'd just like to see her, see what she looks like.'

I thought about Debbie to remind myself what I was doing here. Salford opened a drawer and put a cheque book on the table.

'I want you to speak to Donna for me. I'll pay you. I need to know something about my daughter, however small or insignificant it seems to you. I just want to know something.'

I shook my head. 'I can't do that.'

'Why not? I'm paying you.'

'Find somebody else. I'm not interested in helping you.'

He wrote out a cheque and handed it over. Payable to cash. 'Can you make sure Donna gets this? Call it back pay for Chelsea's maintenance.'

The cheque was for £25,000. 'I'll see what I can do' putting it in my pocket. I doubted Donna would take it, but it wasn't my decision to make. If she decided to cash the cheque, Salford would know about it.

Salford stood up and took a cigarette out of his pocket. 'Smoke?'

I shook my head.

'Probably wise of you. I'm going to go outside and have this. You're going to stay here and wait for me and then we'll talk about what you really came here for.'

Salford poured us both another whiskey. I left mine sitting in front of me. I was starting to feel the effects of the alcohol and I wanted to keep a clear head. I needed to keep asking questions.

'I'm dying' Salford said to me.

I looked at him properly. His skin was pale, his eyes had little colour in them. I put his weariness down to the kind of life he led, but now he'd said it, it made sense.

'The doctor's say there's nothing they can do for me, and believe me, I've had second and third opinions on it. I'll be dead within the year.'

He was in his mid-fifties, which was no age to die, but I didn't feel particularly sorry for the man. How could I?

'This is the time for me to get my affairs in order. I'm not going to bullshit you – I've not been a good person. I've done some pretty bad things, but the one thing I can do is make sure my daughter is sorted.' He pointed to me. 'And you can do that for me.'

My mind was racing, playing with theories and ideas and the things we'd said. 'Murdoch was wrong, wasn't he? You didn't kill his wife.'

Salford shook his head. 'I didn't kill her.'

I slugged the whiskey back in one and stood up, ready to leave. I knew Salford wasn't responsible for my wife's death, either.

TWENTY TWO

I strode through the reception, ignoring the woman shouting at me to stop. I walked straight up the stairs and opened the first door I came to. Not finding what I wanted, I repeated the same thing with the next two doors. Entering the fourth door, I found what I wanted. Johnson was in bed with one of the workers. The room was disgusting; everything looked like it needed a good wash, especially the sheets. The wallpaper was peeling in the corners and the lighting was dim. If it had been designed to hurry up the punters, I'm sure it worked. Nobody would want to spend any more time in this room than necessary.

'We tried to stop him' Margaret said, as she entered the room behind me. 'I wasn't on reception when he came in.' She looked flustered, knowing she was in trouble. The woman appalled me. I turned to her and told her to fuck off. Johnson got out of bed and stood naked in front of me, unsure what his next move should be. He turned to the young girl trying to hide under the bedding and told her to disappear.

He laughed. 'What can I do for you today? Have you being having a think about our meeting the other day? If so, I'm pleased, but it's really not the time for business.'

'I wanted to speak to you before the police pick you up.' He laughed again. 'Why would they be doing that?'

'Murdoch expects to be arrested today.'

'He best have his story straight, then.'

Johnson got dressed as spoke to me.

'I think he has.'

'Good.'

'How did you force him to work for you?'

'I didn't need to force him.'

'His choice?'

'That's right.'

'Not once you'd allowed his wife to run up large debts in the casino. You made it sound like his only way out of the situation was to do as he was told.'

'He could have repaid the money and we'd have been cool. He wanted to get involved.'

'How much pressure did you put on Jennifer? You obviously like to sample the goods?'

'She was a very attractive woman.'

I waited for him to finish buttoning his shirt. I wanted his full attention. 'Did you kill her?'

Johnson laughed. 'Don't be stupid. I don't go around killing people.'

I let it hang in the air.

'She wouldn't touch you, would she?' I said. 'She took one look at you, and she didn't want to know. You repulsed her.'

He took a step towards me. 'You watch your mouth, cunt. You're in my place and nobody knows you're here. You'll be lucky if I let you walk out again. This time I might well bury you alive.'

It was my turn to laugh. 'You went to her house, determined to have your own way with her, and she told you to leave.'

'Is that right?'

'And when she laughed in your face, you lost it, because that's what you do. You killed her there and then and tried to cover your tracks. All because she said no to you.'

'You know nothing.'

Johnson was where I wanted him. He'd turned away to find his shoes, no doubt convinced I was throwing around groundless accusations, no threat to him. I waited for him to turn back towards me. 'You didn't kill Jennifer Murdoch, but you did kill my wife' I said.

Johnson stared at me, momentarily lost for words. 'Says who?'

'Says me. I've been talking to Salford.'

Johnson sneered. 'What would he know?'

'More than you think. He's done, isn't he? He'll be dead soon, but he's not stupid.'

He walked away from the window and sat down on the bed. 'If you think you know, what are you doing here?'

There was a hint of defeat in his voice, the realisation he hadn't always been one step ahead of the game.

'I want to hear it from you' I said.

'You won't make anything stick.'

'Doesn't matter.' I walked over to the window, but there was nothing to see. I thought about Salford telling me about wider business interests. 'Salford saw you coming and let you draw Jennifer Murdoch in at the casino. He gave you enough rope to hang yourself with.' I turned back towards him. 'Why did you go behind his back?'

'Why not?'

'The money? You thought Murdoch was a soft touch?'

'He is a soft touch. In fact, he's surprised me with his weakness. I thought he'd do a little better because it wasn't that hard for him. All he had to do was keep his mouth shut and follow instructions.'

'But Salford was able to see it. He knew Murdoch wasn't going to deliver.'

'Judgement call, that's all.'

'But his call was right.' I waited for him to look at me. 'Again.' Johnson looked like a beaten man. 'You knew he was dying?' I asked.

He sprung back to life, defiance on his face. 'What do you think? I'm sick of being the fucking joke in that place. I'm always his number two, always following orders. Fuck that – I want a piece of the action. I want to be the one calling the shots and making the decisions for a change. Besides, who the fuck are you? You're some failed rugby player who thinks he can call the shots over me. Are you taking the piss?'

I ignored him and continued. 'And you thought this was your chance to step up to the plate?'

'If you don't make your move, somebody else will do it for you.'

'Salford saw the stupidity of working with Murdoch and he didn't want to know.'

Johnson stood up, pacing the room. 'He's gone soft. Has been for years. He wants to be legitimate, but fuck that.' His eyes were ablaze, putting me on my guard. 'It's wrong. It's not how we made our reputations in this city. People expect better of you than opening a fucking casino.' He sat back down and rested his head in his hands. 'Fuck that.'

'My wife was the collateral damage for you' I said, turning away from him. He said nothing. Johnson was nothing. Salford was a career criminal but Johnson had only ever been his sidekick, the required muscle to get the dirty work done. It went all the way back to their days as young football hooligans. Julie Richardson had told me that. What Johnson was starting to realise was that things would never change. He thought he'd found some easy pickings when Murdoch and his wife walked into the casino. He had no understanding of the complexity and the details of the regeneration plan. If he thought he could mastermind such an operation, he was stupid. If he thought he could do it on the back of Salford's reputation and without his knowledge, he was deluded.

I stood up and walked towards the door before turning back to take one last look at Johnson, the man who'd caused my wife's death. He'd go to prison for a long time, but his real punishment would be the knowledge he'd failed. He'd never be Frank Salford. That would be what haunted him. My grieving would come, but seeing him crushed would be some small compensation. 'You're done' I said, as I walked out of the room.

Sarah and I were back where we started; sat with Maria Platt and Derek Jones. This time Gary Platt had joined us. I sipped my coffee, letting the news I'd given them sink in.

'Do you think Donna will change her mind?' Derek asked us.

Sarah lent forward. 'We know she misses Hull. Maybe one day.'

'Soon?' Maria asked.

I sighed. 'I'm sorry, but I really don't think so.' I understood why Sarah was trying to give them some hope, but it wasn't fair.

'Donna made it very clear to us she wasn't happy in Hull' I explained. Sarah had turned away, retreating back into her seat. 'She's built a new life for herself.'

'Where is she?' Gary asked.

It was a reasonable request, and he was her brother, but I shook my head. 'I can't tell you that.'

'We need to know.'

'I'm sorry.'

'Why did she leave, then?' Gary asked.

I knew Sarah was staring at me. I swallowed and thought about how far I wanted to go. 'Her music.' It wasn't a lie, but it barely scratched the surface. They didn't need to know about Salford. I'd argued with Sarah over whether we should tell them about Chelsea. I didn't think we should tell them, as Donna clearly didn't want any contact. I knew it was harsh, but there wasn't an easy answer.

'Was it because of dad?' he asked.

We sat looking at each other. Derek nodded at me, clearing me to tell them what I knew. 'He was a factor in her decision' I said.

'Not surprised' said Gary.

Sarah and I said nothing. I didn't know what they wanted to hear.

'Did she go to London?' Derek asked.

'She didn't quite make it that far' I said.

'But she's alright?' Maria asked.

I turned to her and smiled, thankful she wasn't pushing for information. 'She's fine' I said. 'She's happy.'

Maria nodded and dabbed her eyes with a tissue. 'Good.'

I leant forward again, looking directly at her, trying to get what I wanted to say straight in my head. 'There's some things you can't fix,' I said, 'decisions you can't go back and change.' I was thinking of Debbie. 'You have to live with them the best you can.'

I'd told Sarah what I'd learnt about my wife's death. She had wanted me to go home and let her deal with Maria

Platt. It wasn't an option. I wanted to finish what we'd started.

'Thank you' Maria said. 'I appreciate all your efforts in finding her. I'm pleased to hear she's well. I know I don't have much time left and I can't pretend I'm not upset by her decision, but I need to put my affairs in order. I was hoping you could persuade her and whatever family she has to come home. Even if it was just for a quick visit.' Tears were rolling down her face. 'Have you ever lost someone important to you, Mr Geraghty?'

I nodded. 'My wife.'

'I'm sorry to hear that' she said. 'You know that there are no words to describe how you feel on the inside. You have to put a brave face on things, but it eats you up. I was hoping for a second chance to make it better, that's all. I'll have to live with the guilt of what I've done until I die.'

Nobody said anything until Derek asked if Donna still sung.

'Not seriously' I said.

'A broken dream, then' Derek said.

I nodded and turned to Sarah. We were done. I had Salford's cheque for Donna. We still had one last chance to persuade her to see her mother before she died. I turned back to Maria Platt. 'We've got another case on the go at the moment.' I explained about Jennifer Murdoch. 'If it's any consolation, you've helped me get to the bottom of it.'

She gently shook her head. She'd lost her daughter. It was no consolation.

The rain beat down on the car whilst we discussed the information Sarah had dug out for me. I thought about calling Coleman so he could make the arrest, but he could wait - I wanted to hear it first-hand before the police got involved. Sarah was needed at home, and she pointed out, it was my case, so I should be the one to close it. We agreed I'd drop by her house later on, to tell her and Don how it had gone. I glanced back at Maria Platt's house before starting the car up and pulling away. The Platt family hadn't ever caught a single break.

I waited for his reaction. He stood with his back to me, saying nothing.

'You killed Jennifer Murdoch' I repeated. 'And I know why you killed her.'

He turned to face me and laughed. 'No you don't.'

'Fill me in, then.'

The telephone rang, but he ignored it, instead turning to face me. He shrugged. 'You gave me the information I needed. Ironic, I suppose.'

That much was true and made it all the more sickening. It was the reason why I hadn't asked Don to come along. He didn't need to hear how we'd set the wheels in motion, however inadvertently.

'It must have been really eating you up' I said.

'Like you wouldn't believe. You don't let these things go. You never forget. Or forgive.'

'It wasn't her fault.'

'She was the best option.'

I shook my head. 'It wasn't her fault.'

'You never forgive.'

I threw the photograph at Briggs. 'Tell me about your brother.'

I sat down at the boardroom table and listened. 'Sid was three years older than me. He couldn't wait to go to sea and he was good at it, too. A natural. He was cut out for a life at sea. It was hard work for him, but unlike a lot of the others, he knew why he was doing it. Instead of wasting all his money the minute he docked, he gave most of it to my mum to make sure me and my sister had all that we needed. He appreciated how difficult it was for her, as she would do everything for us. When my father had gone to sea, she had to take his place, as well running the house. It was tough for her. My father injured himself at sea, but there was no sick pay, no pension, nothing. Once he had to stop work, nobody wanted to know us. It was a horrible place to live. The houses were disgusting, and it was so insular. People were happy to inter-marry and live in each other's pockets. It was a closed shop.'

Briggs's experience of Hessle Road was the polar opposite of Derek Jones's. He looked a broken man.

'My brother died' he eventually said. He stood up and walked over to the window. 'He died at sea.'

I knew that much. I got Sarah to dig into the archives. She'd tied up a crew listing from the photograph we'd borrowed from Maria Platt. Records told us Sid Briggs had died in 1969.

'Jennifer's father was the captain when he died' I said.

He sat back down. 'Have you heard of the Christmas Crackers?'

I nodded. Derek had told me about them, but I let him continue.

'Nobody wanted to fish over Christmas. The owners of the boats, though, still wanted them out there fishing, making them money, so they got together the Christmas Cracker crews. Because there weren't many men to choose from, they'd round up whoever wanted to sail. I did a couple when I first left school to prove I could do it. It was a test, I suppose. I hated it because they'd even take homeless dossers on board, just to make the numbers up.'

'What happened to your brother?' I asked.

'It was a bad trip. Sid wanted to go because we needed the money. I wanted to go because I was promised a full time job if I could handle it. It was fine at first, but a week in, Sid had an accident on deck. It was a dangerous job with men working long hours. Things would happen and there was little medical treatment available. He got worse and worse over the following days.' Briggs turned away from me. 'And then he died.'

I was puzzled. 'Why wasn't he taken to hospital if he needed treatment?'

'The Merchant Shipping Act.'

'What?'

Briggs laughed. 'You're missing the point. Jennifer's father was the captain and what he said went. The Merchant Shipping Act gave the captain absolute power. He didn't want Sid to go to the hospital. He thought my brother would just recover, given time.'

'The ship would have to be in radio contact with the office, though? They could have arranged something?'

Briggs laughed again, making me feel as stupid as he obviously thought I was. 'Murdoch's father didn't maintain radio contact.'

'Why not?'

'Because it wasn't in anyone's interest to do so. The ships were out there in competition with each other, trying to find where the fish was. If we made contact with our home base, other ships might pick up the signal. And because we only got paid when we landed the catch, nobody would speak out against the captain. If he wanted to keep our location quiet because we'd found a good one, nobody would argue.'

'So Murdoch's father made a judgement call?'

Briggs punched the table. 'A judgement call?' He was pointing a finger at me. 'A fucking judgement call? If it had been, I could have accepted it. No, Murdoch's father was ambitious. He was young and only in charge of the boat because none of the experienced guys wanted the job. If he messed it up, he wouldn't get the promotion he wanted. Reputation was everything. Even though I insisted we abort the trip and head to Iceland to get Sid the medical attention he needed, he wouldn't. He made us carry on fishing whilst Sid got worse and died. He could have saved my brother if he had wanted to, but he put himself and the catch first.'

I didn't know what to say. I didn't know whether or not Brigg's brother would have survived if he had made it to a hospital. He would have had a chance, though, and Jennifer Murdoch's father had chosen not to give it to him. It had been a cut-throat business, but that was going too far. My uncle had told me that although safety wasn't of huge importance to some trawler owners, the men looked out for each other. It was better to come back with a reduced catch and all the men than the alternative. I should have put it together sooner. The police had hinted the break-in wasn't genuine and that she knew her killer. Naturally, suspicion had fallen on her husband, but Briggs would have had all her personal details on file. The rest we had filled him in on. Once we'd given him her background and maiden name, it wouldn't have been difficult to put together. He'd got more than he expected when he'd engaged us. Briggs had spent decades consumed by bitterness over his brother's death and we'd given him the opportunity he needed to take his revenge. He sat quietly at the table whilst I called Coleman on his mobile and told him where I was.

TWENTY THREE

'**Thanks**' I said to Sarah. It was frozen pizza and cheap wine, but it didn't make any difference to me. It was exactly what I needed. Don walked back into the room after checking Lauren was still asleep.

He picked up the slice I'd been eyeing. 'A good day.'

I picked up my glass and returned the toast. 'A good day.' I asked him when Murdoch had been arrested.

'Late afternoon' Sarah told me. She'd taken the message from Coleman. It sounded like they'd been busy, picking up Murdoch, Taylor and Johnson in co-ordinated raids.

'What about Salford?' I asked.

'No word.' She shrugged. 'He wasn't involved, was he?'

I grunted my agreement. So far as we knew, he hadn't had any direct involvement in the fraud. It didn't ring true, but proving it would be a difficult job for Coleman. I also had to break the news to Julie Richardson. 'Your old mate, Branning, won't be best pleased, either' I said to Don.

Don shook his head and sighed. 'I'll have to let him know. He'll think we let him down.'

There was nothing we could do. Salford had turned out not to be our problem. He'd evaded Branning this far, and it wasn't going to change. I hadn't spoken to Don all day, so I explained about Salford's illness. He digested the news and said he'd make talking to Branning a priority. Branning had lost the war without winning a significant battle. The price Salford was going to pay was not knowing his daughter, however much he wanted to.

'What did Murdoch have to say?' Don asked me.

'He wanted me to find out who killed his wife, even if he was arrested.' I shrugged. 'At least we've done that for him.'

'I guess we were wrong about him' Sarah said. Don looked away from me, obviously not ready yet to admit he'd misjudged the man.

'He's hardly one of life's good guys' I said. Murdoch had jeopardised his life's work. His regeneration plans could have made a real difference to the area and the city. Instead he'd let personal greed and gain taint him. He was going to go to prison a broken man, and he'd deserve everything he got.

'He's not all bad, though, is he Dad?' Sarah said to Don.

I managed not to laugh as Don did his best to side-step the question. The pizza was good – I helped myself to another slice.

'He's probably lucky he wasn't fed to the pigs' he eventually said.

We all laughed. I pushed the memory of Johnson threatening to bury me alive to one side.

Don produced a pad of paper. 'I want to make some notes, so we can tidy things up tomorrow. Maybe we should try to take on less dangerous jobs in the future.'

It wasn't an unreasonable point, but I hadn't expected a simple investigation into an employee's illness to mushroom like it had. I told Don I'd try to choose more wisely in the future. Sarah smiled at me, complicit in the joke.

'What do we need to cover off?' he asked us.

Murdoch had given me a cheque to cover our time. I hoped it wouldn't bounce. 'I think we should make sure Sam Carver's alright for money. Try and make it up to him the best we can.'

'Who's he?' Sarah asked.

'The guy at the casino.'

She nodded. 'Right.'

'What about Maria Platt?' Don asked.

I shrugged. 'There's nothing more we can for her.' I told Don about the cheque Salford had given me for Chelsea.

'Shame there's nothing for us' he said.

I wasn't too bothered. Sometimes you get drawn into cases you shouldn't. However much you tell yourself not to let it become personal, it succeeds in getting under your skin. The Platt family had certainly been dealt a rough hand, and it would have been nice to have reunited them, but it wasn't what Donna had wanted. End of story.

'Is Anastazja still at your flat?' Sarah asked.

I nodded. 'I think she's planning on going tomorrow.' I told them I'd like to give her some of Murdoch's money. He'd been generous, so it seemed the right thing to do. She deserved the chance to make a fresh start. Neither of them argued with me.

We heard Lauren shout for us, so Don stood up and said he'd see to her. 'She probably wants a story reading.' He closed the door behind him.

I poured Sarah and me another glass of wine each and sat back down. It had been a long day and I was starting to feel frazzled around the edges.

'Are you alright, Joe?' she asked.

I nodded and said I'd had better days. 'It's such a mess.'

She moved across the couch and sat next to me. 'I know.'

She was sat so close to me, I could smell her perfume. As well as smelling great, she looked great. I smiled at her. The moment was interrupted by my mobile ringing. I listened to the message and disconnected the call. 'Coleman' I said, reluctantly standing up. 'He wants to meet me.'

I found Coleman sat in the corner of Queens, a pint of lager waiting for me.

'Least I could do' he said, as I sat down next to him.

It tasted good, especially after pizza. I hadn't been keen to move off the sofa when he called, but I couldn't say no, either.

'You'll be pleased to know we got someone for the attack on you.'

I raised my eyebrows. 'What?'

'The ones who stole your mobile' he explained.

I nodded. 'Right.' I'd seemingly been attacked so many times since, it didn't really register.

'Gang of kids, looking for easy pickings.'

I picked my drink up. Easy pickings, I thought? 'It was traumatic.'

'I'm sure it was.'

We both laughed. It wasn't important now.

'You'll make another statement?'

'Whatever.'

'We got some work out of the Murdoch's swingers club you went to. Remember New Holland?'

I nodded. 'The band?'

'That's the one. The singer was at the party, complete with a pile of Class A's.'

I didn't recall seeing him, but the band had been over for nearly fifteen years. I'd read they were reforming and going back out on tour. I assumed it would be interesting as I recalled the split being acrimonious. Coleman told me about the day's arrests. 'I wasn't there for them' he said. 'I was involved with the interviews, so I had to prepare at the station. I'm pretty pleased I missed Johnson's arrest, though.'

'Didn't take it too well?'

'Took four officers to pin him down and put the handcuffs on.'

It sounded about right. 'How did it to go with Murdoch?'

'He came without any trouble.'

'The interview?'

Coleman sighed and sat back in his chair. 'Between these four walls, it's going as we expected. We haven't been able to speak to him yet, as the fraud boys get first crack, but he's not holding out on us. He's got his solicitor with him and he's working through the details.'

'How's he holding up?'

'Couldn't really tell you.'

Murdoch had caused me nothing but grief, but I felt a little sorry for him. He'd allowed events to overwhelm him and Johnson had been quick to take advantage of him. For all that, he'd still made his choice. The regeneration work he had planned should have been his crowning moment, but now it wouldn't happen. The biggest losers were going to be people like the Platts and their neighbours. Just like they'd lost their livelihoods all those years ago when the fishing industry had collapsed. 'How did it go with Johnson and Taylor?'

'As you'd expect, really. I'm told Taylor was relieved to get it all off his chest. You could say he's not cut out for a life of crime.' Coleman laughed. 'Johnson is proving to be a harder nut for us to crack.'

'I can imagine.'

'He's saying nothing, insisting he's an innocent bystander, but we'll keep chipping away at him. We've got plenty of time left.'

'Good.' The city would be a better place if he wasn't on the streets. Over the last few days, I'd been thinking about my future. I hadn't been sure how much enthusiasm I had for carrying on, and although most of the work was routine, the chance to help take down people like Johnson was too great to pass over. It got me out of bed in the morning.

'Will you be talking to Frank Salford?'

Coleman shrugged. 'Couldn't tell you. It's not really my case, but it sounds like he kept himself out of the loop.'

It was probably true. Salford had spent his whole life one step ahead of the police, so I doubted he was going to slip up now. He'd given Johnson enough rope to hang himself and he hadn't been disappointed. It showed who was in charge.

'How about Briggs?' I asked, turning the conversation back to the Murdoch's.

'I spent a couple of hours with him. He's not a very pleasant individual, is he?'

I agreed with him. 'Have you charged him yet?'

'Not yet, but it's looking like a formality. He killed Jennifer Murdoch.'

'Good.'

'I hope us getting Johnson gives you some sort of closure for your wife' Coleman said quietly, before turning away from me.

I was going to mention I had given them Johnson, but checked myself. It wasn't important. I was pleased that they had the right man. He might not have set the house on fire himself, but he had ordered it. Maybe the police would get a name from Johnson, but I didn't care who actually started it. It meant nothing to me. Coleman couldn't look me in the eye; he knew the police had let me down. It had been me who'd chipped away and looked beyond the obvious. Christopher Murdoch hadn't killed his wife.

'No hard feelings, Joe.' Coleman was in front of me, coat on, ready to leave. He held out his hand to me but I just stared at it. I thought about Debbie and fumbled around in my pocket for my wedding ring. Finding it, I put it back on, stood up and left the pub.

END

Lightning Source UK Ltd.
Milton Keynes UK
16 June 2010

155691UK00001B/32/P